No Bed of Roses

NJ LITZ

Titles by NJ Litz

Scent of Fear

———◆———

<u>COMING OCTOBER, 2019</u>

All the Time in the World

For S.A.K.
Love you forever, sweetheart!

Chapter One

WHEN, EXACTLY, IS THE RIGHT time to box up a life?

Dr. Brianna Kincaid stared into the deserted work cubicle with dread. Nine days had passed since her grad student, Megan Harper, had fallen asleep while driving home late at night and caused the car crash that took her life. Bree thought it would depress her coworkers even more if they had to continue walking passed a desk where it seemed like the grad student would be coming back any minute. But now that it was Friday, she was tackling the job of removing Megan's pictures and plants. She had waited to pack Megan's things until her research team had gone home because she couldn't deal with their sadness on top of her own.

Megan's cubicle was a test run, Bree supposed, for the coming weeks. In the five months since her mother's death, her father hadn't removed one thing from the house. Bree and her sister had finally talked him into letting Bree box their mother's clothes and personal belongings.

After tonight, I'll have practice at removing a life little by little.

As she placed Megan's things in a cardboard box, Bree wasn't even sure what she was going to do with them. It seemed cruel to send the grad student's coffee mug or books of crossword puzzles to her mother. And the significance of the fortune cookie prediction "love will find a way" pinned on her bulletin board was known only to Megan.

Pictures adorned one corner of her desk: Megan and her mother at her college graduation. Megan and her older sister, Molly. Friends from Pittsburgh. Parties here at the

Missouri Botanical Garden. Bree picked up a large frame holding a montage of photos of the garden, including one of the more famous sculptures—*Zerogee*—a father, mother and child in an exuberant dance. She always marveled at the way the artist had created the sense of joy in the family at simply being a family.

A phone ringing broke the silence, and it took several rings before Bree realized it was her work phone. She set down the picture frame, and grimaced when she heard it topple off the desk while she ran to her office. She had barely said her name when Emery Ralston broke in.

"Bree, I'm glad you're still there. Come over, will you? There's someone here who needs to speak with us."

Emery didn't even wait for an answer before hanging up. How unlike him, Bree thought.

She turned off her computer, put on her raincoat, then stopped by Megan's cubicle to collect the large box. She picked the silver frame off the floor. Luckily the glass hadn't broken. Bree tucked it in her tote as she picked up the heavy container.

She took the paved path from her building toward Emery's office. Thousands of tulips were at the height of their beauty, but their striking colors were muted by the gray April skies. It had drizzled all day, with a brisk, chilly wind. Despite her coat, Bree shivered. Too many years of living and working in the tropics had thinned her blood, and she was always cold now.

Out of habit, Bree noted what else had bloomed this week—azaleas, dogwoods, and daffodils—then reminded herself that she didn't need to know any more. When she'd returned to the States, she had moved into her parents' home to help her father care for her mother. Every day when Bree had come home, she had gone to her parents' bedroom to tell her mother what the Missouri Botanical Garden had looked like. She would describe the ever-changing landscape to a woman who could see the beauty in her mind even as her body was dying.

By the time Bree reached Emery's office, her arms ached from carrying the box. Emery's secretary had already gone home for the day so Bree set it on Faith's desk. She gave three short raps on the door to Emery's office before walking in. Emery and another man stood as she entered. The guest was tall, with neatly-trimmed dark hair, and wearing jeans, an untucked shirt, and a navy sports coat.

She expected Emery wanted her to give the visitor a tour. The Missouri Botanical Garden, the country's oldest public garden and a world-renowned scientific institution, frequently hosted international guests. Or perhaps he was a potential donor, and Emery wanted her to talk about her previous conservation work in Madagascar.

"Bree, this is Detective Daniel Cusumano. He's with the St. Louis Police Department. Detective, Dr. Brianna Kincaid. She was Megan Harper's supervisor," said Emery as he settled back in his desk chair.

Of all the things Bree could have expected to be brought to Emery's office for, Megan wasn't one of them.

Emery gestured for them to sit as well, so Bree took one of the guest chairs and waited.

"Detective Cusumano needs our help regarding Megan."

"Just routine information, Dr. Kincaid," Detective Cusumano said pleasantly.

Bree nodded, though she suspected there was nothing routine about it. There was no reason for the police to be here about a dead woman unless something was wrong. She was careful not to glance at Emery. From years of working with him, she knew he would be polite and engaged because that's what the job required. As president of the Garden, Emery oversaw a budget of forty-two million dollars in revenue and more than one hundred fifty-four million dollars in an endowment. Long before he began mentoring Bree, Emery had learned to play a wicked game of poker, and never gave anything away.

"I'm happy to help you if I can, Detective," Bree said, "though I didn't know Megan very long. Just since last September."

"Yet you signed for her body when it was released from the morgue."

Bree nodded, trying *not* to remember the morgue with Megan's battered face and body and her unblinking eyes. Bree had faced difficult situations in remote areas of the foreign countries in which she'd worked, but the eerie silence of the morgue and its clinical smells had shredded her soul with their detachment.

"Megan's mother lives in Pittsburgh and has multiple sclerosis," Bree explained. "There was no way she could have made the trip."

"No father or siblings?"

She shook her head. "Her father died when she was young, and her older sister, Molly, cares for their mother, whose disease advanced greatly in the last few months. Molly was the one who called and asked me to do the identification."

How did Megan's mother get up each morning after suffering so much loss? Bree wanted to ask how she stood the sorrow because Bree was drowning in her own.

"What can you tell me about Megan?" the detective asked.

She didn't hesitate. "Megan had tremendous potential. She was quite smart. A hard worker. Reliable. She had a promising career as a botanist ahead of her."

The detective nodded, encouraging her to go on.

"Megan was quiet. Kind. If she made a commitment to do something, you could always count on her. She handled the Toys for Tots drive during the holidays. Her death has been difficult for us."

Her heart flitted toward grief, but she ruthlessly tugged it back.

"Did you do things with her outside the office?"

"Every once in a while. If we went out, it was usually everyone in the department for a quick drink to celebrate a colleague's birthday or maybe the department holiday luncheon."

"You didn't eat lunch together? Or go out to happy hours on Fridays?"

"A twenty-three-year old has a totally different concept of happy hours than a thirty-six-year old, Detective," Bree said drily. "I'm sure that to Megan, hanging out with me after hours would have been like having her mother tag along."

Detective Cusumano asked how Megan had seemed the day that she had died. Had she been excited? Was anything different than usual?

Bree tried to remember. It only seemed different now because Megan had died. But that day, it had seemed normal and routine, and she shared the details with the detective, who surprised Bree when he changed the subject.

"How about money? Did she buy a lot of clothes lately, or maybe take a trip?"

"Detective, she was driving a 2009 Toyota when she was killed. She came from a working class neighborhood in Pittsburgh. If she took time off, it was usually to go home to visit her family."

He nodded, giving her the chance to go on, but she knew from her father how lawyers used silence. She figured it was the same with the police.

After a few beats, the detective continued, "Her purse contained a student ID from Washington University."

"Yes, she was working on her master's degree."

"In fact, she was on the Rachel Kincaid fellowship, wasn't she?"

Bree resisted the temptation to shift in her chair. Apparently pleasant Detective Cusumano had done some homework before he showed up. Either he knew someone inside the university or he'd gone through a lot of red tape to get that information. From her own experience with the university, she knew they wouldn't simply release anything on a student. Suddenly, she was glad she had nothing to hide.

"Rachel Kincaid was my mother. She died in November, Detective, from ovarian cancer. Perhaps you already know that my mother was involved with the Garden for many, many years. She was the chairwoman of the board of directors for several terms.

"She loved this Garden, and when we realized that she was going to die, naming a fellowship in her honor was a natural thing for my family to do. You seem to have done some research before you came so you may already know Molly Harper and I had a connection before my family chose Megan."

The detective tilted his head, again as if encouraging Bree to continue.

"Molly and I ran competitively against each other in national track meets for years in high school and college. Molly was a phenomenal runner." Bree paused as she remembered the two of them going down the final stretch so often together. "She made me a better runner. She just missed the cut the U.S. Olympic track and field team at the Beijing games. An injury two years after that ended her career."

"So you kept in touch?"

"Just a little, mostly through social media."

"Yet you weren't close to Megan?"

Even though he asked politely, only Emery's presence made her stifle a sharp retort. Tamping down her anger had become harder and harder since her divorce and then her mother's death.

"I was working out of the country when Megan began her studies at Washington University. I only met her when I came home last fall to care for my mother. Megan turned out to be talented in botany, so when my mother decided on the fellowship, choosing Megan was an easy decision for my family."

"Did Megan date?"

On her guard now, Bree chose her words carefully. "As I said, Detective, I was Megan's supervisor—and then not really for very long. We didn't talk about our personal lives much. Occasionally I overheard talk about her dates. She was a normal twenty-three-year old."

"Any particular boyfriends or girlfriends that you remember?"

Too many for the wrong reasons, Bree thought, but that felt like betraying a sincere young woman. "I'm sorry, but I try not to pry into the lives of my research team. Megan had a roommate at one point. Perhaps she could tell you more. And Molly is flying in next weekend to pack up Megan's apartment."

"Do you know what Megan planned to do the night she died?"

She shook her head at his question. "Detective, most botanists are boring. We tend to be nerds."

"But you are a group that travels in and out of countries with a lot of drug traffic."

"When we're working, we live in the tents in the middle of nowhere. Nothing glamorous about it. Trust me. Hardly the places where drug lords would hang out."

"And yet most drugs come from plants," Detective Cusumano persisted. "Let me ask you, Dr. Kincaid, do you think Megan did drugs?"

Bree stilled. "Did Megan have drugs on her when she died?" she asked carefully.

Normally, she would have scoffed at such an idea, but the detective's questions made her uneasy. If it was true, Molly would be heartbroken. She never drank, was a vegetarian, and took great care of herself.

The detective told her he couldn't answer that question, but spent another ten minutes asking more of his own, sometimes going back over the same points.

Emery leaned forward, clasping his hands on his desk. "Both the FBI and the St. Louis Police Department have asked for our help in identifying an unusual substance found in Megan's body, Bree. Their databases can't identify it. I'm giving the request to Stephen Almy to run through TROPICOS."

TROPICOS® was the Missouri Botanical Garden's own database, one of the largest in the world used to identify plants from across the globe. Stephen was a strong scientist. Quiet, but sharp. Emery thought highly of him.

"I have a box of items from Megan's desk if you'd like to look through it, Detective. I was going to take it home tonight and go through the stuff over the weekend to see if there was anything worth donating to charity."

"Yes, thank you. I'd like to see it."

Bree led both men to the box she'd left on the desk of Emery's secretary. The detective paid no attention to the mug or the knickknacks. He asked who the people were in the various pictures, and Bree explained the people she knew.

After about five minutes, the detective handed Bree two cards. "If you think of anything else, please call me, Dr. Kincaid. You may wish to give my card to Molly Harper as well."

She retrieved her purse, offering him her card as well.

Detective Cusumano thanked them for their time, shook hands with them both, then let himself out of the office.

She and Emery waited for a few seconds before Bree turned to him, saying, "Do you get the feeling we're under suspicion of something? I feel guilty, and I'm not even sure what for. Luckily, I met Dad downtown for dinner that night," she murmured. "I feel like I need an alibi."

"The good detective knows more about us than he mentioned. From questions he asked before I called you, I'm sure he looked us up on the web," Emery said.

If the detective had looked her up and was looking at staff who'd worked in foreign countries, he undoubtedly also knew about Bree's stints in China and Malaysia as well as

Madagascar. Somehow, she doubted he would have looked into Emery as closely. His numerous presidential and university commendations probably put him above suspicion.

"Let's hope Stephen turns up nothing," Emery said. "If this young woman was doing drugs she may have made a poor decision and paid dearly for it." He headed back into his office. "Do me a favor, will you, and write me an e-mail on Megan Harper and her work? Summarize our meeting with the detective too. I hope to hell we don't get to the point that we need a paper trail, but it's too easy any more to find ourselves on the front page of the *Post-Dispatch*, or God forbid, on the internet."

Bree rolled her eyes. "I don't know how you put up with the politics. Plants are so less complicated." Bree frowned. "Do you think he believes we're running some kind of drug ring?"

Emery sighed. "The last thing we need is rumors about illicit drugs or smuggled plants. We'll be launching a development campaign to raise seventy-million dollars in the fall, Bree. We can't have anything that would interfere with funding for the Garden. Lord knows grants are getting harder to get." He smiled wanly. "I'm getting too old for this."

"Never," she said affectionately.

Emery shook his head. "It will take a younger person with lots of energy to lead this organization."

She knew this was as close as Emery would come to probing if she had interest in succeeding him. He had been director of the Missouri Botanical Garden for twenty-one years, but lately, he talked more often of spending winters in Florida with his wife, and wanting more time to fish with his grandchildren.

He waited a beat. "Are you going to request to go back out in the field?"

She was only back at the Garden itself because she'd taken whatever position she could to get back home to care for her mother. "Soon. I'd like just a little longer with Dad, though. I packed him off to Boston this morning so he could spend time with Carly. He thinks my niece is just as perfect as his two daughters. He's staying with Carly for a couple of weeks." She flashed a rueful smile. "Poor Boston."

They smiled at each other in understanding. "Silence" and "Scottie Kincaid" were rarely ever used in the same sentence.

"Then we arranged to have him visit the firm's offices in D.C. and New York. He's restless and unfocused. We thought the change might be good for him." Bree hesitated. "I'm going to use the time to clear out mom's things."

Emery's eyes softened. He reached out and squeezed her hand. "I know it will be difficult, but when has difficult ever stopped you?"

Right now. I'm so tired of loss. I just want to turn back the clock.

However, she only smiled and squared her shoulders. "Good night, Emery."

Bree picked up the box of Megan's things, and wandered out to the parking lot, nodding absently at the security guard at the Garden's employee entrance. As a scientist, she tried to fashion what she'd just learned into some order in her mind, but the past few years had painfully taught her that bad news never fit neatly into life.

Chapter Two

BREE HELD HER MOTHER'S SWEATER at arm's length. The color didn't suit Bree, but it didn't matter. She would keep a couple of her mother's sweaters and wear them until they were threadbare. She recognized the irony of a woman who did fieldwork in the tropics dragging around beautiful wool sweaters, but she really didn't care about being logical.

It was nearly eleven p.m. She had been methodical and disciplined for four difficult hours, when everything she touched brought back a happy memory—one that would never happen again.

Tomorrow, she would start on her mother's jewelry. She would offer the better pieces to her aunts for sentimental value. She knew her father would like the pearls to go to Carly for her six-month-old daughter, Grace.

She turned back to survey her parents' walk-in closet. It looked so dramatically different—disturbingly empty—with just a third of her mother's clothes packed that Bree sank to the floor. Tears welled in her eyes. She shook her head. No, she would not cry again. She swiped at her eyes and sniffled. She would, however, have to think of some way to minimize the bareness when her father returned so he did not become morose.

Bree rose and carried the first of numerous boxes down to the first floor. She sat the box by the door leading to the garage and headed to the kitchen for a soda. She thought about watching a movie on Netflix, but couldn't work up the interest. It would be easier if she just went to bed and slept off her sadness the way a drunk slept off a binge.

Surely by tomorrow when she was rested, everything would look better.

Bree glanced at the box of Megan's things in a corner of the kitchen. She dreaded having to put one more thing on her list, but she should sort through Megan's personal items and pack whatever she decided to send to Molly and her mother over the weekend too.

She began reading the notes she'd taken off Megan's bulletin board. Most of them could be tossed in the trash. The picture frames were cheap. Bree would donate those to Goodwill. The doll made of multi-colored corn husks from a trip to Guatemala could probably be thrown away too. Of course, she would save the pictures of Magen and her family and give them to Molly when she came in next weekend.

Where was the picture of the various shots from the Garden? Megan's mother might want that for sentimental reasons. Bree moved items around in the box, then remembered she had tossed it in her tote when Emery had called. She fished it out, and her fingers felt the clasp holding the back of the picture in place. It had come loose. She flipped the picture over and found a piece of cardstock wedged between the backing and the cardboard. Magen must have wedged it there to help the picture stay in place. She started to put it back, then noticed it wasn't a blank.

Bree blanched when she noticed the document was dated April Seventeenth—the day Megan died. She couldn't help it. She read what Megan had scribbled.

We will travel the train of tears in life armed with our love.
Amazing!
Together, we will build a house of love.
The beauty we can and cannot see.
Oh, the happy times we will show our child.
Our love is worth a fortune.
If Megan was writing poetry, Bree thought it was a good thing she'd chosen botany instead.

Her phone rang, and when Bree recognized the number

as Molly's, she immediately felt guilty for thinking badly of the dead. For a second she considered letting the call go to voice mail. She had no energy left to give to Molly, who surely needed to talk about her sister and mother. Then the dratted sense of Kincaid duty, drummed into her DNA for four generations, kicked in. Pulling her shoulders back, Bree took a deep breath.

"Hey, Molly! What's up?"

"Hi, Bree." Her voice was laced with weariness.

Bree gripped the kitchen island. Molly was one of the few people who was just as stubborn and had just as much grit as herself. Like Emery, Molly deflected anything that wouldn't show her in a position of strength. She must have been beyond tired not to disguise her feelings.

"What's wrong?"

"My mother has taken a turn for the worst. Not a surprise, I guess, given the shock of Megan's death."

"I'm so sorry."

"No, I'm the one who's sorry. Bree, I have a huge favor to ask."

Bree slumped. She didn't have the energy to do a big favor right now. But saying no really wasn't an option. "Sure."

"I can't leave mom. I can't come to St. Louis next weekend to pack up Megan's apartment, and it's the last weekend before the end of the month. I hate to admit it, but between mom's medical expenses and Megan's funeral, there's—"

Bree interrupted so Molly didn't have to say the family didn't have enough money to pay for another month of rent.

"I understand, Molly. Why don't I get in touch with her roommate, and the two of us will figure something out."

Bree could hear the relief in Molly's voice as she thanked Bree profusely.

"Her roommate's name is Amber, right?" Bree said. "I met her once when she picked up Megan to head to the lake for the Labor Day holiday. What's her number?"

"Well, that's the reason I'm reaching out to you. I can't get a hold of her. I tried calling and texting the number Megan gave us, but the person who answered said she just gotten the number."

"No worries. I can swing by their apartment on the way to the Garden and leave her a note."

"Oh thank you. I'm hoping she calls me. She must be eager to have Megan's things out of her way. I may even be able to get her to take care of everything so I don't have to impose on you."

"Let me handle it for you. You just take care of your mother," Bree soothed. "If there's anything you want from the apartment, send me an email or a text in the next few days, okay?"

"Let me talk with my mom. Most of Megan's stuff can go to Goodwill or maybe other grad students would want it."

Molly offered to text the address of Megan's apartment, but Bree assured her that she had it from her work records. With the logistics worked out, Bree asked more about Molly's mother, but she could tell Molly had no more energy for polite conversation than she did so they ended the call a minute later.

Bree wandered through the first floor of the house, turning off lights, trudging upstairs to her bedroom, and turning on the security system. Once in bed, she stared into the darkness, the silence of the big house making her feel small and lonely.

She turned over on her side and curled up. I am never going to be happy again, she thought with the maturity of a ten-year old. Maybe you all you get in life is so many years of happiness, followed by an equal amount of misery.

She couldn't see the finish line on this one. So she would do what she always did when a race had been a struggle. She would put one foot in front of the other. Just one step at a time until she could see that line.

Tomorrow, she would swing by Megan's apartment to size

up what needed to be done. If she went at it ferociously this weekend, she could sprint into the month of May and out run this stifling sorrow.

Chapter Three

B REE RAN UP THE THREE flights of stairs to Megan's apartment. At nine o'clock on a Saturday morning, she was hoping to catch Megan's roommate before she might run out to do errands. Like Megan, this Amber was a grad student. Grad school was too expensive for a student to be a partier these days, so Bree didn't think she would be disturbing her too early.

The three-story building housing Megan's apartment was in a former Shriner's temple that had been subdivided into twelve living spaces. The building was old, and with students as renters, there was nothing chic or charming about it. Still, it would have cost a pretty penny to rent because it was near both the university and the hospital complex.

Bree knocked on the door. When no one came, she rapped more intensely.

A minute later, a sleepy brunette in an oversized football jersey opened the door.

"What?"

The young woman wasn't Amber. Surely, Amber could not have found another roommate already. It seemed so coldhearted with Megan dead just over a week.

"Is Amber here?"

The young woman closed the door. Bree started to knock again when she heard the woman yelling for Amber. Vexed, Bree counted to ten. Then she counted to ten again before she pounded on the door a second time. This time, Amber answered. Her strawberry blonde hair was wet and she smelled like lemons. Clearly, she'd just gotten out of the shower.

"Hi, I'm Dr. Kincaid. Megan's supervisor. We met once last fall."

"Oh yeah."

"Can I come in? I wanted to talk to you about Megan's things. Her sister was planning to fly in, but can't now so she asked me to —"

Bree stumbled for the right words. 'Get rid of Megan's stuff' seemed so insensitive.

"Anyway, her sister wanted me to see if you cared to have anything of Megan's before I called Goodwill."

Amber's eyes widened. "Has something happened to Megan?"

Bree cocked her head, sure her confusion showed in her expression. "You didn't think it strange that she hasn't come home for more than a week?"

It was Amber's turn to look confused. "Megan doesn't live here anymore."

"What?"

"She moved out at the beginning of the year."

"What?" Bree must have sounded like an idiot. "Can I come in?"

"Yeah, sure." Amber moved out of the doorway to make room for Bree.

The living room was dimly lit because there was no window, though it gave way to a small kitchen with a single window. Two doors opened off the main room. Bedrooms, Bree guessed. One was closed. The roommate's? She probably had gone back to bed.

Amber indicated a beige couch, on which she settled. "What happened to Megan?"

Bree sat. "I'm sorry to have to tell you. She died."

Amber's hand moved to her heart.

"Her car crashed into a highway median. She died instantly. The police didn't contact you?"

"No, not at all, but like I said, she moved out at the end of January."

Bree bit her tongue so she didn't blurt out 'why'. "She didn't change her address on her emergency contacts at work."

Silent, Amber stared at her hands. Then she looked up, searching Bree's face. She was trying to decide whether to share something or not, Bree thought.

"Did y'all decide you weren't compatible as roommates? Is that why she moved out?"

Amber shook her head. "She wanted a place of her own because of the boyfriend."

Boyfriend? Bree leaned forward. "She never mentioned a steady boyfriend at work."

Amber pursed her lips and shrugged.

"You didn't like the guy?"

"I never met him. But she changed when she started seeing him."

Had Megan changed in the months before her death, and Bree had been too wrapped up with her mother to notice a difference?

"What was different about her?"

"She was so—she was like a thirteen-year-old with a first boyfriend. But she was very secretive about him."

Bree was oddly disappointed in Megan. She had seemed so stable at work.

"Do you know his name?"

Amber shook her head. "She called him by so many names. Prince Charming. My guy. They ran into each other at a bar in the Central West End. She'd only been seeing him a couple of months when she said she wanted her own place."

"Did they move in together?"

"I don't know, but I suspect she wanted a place of her own so he could spend the night. She got a loft down on Washington Avenue. "

"Do you have an address? I need to find the place so I can help her family with her things."

"She would never tell me. I don't think she wanted me to show up unannounced."

Bree's heart sank. A guy. Secrets. Drugs in her system when she died. *Oh, Megan, what had you gotten yourself into?*

"I tried to talk to her about him," Amber said. "But she was so head over heels that she didn't want to listen. And we'd only been roommates about six months so we were just becoming close when she started going out with this guy."

Bree felt a subtle gloom settle on both of them. She took a deep breath to shatter it, then stood up.

"Let me give you my card, Amber, in case you think of anything else that might give me an idea where to look."

As they walked to the door, Amber said, "I'm so sorry about Megan. She was very sweet. Smart too."

"Yes, she was both of those things."

"Can I send something to her family to let them know how sorry I am? They must think I'm a horrible person not to have reached out to them yet."

What the heck was Bree going to tell Molly? Neither Molly nor her mother needed more bad news.

"You know, Amber, I think the fact she didn't tell her family she moved would be more than her mother and sister can handle right now. Why don't you give me a week, maybe ten days, to figure this out? I'll call you." Bree turned to leave. "Oh wait. No one has your phone number. That's why I showed up."

Amber rolled her eyes. "I had to get a new number. The old one was the number of some sleazy bill collector before I got it, and I kept getting all these angry, threatening callers."

Bree added Amber's new phone number into her own phone contact list.

"If I can help you clear out Megan's loft, just give me a call, Dr. Kincaid."

"Thank you. If there's anything you really want of

Megan's, let me know. I can ask her sister. I think Molly would be comforted to know someone had a table, necklace, or coat of Megan's."

Amber nodded.

Bree heard the door close behind her as she headed to the stairway. When she settled in her late mother's BMW, she pulled out her phone to search for lofts on Washington Avenue. She found seven complexes. Two of the sales offices were closed. She ruled out the ones with low online ratings. If Megan and her boyfriend had moved in together, certainly they could have afforded a decent place to live, though a loft for two people seemed small. Then again, Megan had been in love.

We're such fools, Bree thought. A guy pays a little attention, and we throw everything over. Guys never do that.

Still, Detective Cusumano had never mentioned the boyfriend. Surely, if the police had talked to him, the detective would not have asked some of the questions of Emery and her that he had. Clearly, the detective had not reached Amber either or she would not have been shocked by Bree's news.

With no one knowing much about this mysterious boyfriend, what if he had cleared Megan's things out of the loft? What if he'd taken advantage of her death and stolen money from her checking account? Or if he was using her debit and credit cards? Bree would have to ask the Garden's human resource department to which bank Megan had had her pay check electronically deposited. She would subtly suggest to Molly that she put holds on all Megan's account for surely Molly had been too distraught and too busy to think about these details.

Bree started the car and headed from mid-town to downtown St. Louis and Washington Avenue.

If this boyfriend had cared about Megan, why hadn't he reached out to Molly? Surely, he knew Megan had a sister and how to reach her. How could he have not known that

Megan worked at the Garden, and not have reached out to her colleagues to share in his sorrow?

Bree blanched. What if he traveled for his job? What if he didn't know she was dead? No, by now he should have been unable to reach her and surely would have called the Garden or reported her to the police.

Unless this man was an addict? A drug dealer? Either would explain the drugs in Megan's system. What if he had been with her during the accident and had walked away when he'd known her fate? So many questions.

Bree got off the highway at Market Street and turned left at Fourteenth. On a weekend morning, downtown St. Louis was deserted, though that would change later in the day when the Cardinals played. She turned right onto Washington, a historic district that was popular again. The buildings dated from the late nineteenth century to the early 1920s and had been warehouses for the local garment district. Most importantly, the buildings featured distinct architectural personalities so when developers revived the area twenty years earlier, young professionals had been eager to live in the apartments and lofts along with all the trendy restaurants up and down the street.

Mercifully, Bree was early enough that the restaurants hadn't opened yet, and she found a parking spot. The office/sales manager of the first complex was cool once she learned Bree wasn't interested in touring any of the units. She also rebuffed Bree's attempts to discover if Megan Harper had rented a loft there.

Bree held her tongue, but pictured walking back into that office with an officer and a warrant to get the information. After all, what was the point of having a brilliant lawyer for a father if he couldn't suggest a legal way to help Molly Harper in her grief?

She walked briskly for two blocks to the next set of lofts. When Bree explained her glossed-over predicament to the sales manager, the woman said, "Wow, I've never heard that one before."

Bree nodded.

"I can't tell you anything specific about any resident. It violates confidentiality."

Bree felt a sharp retort bubbling up, but then the woman smiled. "I can tell you though that we've had one hundred percent occupancy since last summer."

"Ah." So no chance Megan could have rented a loft here just a few months ago. "Thank you. I appreciate your help."

"You know something else that might help you? Most mailboxes for residents are in the lobby. Sometimes people put their name on them. Mostly guys. Women do it less for security reasons. But if she's young, sometimes the younger ones do it because they're so excited to have their first place all on their own."

"Thank you. You've been very kind."

"No problem. I can imagine if it was my little brother who died, and I was far away."

Though Bree was beginning to think she was on a wild goose chase, she was only a block away from the third middle-of-the-road development. If she struck out here, she was going to talk to her father or reach out to Detective Cusumano. She really didn't want to upend Molly's life any further by bringing in the police if she didn't have to. Though the detective had been polite, he couldn't mask the intelligence and shrewdness behind those brown eyes.

When Bree entered the third building, she looked to her right, towards the office, but turned left to see if she could find the mailboxes. She went past the elevator, down a short hall that dumped into a longer hallway that went right. Sure enough, multiple rows of brass plates fronted locked mailboxes that lined the hallway wall. Bree sighed. There were probably one hundred boxes. She scanned them, then heaved a heavier sigh. Very few had names. But they did have small windows. Clearly, getting mail on Friday was a low priority as many of the boxes still had envelopes in them.

Bree's pulse quickened. If Megan had died, and the boy-friend hadn't picked up the mail, then Megan's mailbox should be crammed with bills and mailers. Maybe she could look for the ones filled to the brim, then could figure out if Megan had rented a loft here. She moved up and down the rows. Bingo! Number 403 was stuffed with envelopes. Not just a day's worth, but as if someone had not picked up the mail in a week.

Bree took the elevator to the fourth floor. The floor was well-lit, the carpet newer. Certainly the building was several steps up from the apartment Megan had lived with Amber. *If* this was Megan's apartment. Only one way to find out.

Apartment 403 was only a few doors from the elevator. At the door, Bree hesitated. What if the boyfriend was home? And exactly what are you going to say if he opens the door? She thought. What if he was overcome with grief? What if he was creepy? What if he invited her in? Bad idea to go in. No one knew she was here.

She pulled out her phone, prepping a text to her sister, telling her where she was and why. She kept her phone out, ready to send the message as she searched the doors. Bree also located the stairs, just in case. Most people couldn't outrun her.

She knocked. Nothing happened. She knocked again, then put her ear to the door. She couldn't hear anything. She tried the door. Locked. No surprise there. She was too short to reach the top of the door frame to see if an extra key was hidden there. She knocked a third time. As she waited, she heard the elevator ding and a guy wearing glasses, perhaps in his late twenties, with a backpack slung over his shoulder, stepped out.

Bree smiled—the expression that worked in any country to indicate she was friendly and not a threat.

He headed toward her.

"Excuse me," she said. "I'm looking for someone, and I

think she lives here."

He shrugged as he passed her. Over his shoulder, he said, "Haven't seen her all week."

Bree hurried towards him. "Excuse me. There may be a reason you haven't seen her. She died in a car crash."

The guy stopped.

"Was the woman who lived here named Megan Harper?" Bree asked.

"Megan, yeah. I don't know her last name."

Bree explained who she was, how she knew Megan, and what she was trying to do, though she modified the story a little to leave out the part about Megan's family not knowing that she moved. The guy did not offer his name.

"She was nice," he said. "Fed my snake when I traveled for work."

"Did her boyfriend live here too?"

The guy shook his head. "Not that I know of, though I'm not sure the guy I saw her with once or twice was her boyfriend."

"What did he look like?"

"Can't tell you. I saw the back of his head, but he had some gray in it."

Not at all what she was expecting to hear. Bree cocked her head. "So he was older than her?"

He shrugged. "I really didn't get a good look at him. He turned his face away one time. The other time, he hustled her into her loft when I got off the elevator."

"Did she ever talk about him?"

He shook his head. "Most of the people here pretty much stick to themselves."

"Okay, sure. I don't suppose Megan gave you a key?"

"Nope. Sorry to hear she died."

"Yeah. Thanks."

The guy started walking towards his door, then disappeared into his own place.

Bree walked back to Megan's loft and stared at the door,

as if she could force it to pop open on sheer willpower alone. She let out a huff of exasperation, and headed down the elevator to the rental office.

But the office was dark. Bree read the office hours printed on the door. Of course, it would close at noon on Saturday. An after-hours phone number was listed, but based on her experience at the other two offices, she doubted calling it would get her any further. Better to get proof of Megan's death and some kind of note from Molly as next of kin.

More people were walking up and down Washington Avenue now that the restaurants were open, and, lost in thought, Bree almost bumped into a few as she headed back to her car.

A smart, sweet girl died with drugs in her system. A mysterious boyfriend, possibly older. A sudden move to a new place.

There was nothing good in that scenario.

Frustrated, she jogged the last block to the car. As she unlocked and slid into the BMW, anger thrummed in her veins. She thought she could make a good start on putting Megan's death behind her. Instead, it loomed greater in her mind.

She beat her fingers against the steering wheel while she thought. There had to be something she could do to move forward with the sorrow of the Harper women weighing on her. Then inspiration struck.

Pulling out her phone, she dialed her colleague, Stephen Almy, and apologized for intruding on a weekend. She explained about Molly and Megan. "I understand you're investigating the drug the police found in her system. This is a difficult time for me since I'm connected to both women. I need to feel I'm helping, Stephen. I'd like to make this an urgent request and work with the lab to run the drug through TROPICOS® tonight."

Chapter Four

"THESE WEST COUNTY PRINCESSES ARE such a pain in the ass," grumbled Nick Mancini.

Daniel Cusumano glanced over at a scowling Nick. "As I recall, West County princesses used to be your favorites because they were so easy."

"That was on a Friday night in the back seat of a car. On a Sunday, princesses are just high maintenance. She's going to make us miss the first inning."

Daniel eased his black Jeep into the middle lane of Highway Forty, heading west. As he drove, the silence between them was the sound of two men comfortable with each other since grade school. Nick knew, though, that Daniel was just biding his time until he thought Nick was ready to talk. Loyal Daniel. Loyal even to someone who just showed up on his doorstep with no warning after a four-year absence. Though they had only exchanged sporadic texts and pictures over those years, they fell back easily into a friendship forged by summer nights of playing hide and seek as children, getting each other in or out of scrapes, and discovering girls.

When Daniel got off Lindbergh at Clayton Road and headed toward Warson, Nick grumbled again, "I don't see why this woman couldn't have talked to you on the phone."

"She has an idea she wants to discuss." Daniel glanced at Nick. "She said it's complicated. Apparently, she worked through the night so she could get me the test results I need. Least I can do is give her fifteen minutes for making my life easier. I thought I was going to have to wait more than a week for the results. She intervened to rush the tests to identify the substance the coroner found in the girl's body."

"I thought you said this wasn't a big deal. That this girl who died had no connections."

"I don't know what it is. It feels like a wild goose chase, but I owe Ben. He's a different kind of coroner. Got a quirky mind, and his examine of this Megan Harper turned up that drug. If he says there's something strange about it—" Daniel shrugged. "He's done so many favors for me, I didn't feel I could turn him down when he pestered me to look into it."

Nick snorted. "So what's this Dr. Kincaid look like?"

Daniel smiled. "You used to ask that question first."

"Yeah, it's amazing what maturity does to a man."

"Not your type, Nick."

"Let me guess. A woman in her late forties, glasses, wears big floppy hats to keep the sun off her pale skin. Big-boned girl. Wears her hair in a long braid down her back."

Daniel grinned. "Actually, she's tiny. Thin." With a cop's eye for detail, Daniel said, "Heart-shaped face. Dark blonde hair, which she wears shorter. And these incredible big violet eyes."

He continued, "She's an accomplished botanist. Saved a rare plant from extinction. She's also very composed. People usually fidget and jabber around a cop because we make them nervous. But Dr. Kincaid seemed unruffled. She wasn't friendly, but she wasn't too cool either."

"If this death is suspicious, maybe she's in on it."

"Still have that vivid imagination, I see." Daniel turned right and looked for the address Brianna Kincaid had given him.

They drove past large house after large house on three-acre lots.

"I didn't realize that being a botanist paid that well," Nick said. "Ladue is the priciest zip code in St. Louis."

"She comes from old, old money."

"How much money are we talking about?" Nick asked.

Daniel glanced over at him. "Lots. It was easy to check the family out before I went to see her because there's so much written about them. Grandfather was a Congressman. Great grandfather was a governor of Missouri.

"And her father," Daniel continued as he slowed down, looking for the specific house number, "is one of the best trial lawyers in the country."

Nick stared out the window as old resentments and anger resurfaced. This woman had grown up with every privilege while he and Tory had had to scramble every day to survive. Hell, he didn't even think of Elena and Bernard as his parents, just two adults who screwed his little sister and him over. If not for the thoughtfulness of Daniel's family, they would have gone hungry and known no kindness.

Daniel turned the car into a U-shaped driveway where a two-story house, built of fieldstone with blue trim, sat among one-hundred-year-old trees. A woman, dressed in a t-shirt, running shorts and tennis shoes, was planting purple and yellow flowers. True to the schizophrenia of April in St. Louis, the weather had warmed, though the wind still blew strong. The woman looked like a twig that would snap with a strong wind, and Nick immediately stopped looking. He liked his women curvy.

Besides, he noticed the purple and yellow flowers were very carefully spaced. He didn't trust people who measured things. Control freak, he thought, as Daniel stepped out of the car and greeted the Twig, who could only be Dr. Kincaid.

She pulled off her garden gloves to shake Daniel's hand. Daniel indicated Nick, and Bree smiled politely. She headed into her house, talking back at Daniel over her shoulder as she went.

Daniel leaned down, smiled through the window at Nick, who narrowed his eyes. It wasn't every day that a woman looked through him as if he weren't there. Daniel followed Bree into her house. Nick got out of Daniel's car and trailed them both. Dr. Kincaid didn't even glance at Nick as he joined them in her foyer; she was intensely focused on Daniel.

She offered them something to drink, and Daniel politely declined for both of them. The botanist excused herself to get paperwork for Daniel, and Nick looked around the spacious house while they waited. Lots of hardwood floors. A little too girlie with yellow walls, but at least there weren't lots of knickknacks. He noticed the dramatic photo of a flower in the hallway, and a table with lots of framed photos sat in the foyer. Still, the house wasn't slickly decorated; it had the feeling of being lived in rather than for show.

The Twig came back from the kitchen with a bottle of water and several pieces of paper.

She handed Daniel the papers. "Megan Harper had a poison in her body."

Daniel skimmed the information. "These numbers don't mean much to me."

"Here, let me explain. These represent the composition of the substance in Megan's body." She shared that the substance most likely came from the manchineel tree. "It's a species of flowering plant. It's one of the deadliest trees in the world. All parts of the tree contain strong toxins. Its sap is so lethal that if you are standing beneath one of the trees during the rain and even a small drop of rain with the milky substance in it touches your skin, your skin will blister."

"So why not wipe it out, if it's that lethal?" Nick asked.

She turned to him. "Surprisingly, when it's dried out, it's good lumber." She refocused on Daniel. "The fruit is pleasantly sweet at first, then the person gets a strange peppery feeling with a burning, tearing sensation and tightness of the throat until the person can barely swallow. Then the throat closes up." She put her hands on her hips. "I suspect this is what happened to Megan. It was probably added to her meal, and she didn't realize she'd ingested until it was too late."

Daniel came back with a question of his own. "Where does it grow?"

"Well, there are some in the very southern tip of Florida, but mostly Central and South America." Bree rushed on. "Did you know she had a boyfriend? A mysterious guy that no one seems to know about?"

Nick thought it was to Daniel's credit that he simply nodded.

"Come on, detective. This young woman has no history of drugs. This guy inserts himself into her life. She dies from a poison primarily found in countries with drug cartels. Don't you think this is suspicious?"

How often had Daniel had shared stories of citizens who thought they had a crime figured out, only to screw up the case? Nick could tell this Dr. Kincaid thought she had all the answers. He paid little attention as the Twig began talking very passionately at Daniel, who was listening in that quiet respectful way that made him such a good cop.

Nick looked at the photos sitting on the table in the foyer. They were all of smiling people. Several different generations of the same family. A few of the photos had been snapped at some intimate moments when couples were sharing a bite at some fancy dress event or when a child was on a bike. It was obvious that this was all the same family in some way—and that it was a happy family.

Nick didn't have any pictures of his family. Everything he had left this God-forsaken city for came rushing back at him. All the anger and anguish of his childhood erupted, and the unloved child found the only outlet for it he could— someone who'd had everything he didn't—the Twig.

Daniel's cell phone rang. He answered it, then indicated the call was his department. He excused himself, then stepped outside.

◆

Bree smiled politely at Detective Cusumano's friend. What

had the detective said his name was? Nick. Nick Mancini.

She sized him up while he eyed her. As a scientist, she recognized a superior specimen when she saw one. She had no doubt that he knew exactly how he looked—a dash of innocence, a drop of mystery, and a liberal dose of sex. This Nick Mancini was tall, broad shouldered, but a little thin. She doubted many women noticed; they probably wouldn't get past his face. She grudgingly admitted to herself that he was drop-dead handsome. His large brown eyes gave away his cockiness. Mitch had had that look. At the time, she thought it was appealing. Sadly, she was wiser now. Still, her mother had raised a well-mannered daughter.

"I really appreciate you all coming by. I take it from your red shirts you're headed to the Cardinals game. Big fan?" Bree said, in an effort to get some conversation going. "They're off to a rocky start."

He shrugged. "No, not a big fan," he said finally. "Daniel is."

"Oh." Bree groped for something to discuss and fell back on the old stand-by. "Are you sure I can't get you anything?"

He looked her up and down and said, "No thanks."

Bree's eyes widened when she caught his insinuation. "You don't know what I have to offer," she said evenly.

He stepped closer, but she didn't step back, though he crowded her a little. Bree had to stop herself from rolling her eyes. Like she hadn't been dealing with tall bullies since the first grade. She stared defiantly into Nick Mancini's eyes.

Bree would love to put this man in his place, but he was a friend of Detective Cusumano's. She needed the detective's help. She would not—*would not*—tell this man to go to hell. She felt both sorry for and angry at this man who obviously had no manners.

"So, you plant flowers for a living?" he asked.

She counted to three. "Actually, that's a horticulturalist. I'm a botanist. I study the molecular and chemical make-up of plants."

Nick shrugged again. "Not good at science," he explained.

She just bet that he wanted her to ask what he was good at, and she wouldn't give him the satisfaction.

"Well, there is a lot of Latin," she conceded.

"Yeah, those five and six syllable words are so tough."

She heard the sarcasm again. Still, Bree clung to her politeness.

"And what do you do, Nick?"

"I'm a journalist. I try to stick with one and two syllable words, though. Makes life much easier."

Snake. Slime ball. Those were the one- and two-syllable words that came to Bree's mind, but she smiled pertly. Her sister had told her repeatedly that a woman could never go wrong with a smile. Surely, the detective would come back any minute. She tried to think of some excuse she could give to escape the hallway until he came back.

Instead, Nick spoke up. "Daniel said you live here with your parents."

He said it with such a sneer that she felt defensive, as if she were a wallflower who *had* to live with her parents. He knew nothing about what her family had gone through in the last year. She tamped down a tart reply when Nick moved away to peer at one of her mother's photos—a close-up of a dahlia. She had captured a new blossom, off center, with a lushness that usually stole everyone's breath.

"Sensual photography," Nick said.

Bree frowned.

"Looks like a photographic version of Georgia O'Keeffe," he said, moving into the living room to stand in front of another shot of her mother's—this one of a tulip.

Bree saw only the beauty of the flowers, not the overt sensuality that this man saw. Then again, this man probably saw sex everywhere. Had probably *had* sex everywhere.

"I can see how someone could become fascinated by the curves and the twists of their petals. It's actually very erotic. A woman who obviously knows a lot about sexuality and men."

That was it! He could malign her all he wanted, but when he started to take digs at her mother, she took off the white gloves of a good girl. Her mother had raised her to be respectful, but smart ass men who were so inconsiderate, they didn't deserve her politeness.

"The only man my mother knew was my father," she snapped, with her hands on her hips. "And not every son of a bitch recognizes beauty when he sees it."

Bree was furious with this stranger—both because he'd made her lose her temper and because he was dishonoring her mother in her own house! Strangely, though, she felt marvelous, empowered by the righteousness of the good, the just, and the short. She would never see this guy again so why hold back her anger? She started to tell Nick Mancini about her mother when Daniel stepped back into the house.

"Trouble?" Nick asked.

Daniel nodded. "A seven-year old has been shot. It's the third time a child has been shot in two weeks in this neighborhood. The kids may be being targeted."

Bree could see that the detective was disturbed by the news, and felt a moment of panic. As sorry as she was about the children, she needed to keep him focused on Megan. Bree glared at Nick as if this were all his fault, before she turned to concentrate on Detective Cusumano.

"You don't think it's a bit odd, Detective, that this guy, whom Megan loved, hasn't surfaced at all? Don't you think he would have gone by her apartment—a new place she got when she started going out with him, by the way. It's not a leap to think he'd have a key. Why hasn't he called my office or her friends looking for her? Why hasn't he reported her missing?"

She could see the detective swirling her questions around.

"Maybe they broke up before the accident," Daniel offered.

"And then Megan just happens to die of what looks like a drug overdose? From a really unusual drug? How tidy," Bree said tartly. "I think the boyfriend is involved."

Daniel remained unruffled. "There may be other circumstances of which you aren't aware, Dr. Kincaid."

"Like what?"

"I'm sorry. I can't share details of the case."

"I just did you a favor, Detective."

"If Megan Harper had wanted you to know, she would have told you, Dr. Kincaid. She didn't so I'm going to respect a dead young woman."

Bree clenched her fists, closed her eyes, and pursed her lips. Opening her eyes, she asked. "Was she dying?" Her eyes widened. "Oh my God. You don't think she intentionally took the drug to end her own life, do you?"

"Dr. Kincaid, I have no idea why she had the drug in her system. There could be many reasons, but I'm not at liberty to share more with you since you aren't family."

"I'll get the family's permission. Wait, let me get the text from her sister, Molly, showing she wanted me to clear out Megan's apartment. That's proof that the family wants me involved."

Nick snorted, and Bree glared at him.

"Come on, Detective. I just did you a favor. I need a small one in return. Her old roommate said they met in the Central West End. Couldn't you visit a few of the bars in the area to see if anyone remembers seeing Megan with a guy? I'll help. I'll get you a picture of Megan. I can even go around to a couple of the bars."

"That's not a good idea, Dr. Kincaid. We don't know who this guy is. And there's no proof he was involved, or if there's anything further to this. Please leave it to the police." Bree started to protest, but he cut her off. "Here's what I can do for you. Send the text from Megan's sister to my number. I'll get you Megan's death certificate. I'll check with utility companies to get a verified address for Megan.

Get something in writing and notarized from her sister, and then you should be able to show proof to the landlord that you have permission to enter the apartment."

Daniel edged towards the door.

Bree realized he was not going to help any further as she followed the two men out to the car. Frustration and anger swirled in the pit of her stomach, but she bit her tongue to prevent her from getting into a quarrel with the detective. Not good politics.

"Nice petunias," Nick said as they climbed in the car.

"Pansies" she muttered as she watched them buckled up and start the car. "It's too early for petunias."

Bree went back in the house, and took great satisfaction slamming the door for all she was worth. God, people were so warped these days. She was just grateful that she'd never have to see Nick Mancini again!

Chapter Five

B REE STOOD WITH HER HAND on the door handle to
Megan's loft, which *was* the one she had discovered last
weekend. She looked over at the woman who handled leasing and building maintenance. The woman hovered, though
Bree wasn't sure if it was because she was distressed after
learning about Megan, or still uncertain about Bree because
she wasn't a relative, or because she was just nosy.

"Do you want me to go in with you?" the woman asked.

"I appreciate your help, Deborah, but I'll be okay."

Detective Cusumano had kept his word, and had expe-
dited paperwork so Bree had a death certificate, with
Megan's death ruled an accident. He'd even called the owners of the complex to pave the way for her. His efforts,
plus notarized letters from Molly giving her the authority to
act on the family's behalf, covered enough legalities so she
could at least get into Megan's place tonight.

"This must be difficult," Deborah said. "I also think it's
so kind of you to take care of all the utility bills and other
expenses."

"Thank you. It's the least I can do for the family at this
time. And you've been such a big help too. You have all the
paperwork you need for your records, right?"

Take the hint, Bree thought.

But no. This was a chatty woman.

"Megan was such a sweetheart. Always happy to spend a
few minutes talking. She was such a good listener too."

"Yes, you mentioned that. Well, I don't want to keep you.
I know it's about time for you to head home. I'm sure I'm
going to be several hours tonight, but I will let you know

what I line up over the next few days. As I said, the family wants everything out by the end of the month."

"I wish there was a way I could help more."

Where's an introvert when you need her, Bree thought. She brightened. "I just thought of something you could do. I noticed Megan's mailbox is full. Would you be so kind to retrieve the mail and keep it in your office until the next time I'm here?"

"Of course." The woman finally moved down the hall towards the elevator.

"Thank you so much. I really appreciate it."

When Bree heard the elevator ping, she gave the woman a small wave and watched as she mercifully disappeared. Bree turned back to the door.

When, exactly, was the right time to box up a life?

Apparently when you rented, it was by the end of the month.

At least with her mother, Bree had had time to take her grief out in slivers, analyze it, weep over it, and let it go. But when she opened Megan's door, grief would barrel down on her like a herd of stampeding elephants. She braced herself. Best to get it over with, she resolved.

What she wasn't prepared for, though, when she opened the door was that the loft looked like Megan had just left. Of course, she had expected to come home that night. As Bree walked through the narrow room with several large windows, she noticed a sweatshirt draped over the couch, and a mug sat in the sink.

Rachel Kincaid's illness had kept her bedbound towards the end so her life had become tidier and smaller. And upon her death, there had been closure with a service, a celebration of her life.

There was nothing tidy about Megan's death. No closure either since her body had been shipped back to Pittsburgh.

The loft was shabbier than Bree had expected. It looked like that of a grad student who was paying school tuition and working. Clearly, Megan's boyfriend had not provided lavish gifts.

Bree moved towards the kitchenette to search for trash bags. She would arrange for a junk removal company to haul away the big pieces this coming weekend. Clothes and books and dishes she would pack up and donate. At least tonight, she could throw away papers, toothbrush, and cosmetics. Clearly, she was going to spend the entire weekend here.

Bree started in the bathroom. Only one toothbrush, no guy stuff. So he hadn't lived here or spent the night occasionally? Again, not what she expected, given what Megan's former roommate had described. She shoved all the items into the bag.

She headed up to the loft, where she went through Megan's bureau drawers. Her bras and panties were in disarray, scrunched into piles. Huh, Megan had been so organized at work. This was a side of her grad student Bree had never imagined. She threw all the items into the trash bag, and then moved on to the night stand next to the unmade bed. She threw the Rubik's cube and the Disney princess figurine in the trash. Again, the drawer was a jumbled mess, and a corner of the bedsheet was off the mattress.

Bree stopped, turned around, and surveyed the space again. Too many things were wrong. A picture of the Garden wasn't straight. She glanced back down on the main living space. There were a few books lying haphazardly on the floor, and not on the book shelves. And so far, she hadn't found a single piece of paper. No bills, no old mail.

More importantly, there was no laptop or tablet. No twenty-something student would be without one. Had it been in Megan's car when it crashed? Would Daniel Cusumano have it or would it be listed among her belongings?

Had the neighbor lied? Did he have a key? Had he mentioned Megan's death to Deborah who'd gone snooping when she'd heard the news? After all, Bree wouldn't know if anything was missing.

Or was it the mysterious boyfriend? Had he learned of Megan's death and retrieved his things? If he was going to remove items, why not the television, things that could be sold? Or maybe, just maybe, he had come looking for something incriminating about himself. Then again, there was nothing to indicate that a guy had ever been here.

Deborah had already confirmed that Megan's name was the only one on the rental agreement. What if there was no guy? What if Megan had made him up as an excuse to move out from her old place? Or what if she'd created him simply to save face, so she didn't look lonely and alone?

Bree shook her head, as if that would stop her jumble of thoughts. She needed to focus on the task at hand. She moved back down to the main level. Not surprisingly, Megan had lots of common plants—spider and snake plants, ivy—on the window sills. She also had herbs growing. Had she liked to cook? Bree wasn't sure. She and Megan had not spent much time sharing personal lives. Perhaps because of the Molly connection they felt they hadn't needed to.

The house plants were in good shape. Bree would see if any tenants wanted them because she couldn't bear to throw away a plant. The herbs were another matter. They had not fared so well without water for the almost two weeks since Megan's death.

There was a pretty ceramic blue and white pot that Bree liked. Perhaps she would take it back to her office at the Garden and pot something in it in honor of Megan. When she lifted the pot from the saucer, though, she found a piece of paper. On it was written: Clue #1—Amazing! Where had she recently heard that?

Bree turned over the paper and gasped. It was a sonogram. She recognized Megan's handwriting with the date, which was four weeks before she died. Oh God, had Megan been pregnant? Bree leaned against the window. Oh God. She slid to the floor, and gulped air.

Suddenly, her losses were too much to bear. She would never see her mother or Magen again. Never. Mitch would never be part of her life. She would never again have that wonderful sense of love and purpose that she found in marriage. She swiped at tears sliding down her face.

Alone, Bree could admit to herself that it hurt to think about Megan's baby. Bree felt small and mean for such thoughts. She and Mitch had been trying for a baby when Mitch broke the news that he was leaving her. She cringed now when she thought about how often she'd talked about a baby and how they would have to change their live—when the change Mitch had in mind was a twenty-eight-year old. She'd love to be able to scornfully tell her friends that he left her for a bimbo, but he'd left a PhD for an MD—with a bigger trust fund.

Every time she thought about Mitch, she hurt. Would the memories, the feeling of failure never go away? How could it still hurt so damn much after two years? Getting divorced had taught her survival skills that working in jungles never had; skills that she'd never thought she'd need.

Bleakness seeped into her soul, and Bree felt tears sliding down her cheek. She cried harder. After several minutes, exhausted and drained, her natural sense of order and control reasserted itself. She stood and wiped away the salty tears. She couldn't save her mother, but she'd honored her. She couldn't save Megan, but she could honor her. And her unborn child.

Where was this man, the father of her baby who had gotten her pregnant and then disappeared? If he had cared about her, he would have surfaced by now. Maybe he had been relieved at her death, if he hadn't been thrilled by the idea of her pregnancy. Death had taken care of his dilemma.

Bree frowned. Or maybe this guy had taken care of the dilemma himself.

The poison.

What if he had drugged Megan and was responsible for her death?

Chapter Six

NICK FOUND A SPOT AT the bar of a Central West End night spot, and scanned the place. He was bored and restless. With Daniel working around-the-clock on the case of the murdered children, Nick had spent the past ten days catching up on his sleep, watching television, and eating the meals that Daniel's mother and sisters kept dropping off. He needed *something*. After his time reporting in the Middle East, everything now seemed too small, too trivial.

He thought about leaving in the next few days for his sister's place in New York City. Unfortunately, he'd partied too hard in Europe on his way back to the States, and had had to sell his laptop in Atlanta to get enough for the final leg of his airfare into St. Louis. He needed to pick up some quick cash to pay for another plane ticket to New York, and he refused to impose further on Daniel. Writing for a mainstream newspaper like the *Post-Dispatch* wasn't an option. Been there, done that, and there probably was still one pissed editor of a major newspaper in Miami with a grudge. He could make some calls. He'd written pieces for *GQ* and *Maxim* but freelancing meant months before he'd see any money. He still had his writing chops. Words always came easy, even when nothing else did. He consoled himself with the thought that being here was only temporary; just until he could figure out what to do next.

He turned to order a Scotch, and felt the tenderness in his ribs. They only hurt occasionally now, but with every stab of pain, he thought of Luciana and how he'd underestimated her. The Spanish bitch had gotten her revenge when he tried to leave her. She'd told her husband about their affair, and he'd had his thugs beat Nick.

The bartender brought his drink, and Nick started running a tab. Out of the corner of his eye, he caught a swish of purple, turned, then broke into a slow smile. *The Twig.* He had enjoyed sparring with Dr. Kincaid that Saturday. Surprisingly, it had put him in a good mood. But she was dressed all wrong for this bar. The purple dress looked like something she would wear for a job interview. Clearly, she'd put no effort into her hair, and her face looked like she hadn't bothered with make-up.

He watched a guy slide in the booth, across from her. Nick mentally shrugged. Not the kind of guy he would have expected her to be interested in. Something about his face looked too Neanderthal for The Twig. No accounting for taste.

He turned back toward the bar, nursing his Scotch. Nick smiled at a redhead who smiled back. He found women more eager when they had to work to get him. His smile turned wolfish. Toying with the Twig would be a perfect way to kill time until he and the redhead decided to approach each other. As he made his way toward Dr. Kincaid's booth, he saw her frown at the guy. As he drew closer he heard her saying, "It's been nice meeting you, Brandon, but I'm expecting my friend any minute."

Up close, Brandon's eyes were glassy, and he slurred a line so badly, Nick winced. Still, the guy made no move to leave.

Nick slid into the booth next to the Twig, and put his arm around her. "Hello, darling. Sorry, I'm late."

She started to pull away, but Nick tightened his grip on her shoulders.

Nick suppressed a smile. He could see the wheels turning in Brianna Kincaid's overly intelligent, rigid mind. She'd have to choose between him and the drunk. She glared at him, but finally muttered, "I was getting worried about you. I'm so glad you made it."

Turning back to Brandon, she said, "I'm so sorry, but

Nicky and I have a dinner reservation. We need to leave. Now."

As they slid out the booth, Bree pulled out two twenty-dollar bills and gave them to Nick. "Will you take care of the bill for my drinks?"

Once again, Nick was both a little surprised and annoyed she didn't react like most women. There was absolutely no interest in her eyes when she looked at him, no acknowledgment of him as a man at all. Jesus, even eighty-year-old women responded to him with a twinkle in their eye, and a wishful sigh to be fifty years younger. He'd bet that the only way to get a reaction out of Dr. Kincaid was if he were green and had chlorophyll running through his veins. And her eyes were icy as if she was judging him and found him lacking. Maybe she wasn't interested because she had been this Megan's lesbian lover.

He headed back to the bar to pay both their tabs, then pocketed Bree's change. She was gone by the time he finished. Flashing a smile of promise at the redhead, Nick stepped outside.

"You're welcome," he said as he walked up and stood next to her on the sidewalk.

"I could have gotten rid of him."

"I don't doubt it," Nick muttered.

Bree flashed a tight smile. Nick realized no matter how those beautiful violet eyes might spark, she was not going to rise to his taunts. Much to his own surprise, he wasn't going to let it go.

"Hey, I meant it as a compliment."

She snorted.

"I'm surprised to see you here, Dr. Kincaid."

All he got was a noncommittal 'hmmm'.

"If you want to be a player, your technique needs some work. I can give you a few suggestions to attract the right kind of guy," he offered.

"What makes you think I'm not looking for the wrong

kind of guy?" she said too sweetly.

She caught him by surprise—both at the thought that she could be with a player, and that she had such a good comeback. He couldn't help it. He laughed. "Tell me you weren't president of the student council in high school. Tell me that you've ever been so drunk that you can't remember what you did when you woke up the next morning."

She opened her mouth, snapped it shut, then looked down the street again.

"We both know you're not the bar type, Dr. Kincaid."

"You're so good with quick judgments, *Nicky*. It's a wonder a brilliant observer of mankind like you isn't a millionaire."

"All different kinds of brilliance, *Brianna*."

"Well, don't let me up more of your time," she said as she turned right and started walking down the street. "Feel free to go back inside and find a conquest," she said over her shoulder.

He looked back at the club they'd just left. There was that redhead. He glanced back down the street. Huh, the Twig was walking into a pub. He couldn't picture her in a pub. Seemed a little rowdy for a blueblood. Certainly, there were easier ways to hook up than trekking from club to club. Unless she was looking for a particular kind of guy. Who knew? Maybe he was entirely wrong about Brianna Kincaid. Maybe she liked things rough.

Nick strolled down the street and entered the pub. Maybe she liked college-aged boys because the crowd seemed young. He spotted her purple dress. She was sitting at the bar, watching. No flirtatious smile. No running her hand through her hair or looking like she was enjoying the loud music. She'd ordered white wine, but didn't take a sip. Who ordered wine in a pub that was all about craft beers? Didn't she know that you always ordered what everyone else was having so you blended in?

He started toward her, but then some puppy of a guy approached her. She smiled sweetly and bought him a beer.

She certainly was free with her money. Nick moved to the edge of the bar where he ordered a beer too, and watched as the guy's friends flocked around her once they realized she was buying. She leaned into several of the guys, talking with them, but from the serious expression on her face, it looked more like she was cross-examining them than coming on to them.

They must have been several beers ahead of her, though, because one or two started crowding her, leaning their elbows against the bar, and whispering in her ear. Nick saw a flicker of uncertainty when she realized she was hemmed in, then she spoke to them again and they scattered. She'd probably threatened to call their mothers. Bree gathered her purse and headed for the door.

He followed, curious now to see what she was up to. This time, she went into an upscale restaurant, where she parked herself at the bar that was deserted except for her. He hung back, telling the hostess he was waiting for a friend as he watched Bree order white wine again. She chatted up the female bartender. After a few minutes, the bartender moved away to approach two couples who walked in. Bree sat there primly, studying the diners with an intensity that made him think she was analyzing the place for a research paper.

Then he recognized what she was doing. She wasn't looking for a particular kind of guy. She was looking for *the* guy. He remembered only bits of the conversation from the day they'd stopped by her home, but she'd been adamant about Daniel trying to find some guy. After about fifteen minutes, she left cash, gathered her purse, and then headed outside.

He followed her, though she gave no indication she knew. Surprisingly, she headed back to the first nightclub, where she fished a ticket out of her purse and handed it to the valet.

"You're doing what you wanted Daniel to do," he said as he walked up beside her.

"Are you stalking me?"

"How 'bout I call Daniel, and you can tell him you're trying to get leads on the guy who you think was with your student."

"Don't be silly," she said dismissively.

Nick studied Bree. Those violet eyes were beautiful, but serious—the kind that spoke of hard work and too much thinking. She was fixated with this woman's death. Obsessed people were best in small doses, but Nick recognized an opportunity when it sprang at him. Brianna Kincaid would probably pay nicely if he could turn up information for her. Or maybe he could interest a news outlet in a story, if there was one here. He could imagine the public relations frenzy if the venerable Missouri Botanical Garden was involved in drugs or messy affairs. After all, he had plenty of time, and not much of anything else to do.

The valet pulled up in a silver BMW.

"Have a nice life, Nicky."

Nick started to grab her elbow and then thought better of it. She probably was a black belt in something. "Look, we could work together on this," he said across her roof as she moved to the driver's door and gave a tip to the valet. "I could help you."

He was both bemused and irritated when she looked horrified for a second before she gained control of her emotions. As if she'd found a killer bug in her precious purple and yellow flowers.

"Think about it. Daniel would be much more likely to loosen up with me than you. And did I mention I'm an award-winning journalist? Flashing my press pass gets me into places that a botanist isn't going to be able to go. And let's not forget some people will be more willing to talk with a guy. There. That's three good reasons."

He watched her worry her lower lip. She was so uptight; he didn't want to notice that she had nice lips, full and well-shaped.

"Why?" Bree asked.

"What?"

"Why do you want to help me? You didn't even know Megan."

This was why he didn't like smart women. All the questions. All the talking and analyzing.

"If you're right, an innocent young woman has a family that's hurting," said Nick. "If this guy she was involved with had anything to do with her death, he should be brought to justice. He shouldn't get away with this."

He could see that he'd said the right words if only because Brianna Kincaid looked slightly confused. He loved to bait sincere people. They were so easy. She'd been so sure he was a useless devil. But he knew how to talk to these do-gooders. After all, a devil like him knew that the road to hell was paved with their good intentions.

"Would you like to go someplace quiet and talk?" he asked.

"Your interest is noble," she said sarcastically. "Thank you, but good night."

Why the hell was he doing this to himself? Why put up with this irritating woman? He wasn't that bored. But Nick Mancini hadn't lived by his wits by giving up so easily so he turned on his charm.

"It's obvious that we're very different, Dr. Kincaid. We probably have nothing in common, but that could be really effective. We have different skills. We could make a great team. And together we could make a difference in this case. You seem determined to not let this young woman be forgotten, and that's rare anymore."

Overachievers loved words like 'effective', 'skills' and 'team'. Brianna Kincaid probably kept 'to do' lists under her pillow. And his words made her feel like what she was doing was right.

Come on, Twig. Take a chance.

She searched his face. He worked hard to look earnest.

"I can help you find this guy who did bad by a good girl."

He opened the passenger side of her car. "There's a Star-bucks just a few blocks away on Euclid. We can talk there."

"How 'bout if you follow me in your car?"

"A cop introduced us. How bad can I be?"

"You don't really want me to answer that, do you?"

He had to fight a smile as he pulled out his cell phone. "Call Daniel. He'll vouch for me."

With a sigh, she turned around, gave her keys back to the valet. "We'll walk."

◆

Starbucks was packed on Thursday night; the Central West End drew students studying for tomorrow's exam. Bree watched Nick flirt with the girl making their coffees as she snagged two chairs for them. She narrowed her eyes when the girl waved away his wallet.

He'd looked sincere when he spoke about Megan, but she'd just bet he could conjure sincerity as easily as the sun came up every morning. Tonight, he was charming. That Saturday, he'd been sarcastic and prickly. She wondered if cops could have con artists as friends. She couldn't figure out the friendship. Daniel Cusumano was so professional and polite, even when he was blowing her off. Nick seemed like such a lightweight in comparison.

His sudden appearance had bounced her evening from bad to worse. First, she discovered she didn't own one sexy thing in her wardrobe as she'd tried to find an enticing outfit to wear tonight. Most of her professional attire was casual pants, tops and athletic shoes. The best she could do was this purple silk dress, which wouldn't entice anyone unless he was roaring drunk. Which apparently was what that first bar had specialized in. It was only a little after ten when Nick appeared, and Brandon had been the second drunk to try to pick her up. She knew after just a few minutes that he didn't know Megan Harper either. Then to top it all off, Satan had slithered in next to her. Just as he was doing again when he sat a cup of coffee in front of her.

A steady hum of voices filled the room so she had to lean in a little to be heard, and frowned when she smelled his cologne. Of course, he would smell great—a subtle spicy cologne that a woman would only discover if she got close enough. Bree shoved the thought out of her mind so violently that she flinched. So she didn't look like a fool, she leaned back and pulled a photo out of her purse.

"This was Megan."

To a man like Nick, Megan probably appeared plain. Her face had been too round, not a cheek bone to be seen while her eyes and mouth had been too small. No doubt Nick had dated his share of models, and Megan's face did not have the balance and symmetry of a beautiful woman. Bree felt the need to make him understand why she had been special.

"She was a very kind, gentle person. Very sweet. She never trashed anyone else, and she was always willing to help on a tight deadline."

She expected to see derision in Nick's eyes, but he sat patiently, giving her a chance to go on.

"She was incredibly bright. I've worked with a lot of students, and Megan had the potential to grow into a fantastic scientist. She just needed more time."

Bree stared into her coffee, thinking of everything lost with Megan's death. She looked up and gave Nick a small sad smile.

"I'm really not surprised that she got mixed up with the wrong guy. She chased love the way a toddler chased a bird—always with great certainty that it could be caught and always coming away empty-handed. I mean I understood it. Once you knew her dad had died when she was little, it was easy to figure out that she was overcompensating. Megan seemed almost desperate for male attention. And so she kept making bad choices."

"So she would have been a perfect mark for some guy who recognized a vulnerable young woman."

A guy just like you, Bree thought fleetingly, and then realized that Nick Mancini might be the perfect person to find this mysterious lover.

"I don't think Megan did drugs. At least not until she met this guy. She was very reliable at work." She took a sip of coffee. "One more thing. She was pregnant when she died."

She explained her arrangement with Molly Harper, and discovering the sonogram in the apartment.

"You keep turning up information on this Megan. So how do I know that you aren't involved in this thing?" he said. "Maybe you were the one smuggling something, she found out, and you killed her."

Bree recoiled as if he'd slapped her hard.

"You should never play poker," Nick advised. "Everything shows on your face."

"I happen to be an outstanding negotiator," she snapped. "I deal with foreign bureaucrats all the time."

"Oh, yeah. I can tell that you're a real tough ass. Let me just take a guess here. Elite high school. Probably class valedictorian. You have a big house, and you've got a picture of you and Obama sitting on a table in the foyer of the big house. I bet you've also got a box, maybe a room, of trophies for debate."

"The trophies were for cross country. State champ two years in a row," she added.

He leaned back. "For the record, I don't think you had anything to do with it. I suspect, Dr. Kincaid, if you planned this woman's death that you wouldn't leave any trail."

Bree wasn't quite sure if she should take that as a compliment.

"But it's pretty easy to be noble when you've got so much to fall back on if things don't go your way."

"I have nothing to gain from this. I'm not doing this for me. I'm doing it for Megan and her sister, Molly." She explained her connection to Megan's family.

"First thing we need to do is to get the police report,"

Nick said.

"You think the detective will give it to you? Us?"

"Press, remember? You let me worry about that part. I know how to work the system."

Bells clanged loudly in her head. "I don't want to do anything that will lead to me wearing an orange prison uniform."

"No confidence in my skills, doc?"

"Exactly what would those skills be?"

"I can be very persuasive. After all, you're here with me, right? And admit it. You never thought that would happen."

Her eyes narrowed. She wanted to snap at him for being right, but his smile was so disarming that her anger softened. "Fair enough. Just promise me you won't do anything illegal."

"Absolutely."

He agreed so quickly she checked his hands. No fingers crossed. She checked under the table. His feet weren't crossed.

"What are you—" He cocked his head. "You don't believe me."

"I think charm has its limits."

"So what would you do? Ask Daniel straight out to give you a piece of possible evidence, and you think he's just going to do it?"

"I think he would listen to reason. I find most people can be convinced if you present a good case."

"Really? This works for you?"

"Of course. If you ask any of my co-workers, they'd say that I can make a very persuasive case. I've changed their minds about budgets. I've advocated to put the Garden's energies into this project or that."

"So you think that will get the truth about Megan?"

She put her hands on the table and leaned forward and mimicked him. "Absolutely."

He settled back in his seat. "Well, how about if we pit

my charm and people skills against your superior brain and cool thinking? First one to find out something significant buys the next dinner."

"You're on."

He flashed a cocky smile. She fired back a confident one.

"We need to get that report," he said.

Chapter Seven

NICK WAS LEANING AGAINST THE BMW in the Garden's employee parking lot with a nonchalance so studied it almost made Bree laugh and forget her irritation with him. He'd probably practiced that pose from the time he was twelve or thirteen, she thought. Begrudgingly, she had to admit he did look hot with those long legs encased in jeans that fit very, very well. He had on a faded army green T-shirt that set off his brown hair and those warm chocolate eyes.

She saw two secretaries—moms in their mid-thirties—hurrying through the parking lot to get home. He smiled as they approached, and they slowed. He looked past them to watch Bree so he didn't see them glance back as they continued to their cars.

Bree shook her head. Would her sex never learn?

"You don't even know what I'm going to say yet, doc. So how can you say 'no'?"

"Sorry, I was thinking about something from work," she lied.

New personality, she thought. No sarcasm, no toying with her. No, today it appeared that she was with a good ole boy.

She was a little irritated he had just showed up four days after their meeting in Starbucks, like she had nothing better to do than wait for his appearance. She would not . . . she *would* not. . . let him bring out her waspishness again. She didn't think of herself as a bitch. She'd admit to a certain intensity at times. Normally, she wasn't easily ruffled—until she'd met Nick Mancini.

Or maybe she was angry at herself because Daniel Cusumano hadn't returned any of the three calls she'd left in the last few days, proving the point Nick had made.

He held up a folder. "Let's grab a bite to eat, and we can swap information."

She really did not want to spend more time with this guy than she had to. However, he probably could be as useful as he'd claimed. She'd googled Nick Mancini when she'd gotten home the other night, and discovered numerous articles he'd written. His byline appeared in every warm country with a good beach. Surprisingly, though, his writing was sharp, showing more intelligence than she wanted to give him credit for.

She held out her hand for the folder.

Instead of handing it to her, Nick took her elbow and steered her back the way she'd come. "Let's make two copies. Then we can read it over dinner and discuss some ideas."

Sighing, Bree lead him back to her office. "I'm not even going to ask how you got this."

"Good move. *But* I did get it, so you're buying dinner."

In her office, Bree reached into the little refrigerator she kept stocked for late-night work and pulled out a bottle of water. She offered one to Nick, who shook his head. She reached into her purse to pull out the paper on which she'd scribbled an idea, based on the words she'd found that Megan had stuffed in the back of the picture frame. Bree sipped the water while she walked to the nearest copier to make copies of Nick's report and her idea. When she returned, she handed a set to Nick.

"Let's go eat," he said. "There are some great Thai restaurants around Grand."

Bree started to protest, but Nick again grabbed her elbow, which she yanked away.

"I usually don't have this much trouble getting a woman to go to dinner with me, Bree. I promise, I'll be charming and funny. You'll have a good time."

When she frowned, he said, "Look, I'm going to read

this report totally different than you because I didn't know Megan. You'll find my perspective very helpful."

"You're so smooth with words," she huffed as she retrieved her purse.

They headed out of the building. She didn't say anything when he slid into the front seat of the car. She cruised to her favorite restaurant on Grand, where the hostess greeted her warmly and took her to her usual table, a quiet one in the back. The restaurant had only a few other patrons since it was still early for dinner. She was surprised when Nick ordered in Thai, and ordered the same hot, spicy dish she did. She gave him a questioning look.

"I lived in Thailand for about eighteen months, working for the Associated Press."

"You certainly get around."

Nick shrugged. "I thought for sure you'd go for the Pad Thai."

Ah, there it was. The evening's jab. She ignored it. "Boring, you mean. Actually, eating is one of the things I do best."

"Hmmm, you struck me as more of a carrots and broccoli woman who runs one hundred miles a week to stay so thin."

"Boring—again—and anorexic," said Bree, as she sipped tea. "Nick, you're such a flatterer."

He smiled.

"Actually, I only run fifteen to twenty miles a week," Bree said, "and I have a very high metabolism."

"Not a fan of running," he said. He poured hot tea for each of them. "I hit every bar and restaurant in the Central West End over the last couple of nights. No one ever remembers Megan being a regular. I'll try Clayton area in the next couple of nights."

She was tempted to make a sarcastic comment about how noble it was for him to visit so many bars when she suspected that he felt right at home there. She resisted the urge, then realized he was smiling at her. No, wait, he was laughing at her.

"You're surprised I did it, aren't you?"

"No, no. I—"

———◆———

Nick couldn't help it. She was so easy to tease. "Come on, admit it, Bree. You might even be thinking that I made the whole thing up."

She blushed. "I admire how much time you're putting in."

He watched her try to save face when she was saved when her cell phone went off. "Sorry, I need to take this one. Business call from overseas."

He shouldn't have been surprised when she spoke in French. Of course, she would speak French. She probably spent a year abroad in college. Or maybe she'd had an assignment in a French-speaking country.

What caught his attention was how her voice changed as she talked to the person on the other end, and her face lit up. She wasn't exactly a stunning woman; he'd had more than his share of those, but she was pretty with her delicate features and those large violet eyes. He wondered if it was a guy on the phone because she seemed relaxed and happy. He frowned. She wasn't like that when she was with him. She'd always been so solemn and intense, but here she was smiling into her cell phone. It startled him to think that she might have a boyfriend or maybe even a husband who lived half a world away. She was always so cool and controlled that it hadn't even dawned on him that she might be in a relationship.

When she hung up, Nick tried to sound casual. "Not keeping you from a hot date, am I?"

Just keep it light, he thought. That's all anyone expected of him, and he could play that Nick without a second thought.

She gave him a fleeting smile as she leaned over to pull papers out of her briefcase. "The report."

Apparently, small talk was over. They read, not stopping even when the waiter brought their food. The report itself was short. Megan's car had been heading downtown on Lindell when she crashed into a stoplight. Witnesses who attempted to pull her out of the car found her non-responsive. The autopsy, however, showed little trauma to her head or any of her organs. That's what made the coroner test for other things, turning up the unidentified toxin.

Nick put his copy down, unpackaged his chopsticks, and started in on his food. He looked up to see Bree totally absorbed in the report, and he suspected she was reliving Megan Harper's last few moments, that powerful brain analyzing every word a dozen ways. He reached over and touched her arm. Her head snapped up, and a frown appeared on her face.

"This is good stuff," he said, indicating the food. "You need to eat it while it's warm."

She picked up her chopsticks and started eating.

He flipped the report to the next page that detailed what Megan had in her purse at the time of the accident. Her cell phone and wallet were the only important things. Everything else was junk—a pen, her Garden id, lipstick. No receipts, he noted. That would have narrowed down her movements.

Nick looked up from eating and reading to see that Bree had only eaten a few bites and was absorbed in the report again. He sighed, then reached over with his chopsticks to grab a piece of shrimp from her bowl. That got her attention. She gave him a school teacher look and pointed her chopstick at him.

He indicated the report. "Nothing here that's going to help you find this guy. Best thing we can hope for is that I can get a copy of her phone records. Then I can start calling numbers. Maybe finding this guy is as easy as a phone call."

"There might be another way as well. Megan had scribbled notes on the back of a piece of paper that I found by accident. At first I thought the scribbles were just a bad haiku. But then I found one of the same words scribbled on the back of the sonogram of her baby with the words 'Clue #1.'

She leaned forward. "What if clue number one was the start of some kind of treasure hunt? A scavenger hunt. Megan loved puzzles. What if the guy didn't know about the baby, and Megan was going to break it to him in a clever way? You know, like how they have all these extravagant gender reveal parties."

"Not familiar with gender reveal parties."

"Okay, fine. But I'm telling you this would be something Megan would do. And her notes of all the clues were hidden, just like the sonogram." Bree's eyes were shining as she put down her copy of the report. "I think she planned to have this hunt in the Garden because each clue can be connected to the specialized gardens within the whole Garden. We just have to figure out the clues, and hope something turns up that identifies the boyfriend."

Chapter Eight

"OH, NO PROBLEM," SAID NICK. "Let's see. We just have to dig up, what, one hundred acres?"

"Seventy-nine. But once we figure out her clues, we'll be able to narrow it down. C'mon, think about it. She'd have to make them fairly simple, and choose the most obvious places to hide them if this guy was going to find them."

"Well aren't you the optimist."

Her lips curved in a small smile. "Worse. I'm genetically coded to be an idealist. My parents met in the Peace Corps in the early eighties. I was brought up with the expectation that I would make a difference."

"So you decided to save the world through plants?"

Bree thought she could hear amusement in his voice. She finally put her finger on why she didn't like this guy. It wasn't his insolence that bothered her, but the feeling that he was always laughing at her. She led a life of meaning and accomplishment and here was this . . . this slacker . . . making fun of her.

"Did you know that one quarter of all prescription drugs contain at least one plant derivative? And most people would never guess that one of our projects involves collecting samples of plants for the National Cancer Institute so the NCI can try to isolate cancer-inhibiting materials." She leaned forward. "Plants are not only our food, they're in our fuel, our medicines—we take them for granted or don't realize what would happen to our ecosystem if they start disappearing. Close to half the world's plants are facing extinction. Half. And yet less than one in six has been studied for potential benefits to humans."

She sat back, realizing she'd spoken with the fervor of an evangelist. But he hadn't interrupted her once; he was a better listener than she would have given him credit for. His brown eyes watched her with an attentiveness that made her slightly giddy. She could understand how he would be a good journalist, drawing people out. Or how women could drown in the warmth of those eyes. Stop right there, she ordered herself. She'd proven that she wasn't a good judge of men when she'd fallen for Mitch.

Mitch had had the same quality—the ability to make a woman feel like she was the only woman in the world that he would ever want. The trouble was he never wanted one woman for long. She was never going to fall in love again, she vowed. Nick Mancini was merely a business associate and a short-term one at that.

"Well, I feel better knowing all that," he said.

"You are such a smart ass."

He sighed. "Want me to tell you how I'm really feeling?"

She laughed, and could tell she caught him by surprise. "No thanks. I've had more emotions than I can handle in the last two years. If you share your feelings, then I'll just feel obligated to offer your sympathy, or worse, try to help you."

"Good, then we'll just stick to business," he said.

"Perfect."

"So while you're pontificating, tell me more about the drug in Megan's system. It's one of the few solid leads in this whole mess."

"It's in the poppy family. Like opium. Like I told you and Detective Cusumano, it's found mainly in South America—mostly in Nicaragua. There are several investigators around the world looking at it as a possible treatment for cancer, but I also found a couple of stories on the internet about it hitting both coasts as a party drug. It can be odorless, taste-less—hidden very easily in other chemicals."

"So it's possible that she could have been drugged without knowing it."

Bree nodded. "Which makes it even more important that we find this guy. Because it means her death wasn't an accident. He might have asked her out to dinner that night just so he could kill her. He's a monster."

"You should at least consider they were just trying to get high. Maybe there were two Megans, and you just saw the good one. Maybe Megan got a kick out of fooling you."

"Possibly," she said tersely. She ignored Nick when he moved her entrée to his side of the table and began eating it. No doubt he wanted her to chastise him, and she wouldn't give him the satisfaction.

"Megan's first clue was the most obvious," she continued. "*Amazing.*"

"What's amazing about it?"

"No, no. That was the clue."

Nick looked expectantly at her. "And?"

"Come on. Didn't you come to the Garden when you were in grade school?"

Every elementary school kid in a fifty-mile radius took a field trip to the Garden at least once in life. It was a rite of passage in St. Louis.

"That was twenty-five years ago."

"And what's one of the things the kids always do?"

"No clue."

Very patiently, Bree explained, "They run through the Victorian maze. A-maze-ing. She made it simple. I told you. She'd have to make all the clues simple so this guy could find her whatever little love charms she planned to leave."

His raised eyebrow told her he wasn't convinced. She wanted to prick that skepticism, and she could hear the smugness in her voice when she said, "Of course, charm doesn't go very far in deciphering clues, does it?"

"Well," he drawled, "I'm not going to settle for dinner again when I win."

She wouldn't back down. If anything, her chin went up a

fraction.

"You're so deluded. What do you want to bet?"

"Your BMW for a week."

When Bree laughed at his request, Nick hid his surprise. It was a low, husky laugh that teased a man when such a little slip of a woman was made for giggles. He tried to picture Brianna Kincaid giggling.

"Oh, yeah, I'm going to give you a fifty-thousand dollar car when I barely know you. What's your second offer, Mancini?"

He started to bait her with the suggestion of a night in bed, but instinctively knew she'd turn puritan. Problem was he couldn't think of anything else that didn't involve sex or money.

"While you're thinking, let me tell you what I want." Bree leaned in. "I want you to get me one hour with Daniel Cusumano. I don't care if it's at two in the morning."

"You're a little barracuda, aren't you?"

She amused him because her delicate looks were so incongruent with her relentlessness.

She waved her hand dismissively. "Comes with being the daughter of Scottie Kincaid. Not having spent ten minutes in the orbit of my father, you wouldn't know that he's larger than life. Thankfully, my mother was very grounded."

For almost thirty years, Nick had worked hard to pretend he'd never had a mother. He couldn't even remember what Elena looked like now. All he remembered was that she had been beautiful, and that's what had allowed her to abandon him and Tory. He remembered the smell of her perfume, though, even if he couldn't remember her face. Just like he would never be able to forget his father's recliner, even though he couldn't remember his father's face any more either.

Bree looked at her watch. "You know, we can go back to

the Garden and walk through the maze. We've probably got thirty minutes before it gets too dark."

Nick countered. "You've hardly eaten. We've barely talked about the report or a plan. Why don't we look for clues tomorrow night? It's a long shot with no certainty."

"You can box up your meal and eat it later tonight." She gestured to their waiter as Nick picked up his chopsticks and began eating slowly. Bree frowned.

"Give me your phone and let me type in my cell phone number. Text me the clues. I'll call you tomorrow, and you can tell me what you found," he said.

"This is your idea of teamwork?"

"If it was teamwork, we'd be making a decision together, Bree, not you making it for me. And I suspect neither one of us is really a good team player to begin with."

"So what's your plan?" she snapped.

"I'm going to do some solid background work. I'll check to see if I can find her obstetrician. I'm going to get a list of the phone numbers she called. For all we know, he's in her list of contacts. Any of this is easier than traipsing through a bunch of big green bushes."

Bree took a deep breath as she pulled her wallet out of her purse, then threw a couple of twenties on the table. "I'll go traipsing." She leaned down and looked him hard in the eyes. "And when I find the next clue, I'm going to up the ante, Mancini."

"Promises, promises," he said coolly, never breaking her gaze.

Her smile was wintery. Never looking back, she walked out of the restaurant.

Nick signaled the waiter and ordered a popular beer from China.

———◆———

When Bree arrived in the entrance of the maze, the May sun was beginning to set, splitting the sky into stunning streaks of purple and orange. Until Memorial Day, the Garden was closed to visitors at this time of night, but the guards were used to staff coming and going. She stared at the seven-foot high columns of yews that formed the maze, a garden element popular during Victorian times. The maze adjoined the herb garden behind the house of Garden founder, Henry Shaw, a transplanted Englishman.

Could Megan have stashed her next clue in one of the yews? Buried it in the mulch chips on the paths?

Bree tried to think like her grad student. What would have been important to her? What was such a prominent part of a visitor's trip to the Garden so it would have been easy for this boyfriend? Was it because children liked to run through the maze and Megan was having a child? Or maybe it was about the heart of their journey together. A wrought-iron gazebo sat in the center of the maze. It was the prize for finding one's way through the twists and turns. Bree sighed. It was as good of a place to start as any.

From years of practice, Bree knew her way to the gazebo without any wrong turns. She wound her way through the yews, watching the ground as she went, hoping she'd spot something that looked disturbed. Visitors winding their way through the maze rarely looked down; Megan would have known that.

When she reached the gazebo, she stared up. She stared down. She poked in the clemantis, which was barely winding its way up the wrought-iron since it was so early in the season. If what Megan had left wasn't easily spotted, Bree would have a devil of a time finding it. She just couldn't go around digging up the country's oldest botanical garden on suspicions. Emery would not be amused.

She sat in the gazebo for fifteen minutes observing the surroundings for something out of place. She gave up and retraced her steps out of the maze as the last rays of day faded. Hell would freeze over before she'd admit to Nick that he'd been right. She would have to go home and re-read

Megan's clues to see what she might be missing. The answer was here; she just knew it. And when she found it, she'd make Nick pay with more than just time with the detective. As she headed toward the main entrance, she thought how she could inflict a small revenge on him for being so arrogantly right. When the idea came to her, she smiled in the darkness.

Chapter Nine

———◆———

A ROOM FULL OF TESTOSTERONE COULD be a volatile place, Bree thought.

Emery and his senior science team were debating whether the Garden should enter into another research project with China, and as the only woman in the room, she felt like she was in *Lord of the Flies* right here amid all the white and chrome of the contemporary conference room.

She wasn't surprised when Stephen Almy sided with her position. They often thought the same, but she was surprised when Charles Davidson, head of Applied Research, agreed with her.

Emery must have heard all the viewpoints he wanted and then some because he got his revenge—he turned the meeting over to the finance director. As the guy droned on, Bree felt last night catching up with her as she fought to stay awake. When she'd gotten home, she kept turning the clues over and over in her mind before she finally fell into a restless sleep. If she had any hope of making it through the afternoon, she needed to run on her lunch hour.

With her focus waning, she glanced around the room. Charles wasn't even attempting to look interested, a direct contrast to Stephen, who was always polite and earnest.

These two would be her major internal competition when Emery announced his retirement. No doubt others from the New York Botanical Garden and the Kew in England would apply too because a change in leadership was so rare. Despite her accomplishments, she wasn't a shoo-in, and she wasn't even sure she wanted to leave field work for paperwork and fundraising. Still, she contemplated her rivals.

Charles Davidson was a sarcastic son of a bitch. The Garden was the third botanical garden he'd worked for; he went where he got the best offer and opportunities, a botanical gunslinger for hire. Unfortunately, he was also brilliant, and could turn on the charm when needed. That would count in his favor; donors would love him. He did especially well with women donors. Reluctantly, she respected his work, even as she detested the man.

The more Bree thought about it, though, Stephen might be the bigger threat. If the board wanted someone similar to Emery, then they might turn to Stephen, the Eagle Scout of botany. He was kind, loyal to his research staff and peers, thrifty with his budgets. Also brilliant, though in a different, quieter way than Charles. Wasn't it the quiet ones you always had to watch?

Bree looked around the room. Funny how the team of scientists were similar to the garden they protected. Like marigolds, Stephen and Charles thrived and succeeded no matter how hot the heat. Others were more like impatiens—they did well when sheltered by shade (and Emery), but not the glare of sun or the scrutiny of their methods. And there were those who hadn't done well in one environment, but when Emery had transplanted them to another department, they'd flourished. Until her mother's death, she would have said she was like Stephen and Charles.

Blessedly, the finance director ended his spiel, and everyone began closing tablets, laptops or phones.

"One more announcement," Emery said.

Everyone stopped shuffling. Emery looked over at Jim Weathers, the vice president of The Center for Conservation and Sustainable Development. "Jim's given me his resignation.

"I can't tell you all how sorry I was when he talked to me about this. I think back to what this Garden was like when he joined us. How many times we've sat around this very table struggling with issues, and he helped me find the answer. For the past twenty years, he's been my rock, and his shoes will be hard to fill. Of course, we're planning one heck of a party."

When Emery finished, faces swung expectantly to Jim.

"It's been a privilege to work at such a prestigious and effective organization," Jim said. "Working with all of you has been an honor. But time to make room for a new generation," he said. "I'm leaving by Halloween."

Murmurs of congratulations went around the table.

"His job will be posted, if any of you are interested," Emery said.

Like several others, Bree spent a few minutes talking with Jim before she left the room and headed for the stairways. Charles and another director, Michael Singleton, were waiting at the elevator.

"Nice brown nosing today, Kincaid," Charles said.

Bree gave them a small smile, and continued heading toward the stairs. Her smile grew larger once she passed them. She didn't have to see Charles to know he'd be angrier because she didn't take the bait at his taunting. Why couldn't she show the same control with Nick Mancini?

"Bree, wait up," called Michael. "I'll go with you."

In his early forties, with the lean build of a runner, Michael fell in beside her. "I can't get a run in until tonight. Another meeting at noon," he said ruefully.

Bree flashed him a look of sympathy. Occasionally, she and Michael ran together at lunch.

"I'm going to drag myself out," she said. "I need to re-energize. I stayed up 'til two, reading."

"Must have been good. If it was fiction, Paige might want to know about it," Michael said. "She belongs to a book club."

Bad enough Bree was going to have to share her theory at some point with Emery to get permission to traipse through the Garden. However, she didn't want her colleagues snickering at her so the less they knew, the better. "It's a mystery.

Not particularly well written."

"Not for Paige, then. She's only into books that are depressing."

"And how is your lovely wife?"

Bree hoped her question didn't sound as sarcastic as she felt. Paige had been several years ahead of Bree in high school. They'd had little in common, except that they came from old money, and their mothers served together on the board at the Garden for a period. Paige had been a quiet girl, who with the passage of time, had grown into a remote woman. When they ran into each other at Garden events, Bree had more conversation talking to a column. And the column was more cheerful.

"Are you going to apply for Jim's position?" Michael's voice echoed in the empty stairwell.

"No. What would give you that idea?'

"C'mon, Bree. Everyone knows Emery would like to see you succeed him. Everyone knows you have an inside track, given your history with him."

Bree cringed. Emery had been her professor, then her mentor when she joined the Garden staff. As much of a blessing as the relationship had been, it often came back to haunt her. Her colleagues were jealous like second graders.

"That's a long way off, Michael. Emery still has a couple of things he wants to finish before he sets a time table for his retirement."

"Still, Jim's job would position you nicely when Emery does announce."

They passed the third floor as Bree said, "I'm happier— and better—in the field, Michael. I'll be looking to go back out in the next couple of months."

"What do you think my chances would be if I applied for Jim's job?"

Fleetingly, Bree wished Nick could see her poker face now because she gave Michael a small smile and said neutrally, "If that's what you want to do, go for it."

As they passed the second floor landing, Michael launched into what he thought were his strengths for the job.

"Will you put in a good word for me, Bree?"

"I'm flattered, Michael, but I don't carry that much weight."

He laughed. "Oh, come on. When you were in Madagascar, Emery held you up for the great job you were doing, both in conservation and working with the local government. Must have been the reason Charles took an instant dislike to you."

Bree shrugged, hiding her irritation. She deftly turned the conversation to what Jim Weathers might do with his retirement until she and Michael parted when they reached the first floor.

At lunch, both her body and her spirit protested the idea of a run so she did what she always did when she thought she was being too lax—she pushed herself harder as she jogged through the English Woodland Garden and then the Japanese Garden.

Could Henry Shaw possibly have envisioned that his beloved garden would have become a world-class institution when he started his public botanical garden in the 1850s? That his beautiful garden survived one-hundred-and-fifty years later spoke volumes about the power of vision. Bree thought he would be proud that his beloved park had grown into one of the world's leading research and science centers for plants. But, the sad truth was that while Henry Shaw's vision of a garden had been lasting, his name and his money had not. Several decades ago, Shaw's Garden had become the Missouri Botanical Garden, and the state name brought in state revenue (revenue being one of Emery's favorite words). Shaw's fortune, which had been made in hardware, would not finance even one year of the Garden any more.

Normally when she ran, Bree felt free and strong. Her best ideas came while she ran; she mulled over problems as her mind shifted gears, and she would finish exhilarated. But today, she was stalked by dark thoughts.

Did she want to head the Garden? What if she aspired to it, then didn't get the job? Just thinking about it depressed her. The last few years had felt like nothing but loss. When Mitch had walked out, she'd still had a position of prestige and influence doing something she loved. When her mother was dying, Bree found comfort in the Garden. What if she struck out a third time? What would she have?

She would not let that happen, she thought fiercely, commanding herself to stop the negative thinking. She had always gotten what she wanted by setting goals and working hard—harder than anyone else—to achieve them. Aiming for Emery's position would be no different. She would make a plan and execute it. She was only feeling depressed because she'd had so little sleep and so little success at figuring out Megan's clues. As she ran her second lap, she reviewed the clues over and over again in her mind.

We will travel the train of tears in life armed with our love.
Amazing!
Together, we will build a house of love.
The beauty we can and cannot see.
Oh, the happy times we will show our child.
Our love is worth a fortune.

The Garden was composed of thirty-three specialized gardens and centers, along with the visitor center, Shaw's home, and an amphitheater. Without narrowing it down, Bree could search for years—and be haunted for decades by her failure. There was a cheerful thought.

When she finished, she started her cool down and walked to the wooden observatory that overlooked the maze and the herb garden. Bree stared at the pattern the yews formed, hoping she would see something mentioned in the scribbles she'd memorized. Unbidden, Nick's words came back to her. He *would* look at this differently than her. Perhaps, she thought wryly, she couldn't see the clues for the yews. To

Nick, they were just big green bushes. What galled her was that he'd been right. She was getting nowhere on her own, and each day that nothing happened, the chances of justice for Megan faded.

She wondered if Nick had gone home as she had last night and stayed up, thinking. Then again, she couldn't picture him as a homebody or studying. Success would probably rest on her shoulders.

She mixed the five phrases with 'amazing', and looked down at the maze while she repeated them over and over again until she was singing them like a children's nursery rhyme.

Rhyme time. She blinked. Rhyme thyme. *Thyme.*

What was the clue? *Oh, the happy times we will show our child.*

Oh, the happy *thymes* we will show our child.

The herb garden.

She scrambled down the observatory and walked briskly to the herb garden. Searching through the herbs, she smiled triumphantly when she came to a section of thyme. In the middle of the patch was a statue of a young boy. A child.

Bree glanced around to make sure there were no visitors before she tried to move the statue. Because it was small, she could lift it, and gasped when she saw the vellum envelope with the blue ribbon tied around it. She held her breath, her heart pounding as she picked up the envelope.

Chapter Ten

BREE AND NICK STARED AT the white envelope sitting on her kitchen counter, and then at each other.

She had called him after she found the clue. They had agreed she should wait to open it until they could examine it together, which mean the end of the day, given Bree's schedule. He had shown up at her house with Greek food because, he explained, he'd lived in Greece for three years while he was writing for Reuters.

"You found it. You should have the honor," he said.

Bree took a breath as she reached for the envelope, then stopped.

"Before I open it, I want to change my prize."

"Your prize?"

"Yeah, you know how I bought you dinner when you showed up with the report? And I said when I found the clue, I wanted an hour with Daniel Cusumano. I've changed my mind."

"Ah-h-h-h." He smiled coolly.

She snorted. "Oh, please. It's not a night with you. You know, you spend an awful lot of time inferring sex, Nick. Isn't there something else you can do?"

"Darlin', you have no idea what I can—"

"Oh, please. I'm on to you using sexual innuendo to make me feel uncomfortable. You need a new technique."

Nick started to speak, but Bree plunged on.

"What I want is so boring and tame compared to your *talents* that it will be easy for you to say yes."

She couldn't help but be pleased with herself when he started to look wary. About time that he took her seriously instead of just toying with this investigation.

"I get to ask you twenty questions about yourself. And the answers have to be more than a simple yes or no."

"You only get five questions," he countered as he headed to the cabinets to get plates.

She looked pointedly at the envelope, then back at Nick. And waited.

"All right," he snapped. "But when I find a clue, I'm going to ask for more than the BMW."

Her pulse kicked up a notch, but at least her voice stayed steady. "No problem. I have great confidence in my ability to stay one step ahead of you."

She picked up the envelope, then hugged it to her, closed her eyes and made a wish. *Please have written the father's name on here. Please give us a lead to help put your spirit to rest, Megan.*

Bree slowly pulled the blue satin ribbon off the envelope. She pulled out another sonogram. On the bottom of the paper, Megan had scribbled 'James Robert'. Bree turned over the paper to find nothing on the back.

Handing it to Nick, she said softly, "I guess she was having a baby boy."

"Let's hope the baby is James Robert Junior. That should help when I start calling around to obstetricians' offices."

"James was her father's name. I'm sure she was trying to honor his memory. Robert could be the name of the boyfriend. Who do you know that's our age or younger with that name?"

"No one."

"Right, but it might be the name of this guy if he's in his forties or fifties." Bree pulled out another piece of paper out of the envelope and started to read it.

"Well?" he asked.

"It's a love letter."

He rolled his eyes, but grabbed it out of her hands and started reading out loud.

My Darling,

I know you aren't happy about the baby, but you still have months and months to tell your wife that you are leaving her. I don't care if we're married by the time James Robert arrives. We will be together for the rest of our lives.

"Listen to this bullshit," he said. In an exaggerated voice, he read: *You see into my soul like no other person ever has or ever will. You understand me. You accept me. Some people spend an entire life looking for a love like this, and I am so blessed to have found you early in my life. I hope the baby has your height, your blue eyes, but not your poor eyesight.*

Nick made a dramatic sweeping arc with his arm and then brought his hand back to his heart

"We're all fools the first time," Bree said. She could hear the bitterness in her voice. "Then we wise up. Poor Megan didn't get that chance, and look what it cost her."

"A bit unromantic, aren't you, Brianna? I thought every woman was genetically coded, at least a little, for the hearts and flowers stuff."

"It's a long, boring story." She certainly wasn't going to share it with Nick.

"Great. I'll take your word for it."

She burst out laughing. "You're amazing for all the wrong reasons, Nick."

"Thank you. Wait, now you're frowning? What's wrong?"

"*Amazing*. That was the first clue. The clue that I used to find this was number four out of the five. Either the clues are out of order on her scribbles or my theory is totally off. And if the other clues don't reveal more, then this is a wild goose chase."

"Hey, give yourself some credit. We now know the guy is married. That goes along with your theory he had a reason to want to get rid of Megan. Daniel would tell you that's motivation for murder."

"Yes, but I thought he was a drug dealer, maybe from Central America. If he's the bastard I think he is, why would he be honest and tell her he was married? Maybe he really did love her."

Nick shrugged. "I wouldn't be so quick to think these were star-crossed lovers until we know more." He plunked papers covered with numbers on the kitchen island. "Megan's phone calls for the past three months. Unless the father works at Pizza Hut as a delivery guy, her phone is not much help."

"You called all of these?"

"Try not to sound so shocked."

"That was my 'I'm so impressed' voice."

"Uh-huh. Anyway, many, many calls to mother and sister in Pittsburgh. Lots of calls to various numbers at the Garden, including several to you. A couple of calls to the leasing center for her loft. Probably calling to get something fixed. Hair appointments. We can cross all these off a list of suspects. Most of the others are restaurants for take-out or one-time calls to a bunch of places—utilities, stores."

"Texts?"

"Takes longer to get the information, but her list of contacts is fairly small. Not a lot of guys on it. One's her auto mechanic. I left messages for the others. Let's see who doesn't call back."

He smiled, and Bree couldn't help but smile back.

He rested his hands on the kitchen island. "You know what I would have done if I was this guy?" He didn't wait for an answer. "Burner phone. I'd get a phone just for the two of us. Megan and me."

"That seems like a lot of effort to keep an affair quiet. I mean, guys cheat all the time."

"So maybe a rich wife. Certainly some reason he didn't want their relationship known."

"Or a drug dealer. That might explain why her drawers and apartment looked rifled through when I visited the apartment the first time. He was probably looking for her burner phone, if that's what they did." She stared off into space, picturing Megan's apartment. Bree frowned. "Come to think of it, I thought it was odd that there wasn't a laptop or tablet in her apartment. He probably took both. He had more than a week to get there before I did."

"Maybe he'll be back. I wonder if we could rig up a camera in the hallway."

"The onsite person, Deborah, confirmed the junk removal company took the furniture, the dishes, and her books today. I rifled through the books before I boxed them up, but the only things I found were a couple of receipts Megan was using as bookmarks."

"No special books?"

"You mean like *Fifty best places to live when you move to Central America for your boyfriend?*" She shook her head. "Several new books on parenting, but I didn't see any scribbles that would help us. Most looked like she hadn't even opened them."

Nick fell silent.

"Do you think Detective Cusumano would look into Megan's death now that we've found a clue? It gives credibility to my theory."

"Yeah, but your theory doesn't mean the guy had anything to do with her death."

"Except for the poison," she said dryly.

"You should consider at least one other angle."

The gentleness in his tone made Bree hesitate. He hadn't been anything but cocky or sarcastic since she'd met him. She didn't say anything, but that didn't stop him.

"What if she took the poison herself?"

"No," She slammed her hand against the counter. "She would not have done that."

"Really? This is a love-struck young woman who is pregnant. The guy doesn't want the baby. Her family is far away and has its own problems. What if she was despondent and tried to kill herself?"

"While she was driving? She would never have risked anyone else's life."

"Yet it looked like an accident—so her family's going to get the life insurance money that I bet is part of your benefits package at the Garden. Or maybe she was trying to get the boyfriend's attention in a dramatic way, and she misjudged the amount of the drug or the impact of the car."

Bree shook her head adamantly. "No, no, no."

She glared at Nick, but her anger seemed to bounce off him.

"Sister Ignatius used to give me the same look in third grade," he said. "So if you're wishing me to hell you're about thirty years too late."

Bree took a breath as she fought to rein in her anger. "You probably drove a good nun to drink."

Nick shrugged.

To help return them to an equilibrium, Bree started spooning food onto her plate. She heaped a large helping of lamb onto her plate as if she could drown her sorrow. She savored the spicy, greasy flavor, and it tasted so delicious she didn't even attempt polite conversation with Nick while they ate. When she reached for a piece of baklava, she glanced at Nick, who had stopped eating to watch her.

"I just watched you down two huge helpings of lamb, a Greek salad, and you've got room for dessert?"

"Nick, you're such a flatterer."

"If I wanted to flatter you, Dr. Kincaid," he drawled, "you would not be thinking about baklava."

The heat in his eyes made Bree uncomfortable, until she realized that was exactly what he wanted her to feel. She glared at him, and he backed off with a cocky smile.

"I'll go for a run later to work it off," she said. "After we plan our next move."

"You're a little terrier, aren't you?"

"It's a family trait." She rested her elbows on the island counter. "How about you? What did you get from your parents?"

"Are we starting the five questions?" he asked sarcastically.

"Twenty questions, and quit being a spoil sport. So, what did you get from your parents?"

"A love of travel," he said, then flashed a smile.

Bree cast him a sour look. She should have known he wouldn't play fair or easy, but then again, that was why she needed his help on Megan's case. Still, she wasn't going to let him wiggle out of the agreement. "And why is that so funny?"

"Elena took off when I was six. Is that what you're dying to know?"

"Elena's your mother?" she asked cautiously.

"I suppose you would think of her as a mother. I stopped doing that a long time ago. The day I came home from school and found the note she left for my father."

"I'm sorry. I can only imagine how hard that must have been."

Nick shrugged again and looked unconcerned. She bet he'd learned that move the day after his mother abandoned them.

"Your dad never remarried?"

"Bernard retreated into himself. Night after night, he'd come home and plop in his recliner. Night after night, year after year. Do you want to share my feelings about the Christmas's with TV dinners? Looking for the sad story of the boy who had to learn to braid his little sister's hair? How about the cold cereal for breakfast and dinner week after week?"

What disturbed her wasn't his story, but the calm, dispassionate way he told it. Neither his voice nor his eyes revealed any anger. As if he were talking about someone else's life.

"Look, Bree, there's a big difference between a woman who was born with a silver spoon in one hand and a plan for her entire life in the other, and a guy from the Hill who figures out what he wants to do when he gets up each morning."

She rose, taking their plates to the sink to rinse them off to buy herself some time. Part of her was relieved he hadn't been physically or sexually abused. The other part of her thanked God she'd had good parents who would rather have died than abandon their children—physically or emotionally. Who knew what Nick Mancini could have been if that little boy had gotten the love and support she had?

The other part of her was ashamed of herself. She'd come up with the idea of twenty questions as a way to make him as uncomfortable as he made her. He threw her off kilter. She'd wanted to push back, to let him know he couldn't discount or dismiss her. But making him uncomfortable seemed petty now.

She returned to the table. "I'm sorry, Nick. That was mean and childish of me." She sensed that if she went on, she'd only make him more uncomfortable so she used one of the tricks she'd learned from him—she changed the subject and asked what he'd thought of Megan's clues. He stilled for a moment as if surprised that she'd walked away from her game.

"What I don't get is why she would do something like this in the first place. It seems so—" He searched for the right word.

"Romantic?"

"Is that what you think it is?"

Bree chose her words carefully. "I suspect a twenty-three-year-old woman would think so." She hesitated. "Don't you remember when you were young and finding just the right person was a huge part of your life?"

Their eyes met, and she knew he'd never experienced the ecstasy of simply being with someone or the misery of being apart. Surprisingly, she pitied him now, though surely he was the smarter of the two of them for never having given his heart and had it broken.

"Did you have a Prince Charming?" he asked.

She thought she'd found a man whose love would last a life time. Obviously, she'd missed something because Mitch's definition of a lifetime had been three years . . . until he could upgrade. Until that day two years ago when he'd told her coolly that she wasn't enough . . . that he was leaving her for someone who wasn't so dull . . . so focused on her job . . . who was better in bed.

"Yeah. Except in this case, he turned into a toad when I married him. Look, why don't we go over the clues together?" she suggested. "Two heads and all that."

She pulled a scribbled copy out of her briefcase and passed it to him. She led him into the family room, to a corner with lots of windows and two oversized leather chairs and floor lamps. He borrowed her tablet to search the internet. They settled into a comfortable silence as they read.

◆

Nick loved words—had since he was a child, though he couldn't remember if his love came before Elena had deserted them or if he retreated into them to survive. Reading gave him a sense of intimacy to which Bree seemed oblivious.

He looked at her profile, bathed in soft warm light. With her hair draped around her delicate neck and her skin looking soft and peachy, she was pretty. Not beautiful like many of the women he had known, but pretty. He glanced at her as she stared out the window, thinking, and he smiled to himself. Concentrating put a fierce scowl on her face. He could almost see her brain analyzing all the angles, the way a huge mainframe computer would.

Remember all of her faults. She's bossy. She's flat-chested. And she can outrun you.

But she'd backed off quizzing him when she sensed he didn't want to talk about his family. And of course, now that she'd brought it up, too many raw images threatened to close in. Better to concentrate on Megan Harper.

"I've found fourteen obstetricians near the hospital complexes around the Central West End."

"That's a lot. Are you sure it's going to be worth your time? I really think the best thing is to focus on the clues."

"You'd be surprised what a sympathetic nurse who wants to see two star-crossed lovers reunited might tell me if she thinks I'm the father."

Those huge violet eyes gazed solemnly at him. "You know, I can't decide whether to be horrified at your underhandedness or impressed with your creativity."

"Let's go with the positive. I can also talk to more of her neighbors. Maybe someone else saw him."

"If it works, that's brilliant."

Her compliment should not have made him feel so good.

"I was an investigative reporter when I lived in London, Madrid and Rome."

He grew pensive, remembering the days before too many women, drugs and drinks, when he'd been the top choice of editors. He shifted restlessly in his chair, staring out the windows where the setting sun cast soft light on the garden.

Bree caught his eye and smiled. "Stunning, isn't it?"

Nick only recognized that there were a lot of roses. He had no idea what all the other flowers were. When he was growing up, they'd had no flowers or shrubs to offset the dreariness of his house. The Kincaid family's fascination with flowers was a mystery to him. However, from listening to his artistic sister all these years, he recognized an artful arrangement when he saw one.

"That garden was my mother's pride and joy," Bree said. "None of those flower beds were here when she and my Dad moved into the house. But she spent almost thirty-five years moving dirt here and there. My Dad often said he was grateful the trees were hundreds of years old and couldn't be moved too."

Why did it hurt for him to say, "Your mother sounds like she was an incredible woman"?

"She was very nurturing. Some of my earliest memories are of working in this garden with my mother. I would have been about five. Certainly, my little sister would have been around by then, but all I remember is my mother oohing and ahhing over all the blossoms I brought her, some of which I'm sure were clover or dandelions. She made me think that flowers were the coolest things ever."

He thought the smile Bree flashed was tinged with sadness. "It's why her death was so very hard on my family. And even with all our money, our connections, everything we had, we couldn't stop the cancer. Finally, Mom said enough. She was at peace with what was going to happen. It's the rest of us who are struggling. Even now, months later." She leaned forward. "It's why finding Megan's killer is so important to me. At least, I can do something about Megan."

Bree blushed. Perhaps, Nick thought, a little uncomfortable at having revealed so much about herself. They'd both shared more than they ever intended. Get the story and get the hell out of Dodge, he told himself.

Bree brought them out of the intimacy when she got down to business.

"Let's assume Megan was going to tie most of her clues to flowers and love."

"Great. You're the perfect woman for the job."

"No, actually that's bad. Do you know how many roses, day lilies or irises have the word 'love' in them? I poked around the iris beds because they would have been in bloom as she planned all of this, but I didn't see anything that looked like it had been freshly dug."

"Maybe Megan kept all the clues in a small area so her lover could find them quickly. And let's assume he probably wasn't going to have to dig for them. After all, the Garden is open to the public. Someone would notice and reported him."

"Not to mention Megan would have been in a boatload of

trouble." Bree smiled like cat who just ate a canary. "Guess what's right next to the herb garden?"

Nick dropped his head to his chest, then raised his head. "Let me guess. That maze. Okay, Brianna. You were right."

"I'm sorry. I didn't hear you. What did you say?"

"Words that will never pass my lips again because you're such a poor winner."

She laughed as she got up and went over to a desk. After looking in three drawers, she came back with a pamphlet and a pen. "This is what visitors get when they come. This side has the garden's map on it." She circled the herb garden and the maze.

Nick ran his finger down the list of gardens and attractions. "Number seventeen. Henry Shaw's house. Perfect spot for the clue 'Together, we will build a house of love.'"

Chapter Eleven

"I CLAIM DIBS ON SEARCHING THE bell tower," Nick said.

"Of course you do," Bree said.

They stood in the circular driveway, staring at Henry Shaw's two-and-a-half story home.

"For a rich man, it's a pretty simple structure," Nick said as they headed to the front door.

"It actually was his country home. Which is funny because most of us would consider this mid-town now given how far the metro area stretches. But when he started building in the mid-eighteen hundreds, this was the country. This is where he would come to get away from the city."

Bree inserted the old-fashioned key into the lock. If Emery's assistant, Faith, thought it odd that Bree had requested the key on one of the weekdays when Tower Grove House was closed to visitors, she kept it to herself. And if she thought it odd that Bree had asked if Megan Harper had ever asked for the key, her face didn't betray her thoughts either. Faith was like a sphinx, which is why Emery valued her so much.

"Unless Megan borrowed a key from a volunteer, she probably didn't hide the clue after hours," Bree said as they stepped into the hallway. "If she did it on a day when the home is open to visitors, she wouldn't have had a lot of time to hide it so it should be something fairly obvious."

"Good Lord, those Victorians liked their patterns," he said.

The linoleum floor, stairway carpeting and wall paper had what Bree considered competing patterns.

"Little bit goes a long way, doesn't it?" she asked.

"I'll start in the bell tower and work my way down to the second floor. You start down here and work your way up, okay?"

"Why don't we go through each room together?"

"Afraid I'll slip a lace doily in my pocket?"

"Of course not. You'd go for the silver. It's much more valuable."

He paused for a few beats. "Since you recognize my gifts, I'll be gracious and do it your way. But we aren't leaving until I go up in that tower."

They moved into the formal parlor, which had a patterned rug, a table inlaid with marble, an upright piano, and mahogany furniture with pale green cushions.

"What was it with those people that they went for such excess?" Nick asked as he walked around the room. "There's so much stuff here."

"Yes, but we're not looking for anything from Shaw's time."

Nick looked over at her, and she waited. She knew he was smart enough to figure it out. He may already have, and was just being polite. Nick, polite. Hmmm, no. He was smarter than he liked to let on, though.

"So if this guy was going to find the clue, Megan would have had to make it something he would recognize, but not so modern that staff and volunteers would notice something out of place," Nick reasoned.

"Exactly." She handed him a pair of clear vinyl gloves.

"Good idea. We won't leave fingerprints."

"*Or* we could wear them to protect any of the old precious objects that we touch while we're looking."

Bree expected Nick to lounge more than look, but he surprised her with his effort. They spent the next ninety minutes going from room to room on the first floor looking under furniture, opening silver serving dishes and wooden boxes, and behind pictures and pillows.

"I don't think it's here," he finally said.

"I agree," she conceded. "Maybe we'll have better luck on the second floor."

"True. I assume bedrooms are up there. Maybe this clue has something to do with sex since she seemed so infatuated with this guy."

He said it almost absently as he headed up the steep, carpeted stairs. Where was the Nick Mancini leer? She trailed him and watched him gaze at the foot fifteen-ceilings when they reached the top of the stairway.

"The high ceilings were to combat the high heat and humidity in St. Louis in the summer as well as show off Shaw's wealth," she said.

"St. Louis summers and winters were good training for some of the hell holes I ended up reporting from," Nick said as he headed down the hall. "Notice how everyone always says they love to live here because of the four seasons, but then only mention spring or fall? Never winter or summer."

He looked into the first bedroom. "I'm not stepping foot in this one. All the froufrou wallpaper and patterned rugs are giving me a headache." He moved to the next room. "Okay, I can do this one."

She joined him in the doorway. Except for the patterned red rug, the room had clean lines with pale green walls, dark wooden canopied bed and bureau, and white sheets.

"This was Henry Shaw's room. He died here."

"Well, I'm not afraid of ghosts so I'm good."

He stepped into the room and began going through the bureau drawers. Bree headed back to the froufrou guest bedroom where she began checking behind pictures, the porcelain figurines on the mantel, the fireplace.

Thirty minutes later, Nick appeared in the doorway. "Struck out again."

"So far, I'm not having any luck either."

"Check the small bathroom. There's a balcony off this

floor. Maybe she put something outside. I'm sure few people go out there anymore."

"And then I get to go up in the tower?"

"You have to wait until I can go up with you."

"Okay, mom."

She threw him a skeptical look. "Tell me that you have never been drunk, and climbed out on a ledge, thinking you could fly or jump to a big tree branch."

"Brianna, I'm offended."

"Oh, I'm sor—"

"I haven't done that since I was in my mid-twenties," he said as he disappeared down the hallway.

Bree closed her eyes and hung her head. She went back to searching, but found nothing. She joined Nick on the balcony.

"Nothing?" she asked.

He shook his head.

"Me neither."

Nick looked skyward.

"Fine, we'll go up in the tower, but I doubt we find anything from Megan. There's at least one volunteer on this floor at all time to prevent people from doing exactly what you want to do."

"Maybe she was going to bring him here after hours. Maybe she planned to have sex with him in the tower. You know, a botanist's version of the mile-high club."

She ignored his comment. "Except she wouldn't have access to the key like I do," she said as she headed back into the hallway.

"But I bet if she showed up right around closing, gave a sweet, sincere story to the volunteer . . ." He shrugged. "People like to be nice, and they usually cut people they know some slack."

Bree opened the door leading to the tower steps and started climbing.

Behind her, she heard Nick say, "Take yourself, for example. You're doing this both for Megan and her sister. You have a relationship with them."

Bree didn't respond as she stepped into the tower. The square room was empty except for an old broken cane chair in one corner. The north and south sides of the tower had large arches and Nick drifted to the one on the northern side to look down on the circular drive. Bree examined the chair and the dark corners of the tower.

When she was satisfied the tower held no clue, she headed to the side that looked over the herb garden. Nick joined her.

The diffused sun coming through the old trees surrounding the house bathed Nick in soft light. Those full lips, that thick shaggy brown hair, that strong jaw—it was just too much of a package to ignore at the moment. She didn't even have to see those warm brown eyes to imagine the heat they would send through her.

Oh no, oh no. Do not think of him like that.

She told herself that noticing him as a man was good. She must finally be breaking free of the bitter, hurtful memories of Mitch if she was thinking of another guy. But Nick? Too ridiculous to contemplate. She could feel her face warming, and then he looked up. She was grateful that the light was so low because she was sure she was blushing furiously.

"What?" he said.

"Nothing," she squeaked.

"Find anything useful?" he asked, stretching his long frame.

She shook her head, afraid to say anything.

They finished by searching the basement of the house, which had been converted into exhibit space about Shaw's time period. There were fewer items and they were larger pieces so Bree and Nick examined them more quickly.

"Bree, there's nothing here."

"I don't understand. This would fit the clue perfectly. We must be missing something."

"There are lots of other buildings in the Garden." He pulled the visitor's guide out of his back pocket. "What about this Linnean House? It looks big."

She shook her head. "It's not really a house. Not like this. It started out as a greenhouse meant to overwinter citrus trees and delicate plants like ferns. It houses rare and endangered camellias, including *Camellia petelotii*."

"Quit showing off with all those four-syllable words."

"Oh, sorry. If she'd left a clue like 'tea for two', the Linnean House would make sense because of the camellias. Tea comes from their leaves. But that's not what she wrote."

"Maybe she was still playing around with the clues when she died."

Bree turned back to look at the Tower Grove House. "No, I think it's there. We just missed it."

Nick took her upper arm. "You can go back later. On other days when you're fresher. Search one room at a time. Right now, you can take me to lunch. Let's try the café at the visitors' center."

◆

After lunch, Bree headed back to Emery's office to return the key to his assistant.

"He'd like to talk to you if you have time," Faith said.

Bree knocked on Emery's door and walked in. He was answering emails, and she waited until he finished.

"Slight hitch in our work in Kenya," he said as he indicated the chair across his desk.

"Do you ever get good news emails?"

He smiled wryly. "Rarely."

"So what's up?"

"Someone saw you go in the Shaw house with a man, and that you were in there for quite some time. A private tour?"

Was he inferring she would use the house for a clandestine rendezvous? With Nick Mancini of all people. Still, Bree felt heat in her face, which probably made her look guilty.

"Well, I'm glad someone has time to pay attention to my comings and goings."

Emery offered a little shrug. "It is unusual, given that the house is closed today."

What could she possibly say that would not make her sound foolish? As Nick never failed to remind her, the one clue they had found so far, while inappropriate on Megan's part, certainly did not prove her murder.

Emery leaned forward, folding his hands on his desk. "Bree, is everything alright?"

"Of course." Think quickly, she ordered herself. "I wasn't going to say anything until we had something certain worked out, but Megan Harper's family and I were thinking of making a donation in her honor."

"Hmmm."

"It turns out . . ." Where was Nick with his glib tongue when she needed him? "It turns out that Megan loved the herb garden. So the guy, who's another family friend, and I were in the tower to get a bird's eye view to see if there was anything that would go well as an addition to what's already there."

"That's so thoughtful."

"Well, we wanted it to be a surprise. Otherwise, I would have come to you first."

"Did you get some ideas?"

"Not exactly. In fact, we may want to look at a few other spots in the Garden before Megan's mother and sister help me make a decision."

"Until three weeks ago, I never heard of this Megan Harper. Now her name has come up several times. I'm just sorry it has to be related to her death."

Now that she thought about it, Bree decided, doing something permanent in Megan's honor was a lovely idea. "I know. I'll keep you informed once we have some ideas, but don't be surprised if the guy . . . his name is Nick . . . if

Nick and I look at a few other sites. I'm also going to get him a badge to my building, if that's okay with you. It's a pain to have to go down to the lobby to let him in each time he comes to discuss an idea with me."

"Of course. Thank you again."

On her way out, Bree stopped by Faith's desk. "Glad I caught him when he had some time. Sounds like he's had a busy day. Lots of people in and out?"

"Oh just a few. Marilyn, Charles, Porter, Jim and Michael. That's really not a bad day for Emery."

Marilyn, Charles, Porter, Jim and Michael. Had one of them been the nosy snitch? Life was so much easier in the jungle, she decided. There she only had to contend with snakes that slithered.

Chapter Twelve

NICK WAS SURPRISED TO FIND Daniel at home when he let himself into the apartment. Daniel was sitting on the couch, sipping a beer, pizza on the coffee table, and watching the Cardinals game.

"Winning?" Nick asked.

Daniel shook his head. "Too early in the season. They like to wait until after the All-Star game to start winning. Makes the race to the pennant that much more thrilling."

Nick took off his sports coat, headed to the galley kitchen to get himself a beer, and joined Daniel on the couch. For a few minutes neither one spoke as they watched an inning where the Cardinal pitcher got the batters out in order.

Finally, Nick asked, "How's your primary case going?"

"Not good. We've got cars patrolling all over North County, so he switched areas. Shot a kid in South County. Broad daylight as the boy was getting off the bus. Smart son of a bitch."

"Pattern?"

"All boys. Under ten-years old. Race, location, wealth don't seem to be a factor. You can imagine every family with a boy is calling to ask what we're doing as well as not letting the boys go outside. Some are even keeping their boys home from school."

"What a sick bastard. Military background?"

"Or a hunter. He uses a rifle."

Nick didn't have any energy left to offer ideas. Not that Daniel needed his help. He'd always been the smarter of the two of them. Nick had made up for it by being a better schemer.

After another inning, Daniel asked "Out at the bars?"

Nick nodded.

"Must be a bad night if you're home by ten."

Nick searched for a clever comeback, but the truth slowed him down. He'd checked out a few more bars to see if anyone could identify Megan as a regular, but with no better results. He'd been approached by several women, but after a few minutes of banter, he'd moved on. They seemed too predictable. Too shallow. He took a long swig of beer. God, he hoped he wasn't becoming mature.

"I was following up on a possible lead about Megan Harper," he shared.

Daniel looked over at him. "Dr. Kincaid still hasn't given up? I thought you said all you had was a lot of speculation."

Nick had kept Daniel apprised of the basics of what he and Bree were doing, with the promise that if the investigation yielded any hard evidence that Nick would give Daniel a heads up so he could step back into the case.

"Well, the doc is a smart woman, and she knew this Megan better than you or me."

"So you believe her?"

Nick thought about Bree's conviction and passion and totally unreasonable and unshakeable opinions. Only a fool would believe in her, and Nick Mancini was too wily to be suckered in.

Still he felt he was betraying her when he said, "If wishing could make it so, then yes. But in reality . . ." He shrugged, then frowned. Damn, how dare Brianna Kincaid prick him with her hope and sincerity? He had made it thirty-seven years without a conscience. "If I were you, I'd concentrate on finding the killer of those kids."

"So why are you still giving this some time?"

"Have you ever known me to do anything that didn't benefit Nick Mancini? I'm strictly after a good story I can sell to a major news outlet. Just think of the headline." He put out his hand and fanned it the space in front of him. "Garden of Eden hides treacherous secret."

"Found any connection to drug dealers?"

"Nothing tangible."

"The minute you get something, Nick, you call me. You do not attempt to investigate this yourself and end up in the Mississippi."

"Afraid my sister will come after you?"

Daniel was silent, and Nick looked over at him. Tory had trailed them everywhere when they'd been younger. Daniel had treated her just like any of his other three sisters.

Into the silence, Nick said, "In case you're wondering, she's doing fine, thank you. I'm thinking of heading to New York next week to see her. Or maybe I can get her to fly here, see your mom and sisters, and then we can fly back to New York together."

Daniel shrugged. "Last time she was home, we got into it."

"She said she hasn't been back here for years, and you still remember you got into a fight with her? I know Tory can be sassy; it's the Mancini charm. But the two of you—"

"Your sister is stubborn and reckless."

"I'm reckless."

"You can take care of yourself."

"You don't have to worry about Tory. She can handle herself."

"She was drinking too much. She was sleeping around. She was doing drugs."

"She's an artist. Part of the mystique. You don't have to worry."

"Which is what she told me, but in much more explicit terms. Right before she threw a plate and a glass at me."

Daniel rose and cleared the pizza from the table before taking it to the kitchen. Nick also got up and trailed him.

"Is there something you want to say, Daniel?"

"Nope. Forget it, okay? It was between your sister and me. I'm sure she's forgotten it."

"It's not like you to hold a grudge. And I count on you to protect Tory. When I'm out of the country, I know she would turn to you and your family if she was in a crisis. You're her family."

"You're right. It was all a couple of years ago anyway. At least I know now to duck."

"And whose fault is that? You taught her how to throw a baseball and a football, remember?"

"Right. I'm sure she's matured since I saw her last."

I wouldn't count on it, Nick thought.

Chapter Thirteen

THE OFFICE SETTLED INTO THE silence of machines: The hum of the air conditioner, the occasional ring of the phone, the low buzz of a document being faxed from another site.

As Bree typed her last email—one to Molly Harper about her idea for a sculpture to honor Megan—she was grateful for the silence. She stretched and yawned. Ten hours of sitting at her computer, writing, had drained her. With her colleagues gone for the day, she could research flowers or plants in the Garden that might contain the key words she and Nick had drawn up for Megan. She could probably even take a stroll through the Garden—again—for ideas. She might go back to the maze. She'd gone back to the Tower Grove House and searched again, but turned up nothing. She pulled a bottle of water out of her mini fridge and some almonds out of a drawer so she didn't visit the vending machine.

She almost choked on her water when a voice said, "Hey, I'm glad you're still here."

Stephen Almy stood in her doorway, holding a manila folder.

"Oh, sorry. Did I scare you?"

"You're like a ninja, Stephen. I'm surprised you're still here. It's so nice outside. I think everyone snuck out early."

"I like to stay late. I get more done in an hour after everyone has gone home than I do the whole rest of the day." She thought his smile was a little off kilter and slightly sad, before he asked, "Do you have a few minutes?"

She nodded. "A few."

He settled in her visitor's chair. "I did more research on the project with the Chinese. I think it supports our position perfectly." He hesitated. "I thought you might want to give it to Emery."

"Okay," she said slowly, "but is there some reason you don't want to present it to him?"

"He listens to you."

She stifled a groan. "Well, he listens to you too. He has a lot of respect for your opinion. You know that."

"I suppose. I heard you're going to make a donation to erect something in memory of Megan Harper."
"Where did you hear that?"

"Theo in finance."

"Huh. Rumors certainly do travel. Did you hear how much I'm giving? I hope it's not a million dollars because I had something very modest in mind."

"It's a wonderful thing you're doing. I only knew her to say hi. I can't imagine how hard it must be for those of you who worked with her every day."

"I think the rest of the team is starting to recover. I know we're going to need a replacement for her soon. We've got some proposals coming up, so I don't think it's the right time to start anyone new. Unless you have someone you'd like to recommend."

He shook his head. After a few beats of silence, he said, "Abby left me."

"Oh, Stephen, I'm so sorry." She hoped her confusion at his confession didn't show on her face. They were colleagues, not friends.

"She got tired of me traipsing around the world, leaving her at home to deal with three kids and trying to make do on a botanist's salary." He absently rubbed the back of his neck and stared at the floor for a few seconds. When he looked up, he said, "I'm thinking of taking a job with Jones-White pharmaceuticals. The pay is a lot better."

For the first time, he looked directly at Bree; the lenses of his glasses magnifying his eyes. "I like to think that I would have been one of the few internal candidates who would give you a run for Emery's job."

Poor Emery, Bree thought. Everyone was just waiting for him to toddle off into retirement so the next king or queen could be crowned.

"Stephen, Emery is still a couple of years away from retiring. He's getting ready to launch a new development campaign in the fall. He won't leave until that's wrapped up. It wouldn't be good to change leadership during a campaign."

Stephen flashed her yet another rueful smile. "You're always better at the politics than I am. Maybe I was kidding myself about truly being a contender."

"You're one of the best botanists in the country, Stephen. No one's done more research on how to break dormancy and germinate seeds of threatened species. Maybe Abby will change her mind."

He shook his head. "Problems like this don't just crop up in a marriage in a week or a month, Bree. We've been struggling for a couple of years. She's been getting angrier and angrier until she asked me to move out two months ago. I've had too many quiet nights to think this over lately. I don't want to lose the kids."

Stephen was devoted to his children, coaching their soccer and baseball teams. He never missed a band or ballet concert when he was in town. What could she say?

He pushed the manila folder closer to her. "I've done a lot of analyzing, Bree, and there's solid data here that I think you should present to Emery."

Bree gave a little shake of her head. "I don't know why everyone keeps thinking I've got so much influence over Emery. He hasn't been my supervisor for more than ten years."

Stephen leaned across her desk. "More importantly, I don't want Charles Davidson to get the job, Bree. I can't stand the guy. His research skirts some shaky paths, and the guy's a slime ball. I don't want a superficial egotist like that running the Garden."

Bree wanted to know if he knew more about Charles, but she didn't know Stephen well enough to dish that much dirt. What a pity. It would be nice to know Charles' weaknesses, she reflected, then caught herself. She didn't want to play the game like that. She knew from her father's career at the law firm how ruthless people could be when it came to moving up the ladder. Did she want Emery's job badly enough to slander Charles, to use innuendo to beat him? She wanted to think the answer was 'no', but she recognized that she considered it for a few seconds and that made her shift uneasily in her seat.

"I'll be happy to give this to Emery, but I can't take credit for it. I'll tell him to talk to you if he has any questions."

He rose. "Do me a favor and keep what I told you about my family and my career to yourself, will you, Bree?"

"Of course. Though I hope you can work something out. You're too good to lose, Stephen."

He nodded, started to say something, then nodded again and disappeared from her office as quietly as he'd come.

Bree felt sorry for Stephen. He obviously had the same dream she did. How hard to walk away from that. She gave a small prayer of thanks that she'd never had to make such difficult choices. How did you go on when you lost your dream? Did you make a new one? Did you feel like you were settling? She admired Stephen, though. He knew what was important to him.

Then she wondered what she would have done if Mitch had given her the same ultimatum. She had loved him so deeply. Would she have made the choice Stephen was making? Thank God she hadn't been forced to grapple with that one.

With a deep sigh, Bree returned to her task—researching the database. Her eyes widened when the results popped up of the Garden's inventory of flowers and plants with the word "love" in their name. The database spit out forty-five names; most were in the daylily, iris or rose gardens. More than she would have imagined. She could hit one of the rose gardens and the daylily beds on her way out, though the plants would just be beginning to flower for the season.

Bree started when the phone rang. God, but she was getting touchy. Had it only been a few weeks since Emery's phone call to come to his office had started all of this? She didn't even identify herself before the voice at the other end asked, "So what are we eating tonight?"

She shouldn't be smiling into the phone at just hearing Nick's voice. Uneasy, she recognized that she was beginning to look forward to hearing from him each day. Not good. What would happen on the day when he didn't call or show up again?

"You'll want to take me to dinner, Bree, so you can hear what I found out from Megan's obstetrician."

"No way. You found her doctor?"

"Yep, I ended up having to call nineteen offices because her doctor is in Brentwood, not near the hospitals like we thought. But I finally struck pay dirt. I'm not sharing the info, though, until we eat."

She made a frustrated sound. She needed to pick something he might not like. Then again, he seemed to eat everything because he'd lived everywhere. "Okay, Lebanese, and only if we run afterward. I'm eating way too much food with you lately."

"Bree, the only time I run is if I have to save my life."

She started to lecture him on the importance of exercise for good health and to keep his body in shape, when she wondered what Nick looked like under those jeans and t-shirts. She felt herself blushing and was grateful he couldn't see her. She hoped her voice was steady when she said, "OK, here's my final offer: Dinner and a walk."

His sigh was dramatic. "If I have to walk, then we're eating Russian.”

"Don't tell me. You used to write for the Kremlin."

"No one likes a smart-ass flower doctor, Brianna."

"My apology. I should have said, 'Oh Nicky, you're fabulous!' "

"I've been telling you that for weeks. Though I can understand how you might have thought I was just a pretty face."

As superior as she wanted to sound, she couldn't quite keep the laughter out of her voice when she said, "Quit fishing for compliments. You know you're handsome. It's your brain I want."

He was silent so long she thought she'd lost his call when finally he said, "You know the last person who said that to me was a nun in fourth grade when I was sullen about having to do my science homework. She must be in heaven, laughing right now."

They traded quips and barbs for a few more minutes. Only when she hung up the phone and settled into her chair with a smile on her face did she realize that she should be worrying. Obviously, she hadn't learned a damn thing since her divorce from Mitch. Why was she so drawn to superficial charmers? What weakness in her character made her want a guy with an easy smile, wit, and the moral character of a thirteen-year old? Bree pursed her lips, then picked up the phone to dial Nick to tell him she couldn't have dinner with him tonight because an unexpected project had just come her way.

Then she put the phone down. She never broke her commitments and besides, he finally had something to share. The 'finally' part nagged her. Until now, she'd done most of the work; he really hadn't come up with anything until today. All charm, so little substance. Even worse to a woman who made monthly goals, he was content with what he was. No desire to improve. Don't waste your energy on this guy, she told herself.

Bree rehearsed her lie about needing to work at home on

a project under a deadline as she called Nick back.

◆

Bree had only been home for twenty minutes when Nick showed up. She covered her fib poorly, but if he suspected, he didn't say anything. In fact, he was even more charming than usual at dinner. She noticed that he deferred to her choice of Lebanese food, and he listened attentively when she shared the news about Stephen Almy without using his name. Maybe she had just been tired and hungry earlier in the evening. Maybe she was bringing out a better side of him.

But when he started to share his news, Bree noticed that Nick had the enthusiasm of an eight-year-old on Christmas morning.

"First, I'm claiming your BMW for two weeks."

Despite her earlier lecture to herself, Bree couldn't stop the fleeting stab of disappointment that he hadn't pressed her for something more personal.

"Let's see what you've got first, ace."

"I've got a name and a brief description of the guy based on what Megan wrote on her medical records."

"Oh my God, that's great."

"And I did it by telling the truth. Well, mostly. I told the nurses that I talked with the truth about Megan's death. Just like I predicted, when I found the right office, the nurse was sympathetic. That's when I bent the truth. I told her I was Megan's brother, faxed her the death certificate, and she was willing to help."

He leaned back, triumphant. "Shouldn't be hard to find the father. He's got an unusual name. Asa Gray."

"Asa Gray. You're sure?"

"That's what she put on the forms when asked about medical history of the father."

"Well, he's a father alright."

"You know him?"

"Asa Gray is considered the father of American botany. And he's been dead for more than one hundred thirty years."

"Damn."

Bree could tell he was as dejected as she was. They just kept going in circles.

After a few minutes, he said, "Why did she go to such great lengths to hide this guy's identity?"

"This is why I keep insisting he's involved with drugs. She's doing everything she can to protect him. She fell so in love with him that she lost her way about what is right and wrong."

"Well, he may be a drug lord, but he's a Caucasian drug lord. The obstetrician had a form that asked a lot of questions about the health and family history. She listed the father as white. In his early forties. No major disorders like epilepsy, cancer, etc."

"Well, if she lied about his name, she could have lied about everything else about him."

"But why? Why bother? It's not unusual for a single woman to have a baby anymore. And she seems to hold having this baby as almost sacred so she would want him to get the best care possible. Lying doesn't make any sense."

She stared down at her hands. Not surprising that Megan would believe bringing a life into this world was so important. She had such a tender heart. Pain so raw, so piercing slashed Bree's soul, and she had to keep staring down so Nick didn't see the tears she blinked back. How devastating that Megan had died trying to fill a hole in her own heart, a hole in her life.

"Are you okay?" Nick asked quietly.

Of course, the one time she wanted him to be obtuse, he was too perceptive. She nodded.

"So if the doctor is a dead end, I guess we're back to searching for the damn clues," he said. "I think we should change directions a little and not focus on the house. How about the clue, *we will travel the train of tears in life armed with our love.* Tears could be water, right. And there are dozens of fountains at the Garden. Let's focus on them, okay?"

"You'll put together a list of places to search?"

He eyed her. "You know I'm very fond of short lists."

"But, Nicky, you're so very good," she cooed, and felt an unexpected moment of satisfaction when he blinked. She'd never made Mitch blink. She wasn't sure what to do next. *Nothing. Do Nothing.* Was she cursed that just when she decided he was too dangerous to be around, he became useful. She fell back on the business of justice for Megan.

"Find out anything from the neighbors?"

"You know it's harder to find nosy neighbors these days. No little old ladies staying home and watching through the blinds. I found a few at home late this afternoon, but most of them couldn't even tell you that Megan lived there."

Bree leaned forward. "Most?"

Nick smiled wolfishly. "Ah, Brianna, I knew you'd pick up on that. I found a nerdy, out-of-work software programmer. Programmers are very detail oriented, you know. Just like scientists."

"And?"

"You're ruining my dramatic moment with your impatience, Bree."

She scowled at him, but sat back obediently in her chair.

"This guy never talked to Megan, other than to say hi a couple of times. But one night he was going out as Megan and a guy were coming in." He held up his hand to forestall her. "The nerd noticed only because he thought the guy looked so much older than Megan."

Bree shrugged. "Maybe it was some classmate."

Nick shook his head. "The nerd said he had his hands on her butt, was making a lot of suggestions about what he would do to her later than night, and Megan was giggling. And when the guy saw the nerd, he turned his head away. But the nerd said guy was definitely Caucasian."

Bree frowned, then finally said, "So the guy's not from

South America? I pictured him being foreign because of the poison."

Nick lifted one brow, and Bree quickly asked, "Anything else he remembers about the guy."

"If you're hoping the guy had an accent, the neighbor said no. He said his voice wasn't that distinctive."

Bree rested her face between her hands. Finally, she said, "Let's take that walk. I think better when I'm moving."

"Since I brought your choice for dinner, let's just *stroll*."

Bree rolled her eyes. "Well, here we are again. Me with purpose. You just *ambling* along."

"Yes, but when you *mosey* with me, you'll be able to stop and smell the roses." He sent her an absurdly infectious smile over his pun.

She held out her hand to pull him up. "Come on then before I'm reduced to *shuffling*. You can make it to the end of the driveway, right?"

Mid-May had kissed the day with perfection—temperature in the seventies, and none of the oppressive humidity St. Louis would suffer in June and July. Perfect night for a walk. Despite the difference in their heights and strides, Bree had no trouble keeping up with Nick. Unbidden, an image of her body stretched out against his on a sultry night popped into her mind. Thankfully, the heat and the walk hid the real reason for her flushed face.

They walked in companionable silence for a while, giving her more time to recover.

"You're one of the few people I know who isn't afraid of silence," she observed as they walked. "My ex-husband used to chatter through our entire jog. That should have been my first clue. But, hey, I was in love, and I wanted to make him happy. In the end, he made me a bitter woman."

While she had thought a lot about Mitch, she hadn't talked much about him since she'd come back. She'd been too caught up in her mother's illness, then the family's grief. But now that she had started, Bree found it wasn't quite as painful as before.

When she peeked up at him, Nick looked at her with sympathetic eyes, and she understood why everyone seemed to spill their feelings and thoughts to him. How could she resist him when he said softly, "You loved him with the same intensity that you do everything?"

"Yep," she said. "I thought love would make both of us happy. Together, we would be stronger than we were as individuals. My parents were like that. Each one was amazing, but together, they were incredible. Instead, love made me small, petty, angry, feeling like a failure. I will never fall in love again," she stated flatly.

If she expected him to offer assurances that she would love again, apparently she'd have to wait until it snowed in August in St. Louis—which would be never.

Instead, he said, "I see the irony in having to understand . . . to feel . . . Megan's vision of love to solve all of this."

She nodded. "It should be so easy for me, really. Because I had the same dream once. The same passion for a grand kind of love."

Without realizing it, Bree had picked up the pace until she was almost jogging. Nick had fallen a few steps behind and didn't look particularly interested if he caught up. Perhaps he was hoping for an excuse to stop all together. She felt foolish for talking about such intimacies with him.

"Sorry. You shouldn't have been subjected to that self-pity."

As she expected, he responded with a sarcastic "you are so right. Too sappy for me."

But she was no longer in the mood to banter with him. She was starting to glimpse his gifts. She just couldn't let him throw it away. After all she'd learned about loss, she wasn't about to let him remain dross when he could be gold.

"You know, Nick, I think that underneath your cynicism, there's actually the heart of a very sensitive person."

They'd stopped walking and were standing on the side of

the road, staring at each other.

She was not going to let him wiggle out of this. She'd just revealed things about her life, herself, her heart that she hadn't even told her family, and she was not going to let him charm or jest his way out of this.

Bree stared straight into those warm whisky-colored eyes as she placed her hand over his heart. "I think there's a good man in there, Nick Mancini. And I think you can be even better—at anything—if you decided what you want. You just have to want it and work for it."

She took a few steps back toward her family's house. Then, looking back over her shoulder, she said, "I have to finish that project. I'll leave the keys to the BMW in the car. Just remember if anything happens to it, I'm a vengeful person, and I know a really good lawyer."

With that, she ran home, leaving him alone to think about her words.

Chapter Fourteen

B REE'S FEET BEAT A RHYTHM that matched the phrases chanting over and over again in her mind as she ran through the Garden on her lunch hour.

Together, we . . . Left, right, left . . . will build a house . . . Right, left, right, left . . .

She hoped running would free her mind to think about the clues differently because Lord knew she had gone over them so many times she'd lost count, as if flipping through the scribbles would change the words. That was the definition of insanity, wasn't it? Doing the same thing, but expecting different results? She was so frustrated and angry at herself. And at Megan too—as if that did a lot of good. Unfortunately, she still wasn't anywhere closer to figuring out what Megan had meant. Because she had no idea if any of the clues were more important than the other, Bree had simply started working on them in order just to give her a place to start.

Together, we will build a house of love.

She'd tried the Linnean House, named after the Swedish scientist who formalized the modern system of naming organisms, and the Temperate House, which featured plants from Mediterranean climates that bloomed indoors all year long. No luck. All that was left to explore was the Climatron, a geodesic dome that housed a thousand tropical plants. Only a botanist would think of it as a house, Bree thought ruefully. Looking for a clue in the Climatron would be like hoping you had the winning ticket in the lottery—a real long shot. Still, the Climatron was world famous so the boyfriend might know it.

Frustrated by their lack of progress and haunted by night-mares where Megan asked why Bree hadn't found her killer, Bree had turned to the other clue, *the tracks of our tears*. Tears were wet. Maybe Nick was right, and the clue was in one of the dozen fountains dotting the Garden, Bree thought as she ran.

Bree looked up when she heard squeals and saw at least one hundred children coming down the paved path toward her. From the looks of them, probably fourth or fifth grad-ers on a field trip. She veered right, several feet onto the grass. And down she went. Her fast reflexes were the only thing that saved her from falling flat on her face, and she heard the giggles and snickers of the children. She scowled at them while she rubbed her ankle.

She tried to stand, sucked in a gasp at the stabbing pain, and crumpled to the ground again. She felt the sun being blocked and looked up to find a small crowd gathering. It was hard to have dignity when you'd just shown the grace of an elephant. She stood, trying to put some weight on her foot and winced. One of the teachers flagged down a horti-culture staff member, who radioed for one of the Garden's golf carts, and drove her back to her office.

Her assistant, Cheryl, clucked over her until Bree agreed to down some aspirin, which dulled the pain. News of her fall spread. Emery called to see how she felt, HR called to tell her to fill out an accident report, and Cheryl fussed after her again when Bree hobbled to her father's car. She cursed Nick Mancini for having the BMW.

By the time she reached the couch in her family room, her ankle throbbed. She knew the drill from her years of cross country and track—stay off it, keep it elevated, apply cold for the first twenty-four hours, then alternate hot and cold. She sighed. She always hated the cold part—and that was *before* she'd lived in the tropics and her blood had thinned.

As daylight began to fade, her father called to say he was extending his trip on the East Coast. She didn't tell him about her sprain. He would only worry, involve her sister, and before she knew it, he'd have an orthopedic surgeon at her doorstep. She missed her mother's calm. Her father's sense of drama could sometimes be overwhelming. She did wonder, though, if he putting off coming home because he was reluctant to face the changes she'd made with her mother's personal items.

She would have to sleep on the family room couch tonight. Hobbling up to her bedroom was out of the question. But as she laid in the dark, with her foot on a couple of pillows, she missed Nick. He hadn't come by once since she'd lectured him on growing up during their walk days earlier. He'd texted, left messages, but had held himself aloof.

Who could live with a man like that? He would never have a serious conversation. A woman would have to be crazy to be involved with him. The man was only good for one thing. Sex popped into her head. It had been so long since she'd thought about sex . . . so long that she wasn't even sure she missed it—which was pathetic. Pathetic.

Her sleep was fitful. Her ankle hurt like hell, her heart was heavy and bruised for Megan, and she was all by herself. Tears of self-pity escaped during the night.

In the morning, she took one look at her purple and yellow ankle, and knew the only place she might be going that day was to an urgent care for an x-ray. She phoned her office, dissuaded her assistant from coming over with food. She hopped around the kitchen to fix a bowl of cereal. Then she stared at the couch, which seemed like a long journey back. When she finally limped back to it, she was tired and her ankle hurt worse. She propped it up again, opened her laptop, and hoped to distract herself with work. However, she couldn't concentrate and dozed.

A noise startled her awake. Nick sat at the island, eating breakfast and reading. She struggled to sit up.

"The keys to the Beemer also had a house key. Your assistant told me you fell, sprained your ankle."

"Not my most graceful moment. I'm poor company today, Nick."

"You probably need more drugs."

She thought he had just a little too much glee in his voice when he offered to get some ice. When he came back, he said hopefully, "I don't suppose you're ticklish?"

"Absolutely, positively not."

She thought she heard him mutter 'of course not' under his breath.

His fingers brushed her foot as he gently placed the ice pack on her ankle. She shivered. Surely, it was because of the ice pack.

"You know I should probably warn you. I'm not a very good patient," she said as he returned with his own plate of bacon and eggs, and plopped into a seat near the couch. "I don't get sick very often, so I tend to get crabby."

"Trying to get rid of me?"

Yes. You and your warm brown eyes and long, gentle fingers.

"Just warning you. In case my temper snaps."

"Well, I'll just ride off into the sunset in *my* BMW. Which is a terrific car, by the way."

"I'm so glad you like it," she said dryly.

"A convertible would be nicer, though. Great chick magnet, especially in this weather with the top down."

"Well, next time my family buys a car, I'll be sure to take into account . . ."

"Your partner's preferences?" Nick suggested.

She shrugged. "As long as it's not my husband's, I'm can live with it."

Out of the corner of her eye, she saw him studying her. Best to ignore those probing eyes, so she pretended to be very interested in the page she'd pulled up on her laptop.

"What was he like?"

She looked up, startled. "What was who like?"

"Your ex-husband. What was his name?"

"Mitch," she answered warily.

Nick kept staring at her.

"All right. He was charming. Smart. Attentive." She stumbled over that last one, realizing that she was revealing more than she would ever want Nick Mancini to know.

He got that devilish look on his face that just made it more devastatingly handsome, and she got angry at herself for noticing. She was testy when she said, "It was a good marriage, Nick. We respected each other. Had mutual interests."

"Hmmm, sounds to me like you never had any fun."

Bree blinked. "Well, of course, we did. We enjoyed the same kind of movies and books. We hosted a lot of dinner parties."

He lifted an eyebrow. "Did he make your pulse race every time just because he was close to you? Did you think you couldn't live if he wasn't around?"

Memories of being that in love with Mitch overwhelmed her—memories she had pushed away for so long. For the millionth time, Bree tried to figure out what had gone so wrong with Mitch that he'd looked for someone else. She'd been so sure she'd found her own version of her parents' marriage. She'd been so determined to have the same spark they'd had for forty years that she'd waited until her thirties to marry.

"Wait a minute. Where did you get that language? Did you get it out of some romance novel? Because I'm not buying Nick Mancini as a romantic. I bet you know very little about long-term relationships. In fact . . ." Her turn to study him. "I bet you've never been in love before."

He scowled and became indignant. She thought he started to say 'of course, I have', but couldn't get the words out.

"You haven't," she crowed, and winced as she shifted on the couch.

"Oh for God's sake, Brianna, of course I've been in love."

"Describe it to me. No, wait," she said animatedly, now that the ibuprofen had kicked in. "I'll describe it to you.

Lots of sex, lots of laughs, some drugs or booze. More sex." Bree leaned toward him. "And it lasted three months at most."

"Don't sound so smug," he said coolly. "Your nose is so high in the air, you'll break your neck, and your ankle will be the least of your injuries. Besides, love and marriage are highly overrated."

"We can agree on that. I don't even miss the sex that much."

Nick's look such was a mixture of horror and skepticism that Bree laughed. As she settled down, she said, "What I miss is being held . . . being touched."

She realized what she'd said and wished she could take it back. It was too honest and made her uncomfortable. Thank God, she caught herself before she mentioned the occasional longing and loneliness that swept over her until her heart ached as much as her ankle.

Nick flabbergasted her when he said matter-of-factly, "You know, I'm growing used to your openness. I'll admit it took me aback at first. I didn't like that you talked about your family so much. My family never even talked, so who knows if we would have been open."

"In fact," he said, warming to the subject, "being with you is really comfortable. Even when I disagree with you, like now. You know what I like about you? You pay so little attention to my looks. You treat me like a little brother or like a pal you had on the third grade playground. It's a nice change."

"Thanks." *I think. Did he just label me some sexless female eunuch?*

Bree fell silent, mulling over what he'd said, so he had to ask her twice if she'd gotten any further on the clues. She offered her theory on 'tears'.

"Let me get the map of the Garden you gave me out to of the car so I know what fountains to research." He took his plate and her bowl to the sink, then disappeared.

She must have appeared to be dozing when he came back in. She struggled not to move when she felt him tenderly brush her hair back off her face. Heat flooded her body. If she said a word, she'd give herself away on how that touch made her pulse beat faster, and he'd know he affected her. What a disaster that would be.

"You know," he said quietly, "I thought about what you said when you made me take that walk. You know what I've always wanted to do? I want to write a novel. Even started a couple when I was younger."

Bree had to work to keep her breath even, as if she were sleeping. With her eyes closed, she only had his voice to guide her. She thought she heard wistfulness, irony, even longing—which she understood too well.

"I haven't thought about that dream in a long time. Too many other things came along. Got in the way. God, I don't even know if I can do it. Don't know if I'm good as that kind of a writer. What if my ideas are boring? So I'm not sure whether to thank you or kill you. Partner."

Laying on the couch, not moving a muscle, was actually painful. Was he only baring his soul because he thought she didn't hear him? Eventually, he moved off and she heard him rinsing off dishes.

She felt a stab of sadness and hurt for him. No one had ever encouraged Nick to have a dream, much less go for it. He'd had no mother to praise his writing and put his stories on the refrigerator when he'd been a child. No father who cared enough to cheer him on. When she heard the noises in the kitchen stop, she made a production of waking up.

He moved back to the couch. Gently lifting her ankle, he sat down, balancing her propped-up foot on his knee. She handed him her laptop, and he began researching about the fountains. The heat of his body, his concentration lulled her to sleep. When she woke an hour later, he handed her some maps and pictures.

Nick was in a mellow mood today. Or maybe he was as

reluctant as she was to be alone. They tossed around ideas and got diverted, talking about their travels and what they liked about certain countries. They discovered they'd both been in Ecuador in 2015. He swapped out her ice pack a couple of times, and gave her acetaminophen once.

As lunch approached, he asked, "How does the ankle feel?"

"Better. It's not the worst sprain I've ever had. I probably still should go to urgent care just to make sure I didn't chip a bone."

"Let's go then."

"You don't have to take me."

"Well, you sure can't drive yourself. And you're a bit vulnerable for an Uber or taxi. Besides maybe I'll get to push you in a wheelchair."

Bree rolled her eyes. Then, wheelchair ride aside, she realized he was right. Without her father around, she was on her own. With most of her career spent overseas, she'd lost touch with friends, and she'd been too absorbed with her parents' private battles to reach out since she'd been home.

The realization of being alone hurt a lot more than her ankle. Just the thought of hobbling to the car, driving to the urgent care, more hobbling into the center, possibly sitting there for hours—by herself—made her sink into self-pity.

Bree sighed. "Thanks. I'd appreciate your help."

He made the trip to the urgent care center an entertainment. He told stories almost the entire two hours that it took to transport her, have her foot x-rayed to prove it was nothing more than a sprain, and the drive home. She had to admit he lifted her spirits.

"I'm sorry they didn't have a wheelchair," she said as he helped resettle her on the couch.

"Are you going to be okay here tonight by yourself? I can sleep on one of the other couches, in case you feel worse."

Images of Nick sleeping seeped through her like red wine spilled on white carpet. She imagined he would look even more appealing asleep. She wondered if he would still look sinful, the hint of decadence in his mouth, even without the charming smile to lure a woman? She pretended to consider his offer to buy her some time so she didn't sound breathless.

"Thanks, but I think I'll be okay. If you just bring over the charger for my phone. I can call if I feel worse."

He also dragged over a little table, and topped it with a pitcher of water and glass, snacks, plus all the medicines he'd brought so she wouldn't have to go far if she felt worse. He also checked the house to make sure all the doors were locked.

"You won't be stubborn and tough this out if you start to feel worse, right?"

"What? Me? Stubborn?"

"What was I thinking?" He paused. "It's a big house, Bree, on a big lot. Are you sure you're comfortable here by yourself?"

"It is an awfully big house for one person, isn't it? I wonder if my Dad has been keeping it because I'm here. It would be ironic because I'm putting off going back out into the field because of Dad.

"Two good jobs are about to open up in Asia," she shared. "I'd be foolish not to take one."

"I can only stay a few more weeks," he said. "I'll fly to see my sister and start the search for another reporting gig."

They stared at each other in awkward silence.

She sighed. "Right then. If we can't find anything, then we'll just have to let it—" She couldn't say it.

"Go? You're doing all you can, Bree."

She nodded. "Thanks for today, Nick."

He leaned over and kissed her on the forehead. "No problem."

She told herself it was her ankle that kept her awake. Certainly, it wasn't because she kept replaying the feel of Nick's lips or fingers against her skin. She was sure it meant nothing to him. So innocent and brotherly.

You do not want to fall in love again. You are not good at it. You wouldn't survive the pain.

About one a.m., she decided she had it all under control. Her feelings for Nick were just like his for her—nothing but buddies. But the part about her not missing sex? She might be willing to change her mind on that one.

Chapter Fifteen

———◆———

THE SOOTHING SOUNDS OF THE fountain and the languid heat did nothing to tame Bree's frustration. The trail to Megan's lover was growing colder by the day, and Nick had made it clear he was on a countdown. She was running out of time, if she wanted his help. More importantly, Bree hated the idea of giving up. The injustice of it infuriated her. She knew, just knew, that the answers were hidden in this Garden. Trouble was she wasn't coming up with any answers, only more questions.

Did he make your pulse race just because he was close to you? Did you think you wouldn't live if he wasn't part of your life?

Nick's questions haunted her the most. They swirled around in her mind, playing over and over again like Megan's clues. They intruded on her work during the day and were the last thing she thought at night. Had her marriage ever been anything but her own fantasy?

Bree wanted to outrun her black thoughts, but a glance at her bandaged ankle squashed that hope. At least the bruises were fading. She was frustrated at only being able to hobble around when she felt time running faster than her.

She sat on a bench near the entrance to the Garden, nibbling on her lunch watching children throw pennies into the fountain and make wishes. She saw the coins slowly sinking, and knew exactly how it felt to float down and down. Like those pennies, she'd touched bottom. But lately, as unsettling things had been, she felt like she was kicking back toward the surface. If she could find any evidence that could help Daniel Cusumano nail this guy, she felt she could close this miserable chapter of her life and move on.

She ran her hands through her hair in frustration. Analyzing was getting her nowhere. Perhaps it was time to change tactics, consider a fresh approach. What's one hundred eighty degrees from me? The answer came too easily: Nick.

There had to be another more analytical approach. Certainly, keeping the search quiet wasn't getting them far enough, fast enough. What would happen if she talked to staff who might know more than she did? True, maybe she didn't have Nick's charm, but she was on friendly terms with almost all her co-workers. Nice, polite Dr. Kincaid. She mentally made a list of useful people who might know something special that she'd overlooked: the horticulturalist who oversaw the planting of the spring beds, the head groundskeeper, and the Garden historian.

She pulled her cell phone out of her purse, and after calling a couple of departments, got the number of the volunteer who had acted as the Garden's informal historian for twenty-three years. As she dialed him, Bree concocted a story, then shook her head. Her gift for telling lies had grown so much she was starting to feel like Pinocchio. This is what she got for hanging around with Nick. All prepared, she was let down when the historian didn't answer, and she had to leave a message.

The other two men—the horticulturalist and the head groundskeeper—were easier to track down since they worked at the Garden. Emery had thoughtfully provided her with a golf cart, and she cruised past the most heavily trafficked flower beds at this time of year. Her persistence paid off when she caught Marty, the head groundskeeper, coming off a break in the café.

Marty had been with the Garden even longer than Emery, and his leathery face showed every line from working outdoors for three decades. As soon as he saw her, he told her that he'd repaired the turf where she'd twisted her ankle, but there was a bigger problem because the turf kept sinking. She assured him that wasn't what she was interested in. Instead, she told Marty the story she'd concocted with a straight face and still had a short nose when she finished. Marty meandered his way through her questions as each one reminded him of a story, and Bree had to resist fidgeting or sighing. How did Nick do this?

"Were there ever any other houses in the Garden besides Shaw's? Maybe something that's been torn down or built over?"

Marty thought long before finally shaking his head. "Until the last decade or two, the directors didn't want buildings on the property. They wanted just natural gardens. But, of course, now to stay current with all that hype the marketing people come up with, they're building all over the place."

Bree quickly steered him away from *that* conversation. She knew that many of the old timers disagreed whenever Emery took the Garden in a new direction.

"How about railroad tracks? I know that when Shaw started the Garden this was considered the country."

Marty cackled on that one.

"Hmmm. Only train I can think of is that little model one in the Children's Garden."

Bree's heart beat faster. "I've never noticed that one."

"Yep, it's one of those tiny gardens that are part of the home demo area."

Bree wound down the conversation as quickly as possible, and steered the golf cart to the little garden tucked away amid showier demonstration gardens. As she limped to a bench, Bree could immediately see the attraction for children. Everything was their size. Mother Goose poked her head out of a flower bed. The base of one of the big trees wore stone eyes, nose and mouth if the tree were magically alive and could talk. In the back of the garden was a model of a town encircled by a railroad. Bree clapped her hands with all the glee of a five-year old.

She looked for a way to stop the train, and finally found a switch concealed from little eyes and hands. Checking to make sure no one was coming, Bree struggled to get on her hands and knees without reinjuring her ankle. She probed the four plastic railroad cars for secret compartments.

Nothing. Absolutely nothing. Throwing the switch back on, she stepped back onto the paved area—and spotted the little yellow house.

Together, we will build a house of love.

What the heck. Couldn't hurt to look. Saying a silent prayer, she lifted the house. Not a thing underneath. She tried prying off the roof and swore when it wouldn't budge. With her finger, she pushed open the front door—and it gave way. Her finger brushed cold metal. She turned the house on its side, gave it a shake and a simple gold wedding band fell into the palm of her hand.

Oh, Megan.

She examined the inside of the ring. It was inscribed: Love is the flower of life.

Where was the accompanying a note? Bree stuck her finger back in the house and probed. She didn't feel an envelope, but her finger couldn't reach the top of the house. Bree turned the house upside down, shook it hard numerous times, and then turned it on its side as she stuck her finger back in, hoping any note would have come loose. This time, her finger touched something. She rolled it towards the house opening and out fell a tiny scroll wrapped in blue ribbon.

Bree looked skyward and offered a prayer of thanks. Unrolling the parchment, she found Megan's note.

My love,

I want the story of our love to be one we can tell our kids and grandkids every Valentine's Day. Think how romantic it will be to our children when they learn the story of how you found the treasures and pictures of our courtship through the clues in our private scavenger hunt.

Oh, I know that I sound mushy and totally unrealistic. But I believe that love defines who we are in life. Love is the only thing worth living for. And if you don't have love . . . like Dr. Kincaid . . . what do you have to live for?

Bree blanched when she'd read her name. Megan pitied her. Pitied her! Only the young, Bree fumed, thought love was such a salvation. Anyone who had been married could tell you that it was hard work. And that part about protecting her against all the horrible things of life? Well, sometimes the horrible things of life turned out to be the person you loved. Especially when he changed his mind about loving you.

She replaced the house back in its setting, then struggled to stand up again. She stood back to make sure the area looked like it had never been disturbed. Brianna Kincaid, vandal. There's something no one who knew her ever expected to say. Clearly, all of Nick's bad qualities were rubbing off on her.

The scroll and ring in hand, she limped back into the golf cart and directed it back to her office. As she waited for the elevator, she couldn't believe Megan had written such drivel. God, what a sentimental fool she was!

Then the truth struck her. *How jaded I've become. And how I want to be like her.*

Bree blinked to hold back tears.

Megan may not have loved wisely. She certainly hadn't found the right man. But to love that deeply . . . with that much faith and hope. Bree could remember loving like that once—with all the confidence and sureness of 'forever'. The world had seemed so full of possibilities. She thought about the past few years, which seemed so bleak, and worse, the years ahead, stretching endlessly in front of her.

I would give anything to feel like that again. To have someone pull me into his arms and make everything go away, but us. Just us.

She could hear Megan: *You're a coward, Dr. Kincaid, if you stop believing in love just because you got hurt once.*

So many tears came now that Bree couldn't wipe them away. When the elevator stopped at her floor, she barely made it to the stairwell where she wept for her losses and for her lack of courage.

Chapter Sixteen

BREE FELT LIKE FRODO—WHAT TO do with the ring? When she finished her tear-fest, she sniffled as she walked through the hallways back to her office, gingerly carrying the ring in her last tissue. Everything hurt—her foot, her head, her heart. All she wanted was to be alone.

So lost in her misery was she that Bree didn't see Michael Singleton as he came around the corner. They collided, jostling the tissue out of her hand, and out bounced the ring. They both bent to retrieve it, Michael reaching it first. Curiosity in his eyes, he handed it back to her. She gave him a small smile, tried to keep going, hoping he'd let her pass. No such luck.

"Are you okay, Bree? You don't look like you feel well."

He was being kind. With a red nose and eyes, she probably looked like a lab rat.

"I'm okay. But thanks for asking, Michael."

He gave her a skeptical look, but didn't press. "Find that on one of the paths? You can give it to security. They handle lost and found."

She nodded, moving past him to seek refuge in her office. She grabbed a soda while she called Nick. Even the glee in his voice when she told him about the ring and that Megan indicated one of the clues contained a picture of the infamous boyfriend couldn't put a smile on her face. No point in telling him *not* to come over to her house for dinner, so she asked him to bring a good bottle of white wine. She'd never tried drowning her sorrows; maybe it would work. And maybe she could get Nick to leave early. What a dilemma—trying to get a hot guy to leave her alone. If she weren't so drained, it would be funny.

Bree turned back to her desk to find Charles Davidson standing in her doorway. What was it with guys showing up at her office lately? She could feel her face turning red, matching her eyes and nose. She tried to look composed and dignified, hoping like hell that he hadn't heard all of the conversation with Nick.

"How's the ankle, Graceful?"

"Healing fast." Never show blood to a shark, she thought.

"Interesting conversation."

"How lucky for me that you're such a good eavesdropper."

"Is that the new lover? Is it a guy? Or maybe it's a girl. And here I thought the rumors going around about you couldn't possibly be true."

She could guess what some of the rumors were, or maybe she didn't want to know, but to ask would let him know she cared. Bree shrugged. "I'm a really boring person, Charles. I doubt there are many rumors floating about me."

"Well, I can take care of that."

He flashed a lot of white teeth, and she thought 'wrong fish; he's a piranha'.

"Though to tell the truth, you never struck me as the kind of woman who spent much time with men."

She tried to be mature, but it had been a miserable week, so she was weak and gave in to her mood. "Ah, in direct contrast to you, who I hear spends plenty of time with women."

"I never doubted that you'd be a good opponent, Bree."

"How comforting. Is there a reason you're blessing me with your presence this afternoon? I really need to leave soon."

She realized that while her conversation had the same patter as when she verbally jousted with Nick, it simply didn't have the same feel. She imagined that Nick's jabs could be lethal, but he'd never really hurt her with his put-downs.

Whereas Charles—she could easily see him using a woman and tossing her aside with no regret.

"Emery asked me to drop off this report."

"Thanks. I'll look it over."

"You know, a lot of people think you've got this locked up because you know Emery so well, and because your family is so well connected. Personally, I don't think you've been at the top of your game this whole year. I'm sure Emery's noticed how moody and distracted you've been the last few months."

Bree leaned forward, and with more bravado than she felt, said, "Charles, you'll have to do better than that. I grew up learning intimidation tactics at the dinner table."

She had to give him credit, damn it. He was confident, almost cocky.

"May the best man win. See you around, Brianna."

Did he know something she didn't? She didn't doubt he'd drop some well-timed innuendos to Emery. She wouldn't be at all surprised if more gossip, started by Charles, floated through the Garden grapevine. As she packed up her messenger bag, she made a mental note to call Emery for lunch.

She slunk home and shucked her jeans, blazer and top for the oldest, baggiest t-shirt and running shorts she owned. She heard Nick call from the first floor, and she gimped downstairs.

He'd brought tenderloin medallions, and was opening a bottle of wine when she came into the kitchen. Bree pulled two wine glasses out of the cabinets. "Fill mine to the top."

He raised one eyebrow. "Listen, in that outfit you don't even look like you're old enough to drink."

She snorted, then found her bag to carefully pull out the ring. She held it up, using her fingernails. "Do you think Daniel Cusumano could run this for fingerprints? I realize it's a long shot."

He handed her a glass. "I can ask. If I see him. They're working round the clock on the murder of those boys."

"I can't bear to think about it. Those parents must be going crazy."

"Wearing Daniel down too. He never says anything, but I know he's getting by on four hours of sleep most days."

"I'd worry more what it's doing to his soul. It has to be rough after a while. To see the horrible side of people."

Nick watched her taking continuous large sips and frowned. "His dad was a cop. Daniel knew what he was getting into."

"Well," she said too brightly, "at least *we're* getting closer. Two down, four to go. And if we're lucky one of the photos will be of her great love, and at least Daniel can have a conversation with the guy. If he can find him."

———◆———

Bree looked so hopeful, Nick didn't want to bring up all the reasons why this was looking more and more hopeless. She seemed fragile tonight. Frankly, he was a little uneasy at how much wine she was drinking. He had no idea if she'd be a friendly or morose drunk. He doubted if she knew either.

"I've never seen you drink anything but water or maybe an occasional soda. Take it easy, okay?" He made himself at home in the kitchen, getting out plates and utensils. "How's the ankle feeling?"

"It hurts. Everything hurts."

He thought about teasing her and asking if she wanted 'Uncle Nicky' to kiss it and make it better but the flatness in her eyes stopped him. He felt the same helplessness that he'd felt when he and his sister were little, and Tory had needed something he didn't know how to give or get.

"You know, most people wouldn't have made it this far, Bree. You had very little to work with."

She took a final swig of wine and held out her glass for more. "I know you're trying to make me feel better."

"Doing a great job, huh?" He thought about picking a

fight. Her fuse would be short right now, and a fight would take the edge off the sadness clinging to her like scared child holding tight to her mama. Instead, he steered her to the table and forced her to sit down. He dug in to his tenderloin, but after a few bites, he noticed she was merely moving her food around on the plate.

"You know you can't get up from the table until you've eaten all your food, Brianna."

He frowned when she didn't return the jab.

"She was so in love, Nick. She had such faith in its power."

Nick knew better than to roll his eyes. It never paid to cross a woman who was fervently discussing love, especially this woman. He watched her warily, searching for a safe topic when she fell silent. Didn't matter what he said, as long as he said something. "You know—"

She interrupted him. "I want that feeling back. I want to fall in love again. I want to have love like Megan. To love forever. Like my parents.

"And instead, you're eating dinner with a bitter woman. A woman with a shriveled heart. Who's going to grow old all alone. A woman who's going to end up with thirteen cats and a family who whispers about 'poor Aunt Brianna' at holiday dinners."

"Give me the wine glass."

Panic shot through him when she looked at him with eyes so mournful and lost. Too late. Tears pooled in those pale violet eyes.

"What's the point," she whispered, "if you don't have anyone to love you?"

Oh shit, he thought, right before she started sobbing. For a second he was so stunned and scared that he froze. Then he moved to her, pulling her up into his arms, where she went willingly. Her sobs twisted his careless, feckless heart.

"It's okay, baby. Cry all you want."

Part of him knew exactly what to do. After all, he'd held his share of women. He felt her trembling even as he knew she was trying to stop. A feisty woman like Bree would see tears as a weakness and to cry in front of a smart ass like him would be as painful as the sobs wracking her body and the sadness piercing her heart.

He stroked Bree's hair, murmuring little phrases that meant absolutely nothing. What was important was the soothing sound of his voice . . . the warmth of his arms until the world seemed safe again.

He could take her to bed. Between the wine and the tears, she wouldn't resist. And for a few hours, he would make sure she found relief from her deep unhappiness. Until tomorrow. Everything would be different if he slept with her. He hesitated, and cursed himself for doing so. He liked Bree. Really liked her. The only other women he had a relationship with like this were his sister and Daniel's sisters.

He felt her sobs slowing, but he tightened his hold just a little, and remembered what she'd revealed about being touched. He laid his head on top of hers. Her hair was soft and silky. He wanted her to feel secure and protected so they simply stood, locked in silence and each other. He found he was strong enough to absorb some of her misery.

His body protested when she finally pulled away. Bree sniffled and blinked as if she were trying to hold back more tears. Good. She seemed to be working her way back to control. He went to the refrigerator, looking for tea. Best to get everything quickly back to normal so she wouldn't spend time apologizing. With her sincerity and sense of duty, Bree's apology would be long and awkward. He needed to make a graceful exit—as soon as she was okay.

"How about a really hot bath?" he suggested.

She hesitated and for a second, he thought she was going to ask him to run the water and get in with her. Worse, out of sheer habit, he might say yes. This time, she rescued him—from himself—when her resolve kicked in. She nodded.

"I'll put this away. You can eat it later if you want. Do you have a girlfriend you can call?"

"My sister. She lives in Boston, but I can call her at any hour. My sister is a crazy person. She'll make me laugh."

"Does she know what we're doing?"

Bree shook her head. "I didn't exactly think telling my father or my sister that I was chasing a possible drug lord who probably killed someone close to me was a good idea."

"Always thinking." He walked over and kissed her on the forehead. "Things will look better in the morning."

She looked unconvinced.

"There's someone out there who was meant just for you. You'll find him. You'll fall in love again."

He couldn't believe he said that, but he knew it was what she needed to hear. Though from her skeptical expression, he didn't have a lot of credibility as a love seer. He gently nudged her toward the stairs. "Get going."

She grabbed for the wine, but he got to the bottle first. He handed her the glass of iced tea instead.

"You're a really mean person," Bree said.

"Yep, I've been known to pull the petals off daisies for no good reason."

He watched her drag herself upstairs. Women. While he could make love to them, he would never understand them. Funny, but he really didn't think of Bree like he usually thought of women. He could admit he liked her, even admired her. He would even miss her when he left.

Chapter Seventeen

BREE KNEW HE WAS THERE even before she looked up.

She was organizing her desk for the next day and must have subconsciously picked up on the raised female voices outside her office; their chatter, an early warning system that something was different. When she looked up, Nick was leaning against the doorway of her office in the same careless pose he'd staged weeks before when she found him leaning against the car. She'd laughed then. Now she thought, this is a dangerous man. How ironic to have worked in jungles with poisonous snakes and bugs, only to run into real danger in her own office.

Nick was smiling. And she automatically smiled right back. Until she remembered last night's tears. Then she felt foolish.

"Don't," he said, settling into the chair across her desk. "Don't apologize for last night. It's okay not to be perfect, Bree."

He said it matter-of-factly, as if holding a wailing woman in his arms was an everyday occurrence.

She'd always been such an achiever, always out in front, that she wasn't quite sure how to gracefully accept his offer of being normal. She was both grateful and stung. She tried to think of a quip to keep the atmosphere light, but then she really was a woman meant for a crisis, when strength counted. He had read her too well, and she felt uncomfortable with the growing intimacy. And neither one of them had taken off a thing last night.

She wondered if it would have been less awkward if she

offered him her body then. Had Nick ever turned down an invitation like that? Not likely, Bree thought. It wasn't her body she was afraid to give him. Undoubtedly, Nick would be really good in bed. What bothered her was that he knew parts of her soul that no one, even her family, knew. It would have been easier if she'd slept with him. She worried her lower lip. Her feelings for Nick now were so confusing. And complicated. Which didn't stop her from glaring at him when he walked over to her office mini-fridge and pulled out a soda—her last soda.

"I worked hard all day." He didn't even look guilty as he took a long drink. "I went back to Megan's loft and chatted with the building manager, Deborah. She said Megan paid cash for a year's rent."

"Damn, damn, damn. Another dead end."

"Yep, this guy's gone to a lot of trouble to cover his trail—and he's covered it very well."

"He's a good planner. Even caught up in a love affair, he's taken lots of precaution. Which means he probably planned Megan's murder very carefully too."

Bree rubbed the back of her neck with both hands and gazed down at her desk while she thought. "If he just wanted a hot relationship, he probably would have chosen someone different than Megan. Maybe she made him happy."

Nick shrugged, but Bree forged on, "Until she announced she was pregnant. And then for some reason, he feels he has to kill her."

"Because he's got something to hide."

"Aside from the obvious—a pregnant girlfriend. Because . . ."

Nick picked up on where she was going. "Because she's threatened to go to his wife. And for some reason, he needs to stay married."

"Money?"

"Or maybe she knows a secret that he told her after the best sex he'd ever had. And if she shares that secret, she can ruin him."

She supposed it was something that she didn't blink, frown or sputter when he managed to tie all this back to sex. She answered his question with a shake of her head. "Except the two notes don't have that kind of tone. She's reverent, not wrathful."

"I ran the inscription in the ring on the internet," he said. "It's a quote by D.H. Lawrence. Not exactly a guy noted for flowers. Although there's probably a pun in there somewhere about deflowering."

"But of course you won't go there."

"Hey, I'm not the one who inscribed a wedding ring with a saying from a guy whose works were banned in the U.S. because they were considered pornographic. Maybe you botanists are a little wilder than I thought."

"Here's how wild we are. Let's go to dinner and talk where to look next."

Nick groaned.

"Quit whining. You're getting another free meal," she enticed.

The Garden was close to the Hill, the quaint Italian section of St. Louis. She started to say they could get lasagna like his mother used to make, but stopped herself in time. The only lasagna he'd probably had as a child had come from the frozen food section.

"How about a big burger? It's the only food we haven't eaten lately."

They negotiated palates as they walked to "their" BMW.

After they ordered, Bree pulled out the visitor map to the garden and smudged spreadsheet from her tote.

Nick arched one eyebrow. "You color-coded the possibilities?"

"You didn't?" she asked too sweetly. "We can rule out large bodies of water, like the lake in the Japanese Garden. It's huge. Too much for the boyfriend to cover. Same goes for the reflecting pools between the Climatron and the events pavilion."

She studied the map. "I love the Shapleigh Fountain, but so many kids play in that circle of water jets that it's hard to believe anything would survive this long without being discovered. For the same reason, I don't think she would have hidden it in or near the waterfall in the Climatron. Too many people." Bree shook her head. "No, I think she would have chosen a spot that not everyone who visits the garden would take time to see."

Nick pointed to the Boxwood Garden. "What about the fountains here?"

Bree smiled. "Those are some of my favorites. Have you ever watched a child chase the sprays? How can that water jump from fountain to fountain to fountain to fountain? Magic."

"Great way to wear out the little darlings."

Nick's comment seemed absent-minded as he circled the Boxwood Garden and studied the map. Bree wondered if he ever thought of kids. Not that she was going to bring up the subject. She had no need to know, though there probably was a long trail of women who'd had wondered that very thing over the years.

"What about the fountain in the Temperate House?" Nick asked as they moved their papers to make room for the food that the waitress sat before them.

"I agree that it's a possibility. There's also a fountain in the Ottoman Garden. All of those are small and intimate. They would have suited Megan's purpose perfectly."

Probably renewed by her success in finding the ring and these new possibilities, Nick watched Bree dig into her burger. He enjoyed Bree's eclectic taste in foods. There weren't many women Nick could drag to a Brazilian eatery one day and a Greek diner the next. He ran through all the meals they'd shared, and realized they hadn't tried a nice French meal. He'd have to suggest that for the weekend.

He slowed when he realized he was making plans. Shit,

the worst of her was wearing off on him. Only temporary, he reminded himself, looking at the source of his discomfort. He noticed she'd put on a little weight since they'd start investigating, and it looked good on her. She'd been so thin, almost brittle. But she was filling out that flirty little pink dress much better than he'd ever noticed. Until now, he'd seen her mostly in pantsuits, jeans or running shorts.

"I wonder," she said as she dipped a fry into ketchup, "How this guy could kill knowing he'd created a child."

Nick felt tired and shifted in his seat.

"What kind of person could do that? Killing someone in defense or in a moment's passion I might be able to understand."

Suddenly, his stomach clenched.

Bree stopped, her burger in mid-air, and threw him a quizzical look.

"Not feeling too well," he explained.

He heard Bree droning on, but he couldn't quite make out the words. He blinked and saw two of everything. He closed his eyes, opened them again. Still two of everything. Worse, now he felt like he was on fire. Damn it, he hurt. He thought he heard Bree screaming at him. The pain was only getting worse; his body was being pricked by a thousand hot needles. Then the double images started to fade to black. But no pain now. Just warmth. And drowsiness.

Death was easier than he thought.

Chapter Eighteen

Nick heard the beeping as he slowly surfaced from the fog. It hurt to breathe. He couldn't think, and his throat felt like it had been bored out with a roto-rooter. He hurt fucking everywhere. He opened his eyes for a few seconds and realized that he was in a hospital room, hooked up to several machines. He hoped that was good, and then he closed his eyes again to drift back into the fog.

The next time he woke up, the beeping was still there, but his eyes stayed open long enough to see Tory. His sister smiled and squeezed his hand. He squeezed back and retreated from the pain into a deep sleep.

Bree heard Nick stirring, but he didn't wake up. She gazed at him through bleary, gritty eyes; she had so little sleep the last two days. At first, she was afraid if she slept, he wouldn't wake up. Watching Nick . . . worrying if he would make it . . . brought back memories of sitting by Rachel's side at her death bed. Bree was as exhausted and limp as the Thai noodles Nick liked to eat.

Though she knew he was out of danger now, he looked pale, like a vampire. She had studied his face as she had so many times for the last forty-eight hours. For the first day, she had watched with fear. Once they knew he wasn't going to die, she had started to study it out of boredom, because what else was there to do when you were sitting in the hospital for hours and the patient was sleeping?

It was a strong face, she decided. Handsome, for sure. She'd noticed that, reluctantly, from the very beginning. Nick projected such an air of nonchalance that it was easy for everyone to see the charmer. Normally, she never would have looked for strength because the Nick she knew always took the easiest way out. But Bree discovered his strength in the hardest way possible these last few days. The doctors said that he had been fighting to live in those first few critical hours when it could have gone either way.

She waited for the tell-tale feeling of sadness that had been with her the past several years, but what she felt instead was anger, maybe even rage. She was going to find this guy who tried to kill her and had caused Nick so much pain. Years later she would say it was the rage that fueled her; made her stop looking at everything rationally to come up with the theory that horrified her.

He woke faster this time. Thank God, no beeping, but the lights seemed bright. He was going to be disappointed if this turned out to be Hell. He'd always thought Hell would be dark and smoky like a honky-tonk. He could hear voices but he had to wait while both his vision and brain cleared. He recognized Tory's sultry voice, and could hear the same quiver of fear she tried to mask when she was four and realized Elena had walked out on them.

"Hey," he croaked.

His sister and Daniel Cusumano's mother, Marie, moved into his view.

"Hello, handsome," Tory said, leaning over and kissing his forehead.

"Hey, baby." His speech was slow and slurred as he asked, "Was it that close that they sent for you?"

"I know we talked about visiting, but I think this is an extreme way to get me to come, Nicky."

She kissed his forehead again, as if she were trying to

reassure herself.

He reached over to squeeze Marie's hand, and she patted his arm.

"I'm really fuzzy, Tory. How long have I been laying here?"

"Two days. You were poisoned. Do you remember any of it?"

"Not really." He struggled to recall anything. Bits and pieces floated back, but they were all surreal. "I remember hearing Bree's voice fade out and then everything went black."

Tory took his hand in hers. "Brianna Kincaid called 911, and the paramedics got you to the hospital in time. She guessed what the problem was so the doctors looked for that poison, and that probably made the difference. They were able to pump it out of your system, and give you a drug to counter the worst of it."

Marie chimed in. "It was touch and go for a while, Nicky."

"I believe that. My head is still pounding and my stomach—do I still have one?"

"Want me to buzz for the nurse and get you something?"

Nick shifted in his bed, sitting up and wincing at the same time. He tried to smile, though he wasn't sure that's what he did; his muscles felt paralyzed.

He hadn't seen his sister for more than three years, but she looked much the same if you didn't count the dark circles under her eyes. She'd always been a pretty little girl, but Tory had grown into a beautiful woman, even when she appeared this tired.

"I'm sorry, but I'm getting groggy again," Nick said because he decided they needed sleep more than he did.

Nick thought Marie's tactful offer to get the car was an excuse to give brother and sister a few minutes alone.

"You staying with them?" he asked his sister.

She nodded as she pulled a chair next to his bed and sat. He saw her blinking back tears.

"It's OK, Tory."

"I'm sorry, Nick. It's just that on the flight here, I pictured myself all alone. Even though I don't see you much, I always know that you're there. And suddenly the thought of you being gone just knocked me off my feet. It helped to have Marie. And this Bree. She's a very calm, steady person."

He frowned. His mind reached for something, but couldn't quite make it break through the haze. He finally noticed his sister's speculative gaze.

"I still feel like shit," he said quickly to stall any questions about Bree.

"Okay. I'll be back tonight for a little while," Tory picked up her purse. "You should know that Bree's been here every day, Nick. Daniel and Marie had to force her to go home a couple of hours ago."

Nick took her hand in his. "Promise me that you and I will always be spontaneous. People like Brianna Kincaid, with their overly developed sense of right and justice, are the biggest pains in the ass you can possibly imagine. Promise me, Tory."

◆

Nick had too much time to think. He slept when it was day and was wide awake at night. The first night Tory was assigned to 'Nick duty'. He had no qualms about keeping her up to keep him company. She kept irregular hours with her art anyway. She told him about her coming show and her successes, dealing with deadlines and patrons she couldn't stand. Despite her success, she was still his little sister and adored him the same way that she had when she'd been eight, and Nick was all she'd had then. He wanted to ask her if her memories were as painful as his, and if it had influenced all her decisions since then, but he couldn't bring himself to do it. He couldn't stand to wipe that worshipping look off her face.

He still slept more than he was awake, and in those brief

stints, his brain churned over the fact that he could have died. And then remembered the one thing he'd been struggling to think of.

He came awake abruptly this time, a dream of the emergency room coming at him with the ferocity of a chain-saw murderer. He must have shouted in his sleep because Bree was by his bedside when he opened his eyes. The fear in his dream made him more alert than the other times he woke up, and he saw both tenderness and guilt in her eyes for just a second before she shuttered them to go into nurse mode.

"Are you OK?"

"How to answer that one," he said sarcastically.

"Well, your sharp tongue obviously hasn't suffered any of the effects of the poison."

"I'm so glad you bring that up, Brianna, because no one else quite knows the answer or will tell me—how could someone have poisoned me?"

"The soda."

"What?"

"The can of soda you drank in my office before we left. Daniel's been investigating. He ruled out every place except my office, and that was the only difference between you and me in the time span in which the poison kicked in. We were able to retrieve the can out of the trash. There was a tiny hole by the tab. As if someone had used a syringe to inject poison into the can but so subtle that the drinker would never notice it. Daniel ran tests on it. It was the same poison used to kill Megan."

"Why am I not dead?"

"Two reasons. Remember I took the can away from you after just a sip or two because I was so irritated with you for opening my last can so you barely ingested any of it. And do you recall what I told you and Daniel the first time we met? The poison starts out sweet so the sweetness of the soda masked it." She offered a weak smile. "The paramedics and the doctors were able to give you enough meds to counteract the poison to some degree."

"Permanent damage?"

"Not any more than you've already done through your abusive lifestyle."

"Well that's comforting."

Nick was silent as he tried to absorb everything she was telling him. One of the machines he was hooked up to started beeping. He looked at Bree.

She reached for his hand and squeezed it. "Your heart rate is increasing. Take deep breaths."

He watched the number on the machine decrease. Keeping one eye on the machine, he asked, "Has Daniel come up with anything?"

She shook her head. "Unfortunately, the bastard who did this was smart enough to wear gloves so there were no fingerprints."

"I assume the mysterious lover is the prime suspect."

She nodded. He watched her face as he said very calmly, "Now, just how would this guy know I'd drink that soda?" His eyes narrowed. "Oh wait. He couldn't have known. He was trying to kill *you*. And I was just at the wrong place at the wrong time."

He cursed in several languages, glaring at Bree, who had gone still.

"You're right. I'm sorry, Nick. I never should have dragged you into this."

"You're damn right you shouldn't have. But I'm going to find this bastard," Nick promised. "And I'm going to break every bone in his body."

"Listen, I've had more time to think about this than you have and I have a plan," she said, leaning in.

He bent closer to her—as close as all the tubes would let him stretch. "Your plan is what almost got me killed. But for sheer luck, I'd be dead now, Bree. Dead."

She paled so much that he thought he'd have to ring for the nurse for her.

"I'm so sorry," she whispered.

Nick realized he was overstepping bounds, but he hurt so damn much and he was so pissed.

"Sorry doesn't make me feel much better. I feel like my body's been pulled apart and put back together all wrong. And my health insurance sucks," he yelled.

"Nick, my family will take care of—"

But he didn't want to listen to reason. "Do you think that finding this guy is going to bring them back, Bree? Because it won't. You can't get Megan back. And you can't get your mother back. Ever. So let's just be honest here. Maybe it's never been about Megan at all. Maybe it's really always been about you—the rich girl who found there was something she couldn't control in her perfectly planned world."

He didn't think that he could feel any worse than he already did, until a tear slid slowly down one cheek. He watched for a second as her small, lithe body shook, even as she made no sound. The anger drained out of him, though the throbbing felt ten times worse.

"Bree," he said, reaching to touch her hair.

But she jumped up and fled the room.

Fuck! He'd screwed that up. He slammed his hand down on the bed, which tugged on his IV and hurt even more. He buzzed the nurse to look for Bree, who couldn't be found on the floor. She didn't answer her cell phone either. Nick finally fell into a fitful sleep where he dreamed of salty raindrops.

Chapter Nineteen

W HEN NICK WOKE AGAIN, THE sun had long set, leaving his hospital room dark and chilly. The machines still beeped consistently. He wasn't as groggy as the other times he'd awaken, and this time, he could feel his hands and feet tingling. Thank God. The poison must be leaving his system.

He reached for the pitcher of water on the table tray next to his bed, then cursed when he couldn't get the cellophane off the cup.

"I'll get it," Bree said quietly, rising from the chair where she had blended into the shadows. She moved around his bed, then ripped the plastic off.

He regarded her warily as she poured him a glass of water. She wouldn't look at him, and her movements were subdued. *Damn.* He really wanted to be mad at her. He took the cup she offered, then put his hand on her shoulder.

She trembled. Her violet eyes, filled with concern and regret, finally met his. "I'm sorry, Nick," she whispered.

She gestured to a bud vase, with a single yellow rose and a sprig of exotic greenery, sitting next to the pitcher.

"I know a rose isn't the usual thing to give a guy. But in the language of flowers, a yellow rose can mean 'I'm sorry'."

He struggled to recall another woman who'd ever made up with him with something besides sex. When he started to speak, she put her finger on his lips. They started to tingle too.

"You were right, you know. Little Miss Justice. I was arrogant, just making myself feel better. And I almost got you killed."

Tears pooled in her eyes, but he could tell she would not permit herself to cry again.

What the hell could he say to that? The woman was infuriating. Not to mention opinionated, feisty, and too smart by half. *That* woman needed to be taken down a notch, and he could handle *her* by now. This humble one not only surprised him, he admired her courage. He looked carefully to make sure she wasn't saying the words she knew he wanted to hear just to take the wind out of him. After all, that's what he would have done. Instead, he looked into those large sorrowful eyes, baring herself for his rejection. He couldn't bring himself to fire back any zingers; that would flay her. He sighed.

"You're forgiven." He patted a spot on the bed with its scratchy, bleached hospital sheets.

"Thank you." She perched on the edge, like a finch that would take flight at any sudden movement.

She looked fresh and soft, but so serious. She worried her bottom lip—those full lips he'd noticed from their very first meeting. He wished she'd stop because he found himself wanting to nibble them. What was wrong with him? He was half dead, stuck in a hospital bed. Nick could only blame it on the drugs.

"I really wanted to bring you a bottle of Jack Daniels, but it would only make you sicker so I settled for the flower."

She traced her finger against the delicate petals. The sight stirred him in a way he knew she never intended, and he had to remind himself he was too ill for sex. This was Brianna Kincaid, for Christ's sake.

"Roses really are the most beautiful flower," Bree murmured. "They're my favorite. Though no one gives them to me. I guess because I'm a botanist, people feel they have to give me something unique for me to appreciate it. Really, I'd rather just have a simple, elegant rose."

She was nervous. It wasn't like her to chatter. Lecture him, maybe; pontificate, for sure, but chattering told him she wasn't sure he'd really forgiven her. Seeing Brianna Kincaid unsure was a new, and very satisfying, experience.

He took a breath. His temper had picked a lousy time to show itself earlier. Nick wanted to say he was sorry for yelling at her, but the words simply wouldn't come. Probably because he was so out of practice. He couldn't remember the last time he'd apologized to anyone. He wanted to thank her for coming back, for being enough of a friend to take his bad moods and still talk to him again, but having a woman friend was such a novel experience, he fumbled. Uncertain, he went with the safest subject he could think of—murder.

"We're going to find the bastard that did this," he said grimly.

Bree put her hand over his, and her warmth chased away the hardness of his own words. He stared at their hands. It was the first time they'd touched when neither one was in distress.

"Yes, we will find the bastard. But first, let's get you well. The doctors expect you to make a full recovery."

She smiled. "Although you may not remember that when you wake up next time. Your record for staying awake has been a whopping fifteen minutes over the past two days. We keep having many of the same conversations because you aren't remembering much.

"The doctors warned us you'll probably have to stay another day until they're sure there are no complications. They also said you won't feel good for at least another week. Don't worry, though, we have a plan. And if it makes you feel safer, I didn't come up with this one."

He smiled, and noticed she looked relieved.

"I need to go," she said softly, easing off the bed. "I'll stop by tomorrow after work to see how you're doing."

He caught her hand, not wanting her to leave. He felt like hell, but lately he'd felt better when she was around. "Stay."

She hesitated, then shook her head. "You still need to take it easy and rest."

Bree leaned over to kiss his forehead.

She smelled like the rose—fresh and subtle. He was used to women proclaiming their femininity with perfumes—sometimes subtle, sometimes powerful—but this woman smelled natural. He wouldn't admit the rush her understated scent gave him.

Later, he would tell himself it was the drugs and having come so close to dying, but now, he wrapped his hand around the back of her head and redirected her kiss to his lips. He tangled his fingers in her hair, so thick and soft, as he heard her faint gasp.

The sweetness of her mouth took him by surprise as he nibbled on her bottom lip. He kissed her gently, a feathery kiss. He knew she was attracted to him. She was a highly disciplined woman, but every once in a while, she couldn't hide the longing in her eyes.

Bree leaned into him, just a fraction, and opened her mouth enough for him to deepen the kiss. He felt her eagerness, her desire, even as she tried to hold back.

The steady beep of the machine was replaced by the pounding of his heart as his hand caressed her cheek, then trailed a slow path down her neck. So silky, he thought through the haze that was overtaking his mind and body. He brushed the tips of his fingers across her breast, then wrapped his arm around her waist and pulled her against him. Nick couldn't get her close enough. He wanted her in the bed with him, to feel her lithe body pressed to his.

He left her lips to devour her neck and stoke the growing passion. She tilted her head to give him better access. The pulse in her neck would call her a liar if she tried to deny she wasn't aroused.

When the nurse entered the room, chattering about giving him his next dose of medications, Bree jerked away as if he'd scorched her. The nurse couldn't have missed their intimacy, but kept talking as if she noticed nothing. Bree stepped back as the nurse came to the bed, but Nick's eyes never left her as she touched her fingertips to her lips. For a moment, they just stared at each other, so unsure now that the touch had been broken.

"I'll let you get some rest," Bree said, but she didn't move.

"Bree . . ." He held out his hand, but it must have been the heat in his eyes that sent her scurrying to the chair to get her purse instead of reaching back to him.

She kept talking as if nothing had happened between them, but she wouldn't meet his eyes again. "We're taking turns sitting by your bedside. Your sister is coming tomorrow morning."

She gave the nurse a small smile, then said good-bye to them both, and walked out of the room without looking back.

Damn. What just happened here?

He took the pill and glass of water the nurse gave him, and grunted when she sailed out of the room, encouraging him to ring his call button if he wanted another dose during the night.

Shit. He couldn't decide which was worse—yelling at Bree or kissing her.

He glanced over at the yellow rose. She was as delicate as that flower, though it took a long time to discover that fact.

He would never apologize for what just happened, though tomorrow he could always claim it had been the meds if she acted uncomfortable. Still, he'd been an ass to scream at her earlier. Maybe he'd have his sister order a dozen yellow roses and send them to Bree's office. He should get big brownie points, though he'd have to be careful that she didn't get the wrong idea. That made him smile. Nothing might terrify Brianna Kincaid more than thinking a party boy like him was interested in her.

Nick frowned. Bree would never think that. Her thoughtless ex-husband had convinced her that she had no sex appeal. And because she was convinced she could never be sexy, she never tried. Her mind was so focused on finding the killer or on her job or her family that she never took time to think about pleasure.

She had potential, though. He'd slept with enough women to know Bree had potential; it was just deeply buried. For a few seconds, when she'd let her guard down, he'd felt the passion waiting to be unleashed. It *needed* to be unleashed. Instead, she'd kept a tight lock on her heart since the divorce.

He wanted her to be happy. The thought surprised him. True, she could be annoying, but she'd grown on him. In fact, he enjoyed spending time with her. She didn't require him to be constantly charming and entertaining. Unlike all the other women he'd been with, she didn't measure him based on how good he was in bed. Instead, she listened to him and paid attention to his ideas.

He had his first woman friend—whom earlier he'd crucified for caring about right and wrong, for trying to make something better. What an ass he'd been. Maybe he'd send two dozen roses; that should make her feel better.

No, he thought slowly, if he really wanted to make her better, he would restore her confidence in herself as a woman. Nick smiled. Who knew women better? He laughed out loud when he thought of sex with Bree—he couldn't imagine that she'd be much good at it at this point, compared to what he'd known. But the issue wasn't sex; it was to banish the haunted look in her eyes. He felt both noble and a little disquieted. It wasn't like him to think of anyone but himself. And damn if he was going to change that, but Bree was a special woman—a friend. He'd give her the greatest gift he could give.

Nick fell into a deep sleep, planning the seduction and pleasuring of Brianna Kincaid.

Chapter Twenty

B REE CLIMBED THE THREE FLIGHTS of stairs to Daniel's apartment like Joan of Arc walking to the stake. She wondered if Joan had felt the same sense of doom or if she'd been calm and resolved. Personally, Bree was going for light and casual when she saw Nick, but she was afraid her luck was about to run out. She could almost feel the flames licking at her feet.

She had taken her share of shifts caring for him since his release from the hospital five days earlier. To get the extra time off, she'd had to come clean to Emery about what she had been trying to do for Megan Harper, and why she needed more time off in addition to the emergency amount she'd requested last week. She was certain she'd used up all of the favor she held with Emery, but it had been necessary to help Nick recover.

Most of the time, he'd slept or been confined to bed so Bree hadn't the heart to share her new theory about Megan's killer. She'd kept her disturbing thoughts to herself, losing sleep, but she didn't feel she could wait any longer; they needed to set a trap to flush the killer out.

She stopped on the second floor landing. *Be honest with yourself, Bree. The killer isn't the only thing disturbing your sleep.*

Nick couldn't realize the havoc he was playing on her senses. Because he was still recovering, she'd sat by his bedside, and they'd talked. Should have been so simple. How much trouble could she get into talking? Talking was one of the things she did best, after analyzing and planning. So why did she feel so confused when she left him? They'd talked about their sisters, the countries they still wanted to visit, favorite movies and music.

One day he complimented her on a new necklace because he thought it was pretty. She could still remember the warmth of his hands when he'd lifted it to get a better look. Had he been able to feel her pulse pick up?

She'd also been dumbfounded when two dozen pink roses showed up on her desk. The card read: In the language of flowers, there is no color for 'dumb ass'. I'm sorry.

She couldn't deny the boost she'd felt when the guard had called to tell her flowers had arrived for her. Two dozen roses. Her stock had gone up with the other women in the office as they sighed over the blooms.

At least her prayers about that kiss had been answered. She had prayed Nick wouldn't remember the hospital room kiss, and he hadn't brought it up yet. Not like Nick to hold back a sarcastic or taunting remark if the opportunity presented itself. Perhaps he had been so drugged, he thought he'd dreamed it. Or worse, maybe he was repulsed by the incident. She just hoped the only topic they would talk about tonight was Megan's killer.

She let herself in with the key Daniel had given her. Did she look like a startled deer in the headlights when she found Nick dressed, sitting on the couch, watching Netflix? Fortunately, he didn't seem to notice as he greeted her with a smile. She struggled to breath. He looked so damn good.

Thirty minutes. She would only stay thirty minutes since he looked like he could take care of himself. Then she'd make a hasty retreat back to her house where it was safe. No tall, heart-stopping men hanging around her family room. She took a deep breath. She could do anything for thirty minutes.

"Feeling a lot better?" Even to herself, she sounded overly perky.

"Oh, yeah. The shower felt great."

"You look better each day, Nick."

Not surprisingly, he'd lost some weight, which had only

sculpted those high cheek bones more. No, no, no. She did not want to think about Nick Mancini like that. She'd lost so much sleep the last few days over a simple kiss. One kiss. One fantastic, searing kiss. Oh God, is this how it had started for Megan?

And the truth was she knew that kiss was nothing compared to what she imagined Nick Mancini could really do. The kiss had been so gentle, which was why she didn't understand how she could still feel butterflies in her stomach. Thank God the nurse had entered Nick's hospital room. Bree would have made such a fool of herself otherwise.

Nick looked questioningly at her. "Are you coming in?"

"Oh. Oh, sure." She finally noticed the table set for two and frowned.

"I'm tired of eating eggs and toast so I ordered a really nice dinner."

He turned off the TV and took her arm, steering her to the table. A bottle of white wine sat chilling next to the table, which was set with delicate china, candles and an exotic arrangement of hydrangeas and lilies.

He took off her suit jacket and said, "The caterer left the food warming in the oven. I'm still a little weak. Do you think you can set it up for us?"

She wanted to protest that she couldn't stay, but he looked so hopeful. She was dismayed to find chicken crepes, risotto and all her other favorite dishes that they'd talked about in the last week. He'd obviously gone to a lot of trouble to say thank you for her caregiving when all she wanted to do was run away.

She blinked when she stepped back into the main room with the plates. The room seemed dimmer. Had those other candles by the TV been lit when she'd arrived? She must have been so preoccupied that she hadn't paid any attention.

"I've decided not share my story about the poisoning with the press for now," he said as he held out her chair for her.

Bree put her hand to her heart. "Thank you. It would absolutely destroy the Garden's reputation if the poisoning became public. With all the social media, just one incident can undo so much good. And it really was all my fault. If I hadn't been poking into Megan's death, it wouldn't have happened. I don't want to see the Garden and Emery and the staff suffer because of my efforts."

She didn't want to admit that she was tense every time she walked into her building now. As she approached her office each morning or when she came back from a meeting, her heart beat faster, and she struggled for breath. She was afraid. Afraid to be in her own office. Afraid to touch her keyboard, her pens, to sit in her chair. Afraid the murderer had slipped in while she was away, and was going to try again. She couldn't trouble Nick about that, though. He needed to focus on his recovery.

Five minutes into their dinner, she had a hard time remembering she was in a hurry to leave. The chicken crepes melted in her mouth while the risotto was an exotic complement. His choice of wine was exquisite. He told her he had picked up a great knowledge of wines while working for a magazine in France. She didn't have the heart to tell him about her theory when he was so clearly enjoying his first nice meal in a week. They lingered over dessert of strawberries rolled in sour cream and brown sugar.

She insisted on clearing the table and his hands accidentally closed around hers as they both reached for a plate at the same time. His brown warm eyes held hers, startling her with the intensity of his gaze. She wanted to look down, to pretend that she hadn't seen his smoldering, unsettling stare, but she couldn't break his pull. His look confused her and made her feel helpless. She realized that she was holding her breath. Any minute he would shatter the mood, by breaking into a joke. Please, she thought, make an innuendo about sex so I can get indignant.

Finally, she forced herself to break the connection. She

tried not to stumble as she moved into the kitchen. She heard Michael Buble come up on his playlist while she cleared the dishes. She recognized it as his duet with Laura Pausini, one of her favorites.

When she returned to the main room, Nick smiled at her, then held out his arms. "I can't sit any more. I need to move a little. Come dance with me."

"I'm a ter-terrible dancer," Bree stammered.

"Well, I don't think you have to worry about us doing a tango."

She envisioned wrapping herself around Nick and sliding down his body.

"You know, I really can't stay. Now that I can see how much better you're doing, I'll scoot out of here in the next few minutes. Got to attack that pile of reading that's been building up for the past couple of weeks. But thank you for that fantastic dinner."

She felt time slow down, and her heart speed up as he sauntered over to her.

"Don't leave me," he said, wrapping his arms around her waist. "I need you."

She knew she should resist as he pulled her against him and laid his head on top of hers.

"Nick," she whispered, but she didn't pull away. She couldn't. The heat of his body made her want to curl up around him. Oh God. She was sure her legs had turned to jelly and she'd fall if he let her go.

Nick didn't say a word, simply held her as the music surrounded them, and they swayed in the candlelight. She should feel safe and comfortable with him, but her heart pounded so hard and fast she thought she might die.

He stopped dancing to cup her face in his hands and kissed her. So sweet. The merest brush of his lips. The warmth of his breath as he moved across her jaw and down her neck.

"Nick, I don't think . . ."

She trailed off when he lifted his head and placed a finger on her lips. She felt the jolt zip down her body.

"Not thinking would be perfect now, Bree."

She savored the next kiss. She should not be falling for this, for Nick. He was so practiced at seduction. What chance did she have? she thought helplessly. But she couldn't deny that she wanted this. Couldn't deny that his touch ignited a hunger in her.

Then he deepened the kiss. It was the kiss that girls dream about from the time they discover boys. She couldn't collect a single thought. And what's more, she didn't care.

Bree wrapped her arms around Nick's neck. She felt ripples of excitement wash over her as his tongue caressed and cajoled her. One of Nick's arms gripped her tightly around the waist while the other moved through her hair, his kiss becoming more demanding.

He eased her towards the couch, then down on it and began removing her blouse slowly, button by button. She struggled to breathe while sanity made a tiny last stand. He gave her a small knowing smile.

"You bastard," she muttered.

He laughed. "Let's see if you still feel that way in an hour."

They stared into each other's eyes as he finished her blouse. She'd always thought his eyes dreamy, but all she could see now was the heat in them. She felt lightheaded, knowing that heat promised heaven.

With a smooth motion, he undid the clasp on her bra, then teased her breast with his tongue. Her entire body tingled, then started begging.

Like a mad woman, she tugged at his shirt, pulling it off until his warm skin met hers. She met his kisses with a fierceness she hadn't felt in so long. As their passion built, they clawed at each other's pants until they were freed and naked. He deepened his kisses while at the same time kicking up the urgency. He was like the match setting the kindling around her Joan of Arc pyre on fire, but Bree didn't want to question; she didn't want to doubt—either him or herself. She just wanted to feel, to revel in the sensations that he caused.

"Don't make me beg, Nick," she panted.

He smothered a small laugh against her neck as he settled between her legs. She writhed, impatient and eager, until he entered her. She met his thrusts with raised hips, craving her release after so, so long. She spiraled higher and higher until ripples of sensation washed over her, and she cried out when pleasure shattered her. She was dimly aware when he came.

They collapsed against each other, breathing hard and slightly sweaty. Nick took her face between his hands, searching her eyes. She broke into a slow smile, which he wiped off her face with a long kiss. Tenderly, he pulled her toward him, tucking her under his chin and they drifted into an exquisite sleep.

When Nick woke up, he was surprised to find Bree gone. He expected her to want to talk about what had happened, to draw boundaries, to overthink it. He smiled. The woman surprised him more than he would have anticipated.

She didn't kiss with the skill of so many of the other women that he'd slept with, but that didn't surprise him. This hadn't been for him. He wanted to pleasure Bree and wipe away those doubts that she had about herself as a woman.

If he counted her fierceness to love, she was probably more woman than he'd ever known. He realized that he trusted Bree as he only trusted Tory and the Cusumano women, but after tonight, he certainly didn't think of her as a sister or mother-figure.

He swung out of bed, a little sore, but the sex had re-energized him, and there was no reason left to lay in bed. He had a killer to catch.

Chapter Twenty-One

"I THINK THE KILLER IS SOMEONE I work with."

Bree winced. She really hadn't meant to blurt out her idea, but she was so nervous being around Nick now, she couldn't help it.

Since they'd slept together last night, Bree thought Nick would avoid her like the plague; she steeled herself for excuses, even as she worked on her own. To say she was confused about him would be an understatement. She was both angry with herself for letting him seduce her, and thrilled at the experience.

Then he surprised her—no, shocked her—by showing up at her office, with a bouquet of calla lilies and a wicked grin on his face. It was either blurt her theory or make a big puddle at his feet.

Well, her statement certainly killed his grin, and, she suspected, any possible thoughts of a sexual encore.

He stepped in her office and closed the door. "You have my undivided attention."

"I had a lot of time to think while you were recovering, Nick. I now think the chance that the father of Megan's baby was a drug lord is small. After all, if he wanted me dead, there were easier ways to do it. He could have just had me shot in the parking lot, run my car off the road. There would be no connection to him. With the poison, he would have had to find some way to get into this building, know which office was mine, and most importantly, he'd have to be someone who knows my habits. I put in long hours here. If he popped in during the day, surely my assistant, Cheryl, or others who sit near my office would have mentioned a stranger in my office."

"So he came in at night, after everyone was gone."

"Exactly. But again, to be strolling around the grounds or have access to this building after hours, he'd have to have a badge."

She waited patiently as he sorted through the ideas and caught up to her.

"Megan's clues fit better with someone who works here too," Nick said. "That's why so many of the clues are tied to botany. Because her lover would understand them. The inscription in the wedding ring wasn't about D.H. Lawrence. It was the reference to the flower of life. The reference to Asa Gray as the father. It was probably some little inside joke they shared. "

She nodded. "She also mentioned me by name in one of her clues. Why not just refer to me as 'my supervisor' or 'my boss' unless the guy would understand the reference to me. Botany ties everything together, and can help us when we find the next clue."

He didn't respond.

"I've had more time to think this through than you have. What if I start wearing a locket and say that I found it among Megan's things and her mother wanted me to have it? I could put out the rumor that I'd found out other very interesting things and see what happens. Or who, I guess."

He stared at her.

"What?" she asked.

"Someone just tried to kill you. Me. Us. Now that my initial anger has passed and I'm thinking more clearly, don't you think we should leave this to Daniel? Safe to say, we all agree that you were right about Megan's death not being an accident."

Logically, she understood that what he said made perfect sense. When she'd sat next to his bedside during the touch and go of the first twenty-four hours, she had dozed and repeatedly startled herself awake with the nightmare of being poisoned. If her nightmare wasn't of her or him struggling to breathe, it was her father, sister, Emery.

This killer had now harmed two people about whom she cared so logic was losing to her emotions. She stalled for time. "Realistically, how much time do you think Daniel will be able to give this?"

"This nut job tried to kill his best friend. I'm pretty sure he's going to make time."

Nick leaned in towards her. "This is not a game, Bree. Not a puzzle for that brilliant mind of yours to solve and then move on. It's pure luck that I'm not dead."

She opened her mouth to respond, but Nick was on a roll.

"Megan's killer clearly is very adept with poison. He's an intelligent person, Bree. Methodical. He knows who we are. We don't have the slightest idea who he is." Nick looked up at the ceiling, then around her office. "For all we know, he's got the place bugged, and is listening to our conversation so he can stay one step ahead of us."

"I'll hire someone to sweep—"

"You're not listening."

"We're so close," she persisted.

"No, we're not. All we have is slivers."

"I'll take more precautions."

"Like what? Are you going to start carrying a gun?"

"Not crazy about the idea, but I know how to shoot."

"Really? Not something I was expecting a Ladue girl to know."

"I've worked overseas in remote areas, remember? Places where there are bandits who will kidnap you for ransom."

"Are you listening to yourself? This is St. Louis, not a jungle. If you need to carry a gun to protect yourself from this guy, it's too dangerous to continue."

"I find it ironic that you of all people should be lecturing me."

"I'm a careless man, not a stupid one. There's a difference."

"Huh." She cocked her head. "That's a fine line of distinction."

"Exactly. I knew you'd see it. Because someone in this relationship has to be the adult, and you're it. So act like the smart woman you are, Brianna, and walk away. Now, promise me you won't pursue this any further."

She searched for a way around his request, an answer that would not commit her to her word.

Nick slammed the calla lilies on her desk, and she scooted back in surprise.

"Promise me."

The ire in his eyes and the heat of his tone told her he wasn't going to let this go. She didn't know how to deal with a man whose concern was clearly overriding his judgment.

"O-Okay. I promise."

"Repeat after me. I will not purposely go looking for any more clues. Come on. Say it back to me."

She rolled her eyes, but played back the words he wanted to hear.

"Good." He picked up the flowers. "These are for you."

She thought it wise not to say more than a quiet thank you.

"Marie is hosting a family dinner in Tory's honor on Saturday night. She has to fly back to New York on Sunday. You're invited."

"Don't you think the dinner should be just you and your sister and the Cusumanos? A chance for you to all catch up?"

"Marie wants you there. You impressed her."

"I'm sure it's because I can put up with you."

A small smile appeared on his face, and Bree relaxed slightly. Back to their familiar patter. She welcomed the return of their normal relationship, given everything that had happened over the past two weeks.

"Is your father still out of town?"

"Only for a few more days."

Her pulse race when he walked around her desk, pulled her up, wrapped his arms around her, and kissed her. She should push him away. A small shove to let him know he couldn't manipulate her. Lord knew she needed to regain some control of him, of this . . . this thing she was feeling.

Instead, he stepped away from her, and her body felt bereft.

"Okay if I come by tonight?"

He was giving her a chance to draw a line. If she wanted to walk away after just one night, he would let her. She surprised herself when her voice held steady as she said, "That would be fine."

"See you soon then," he said as he opened her office door and disappeared.

Bree wondered if her colleagues were gossiping about Nick, the closed door, and all of the time she'd taken recently. As she pulled a cheap glass vase off her bookcase shelf, she found she didn't care about her reputation.

But she did care about her own heart. Didn't she ever learn? Hadn't it been painful enough with Mitch? What was the weakness in her character that attracted her to men that were poorly suited for her?

As much as she decided she was willing to take a chance on love, she recognized it wouldn't be Nick. He was just too free-spirited. She need someone to love her who would stick around. Someone who would build a good life with her. Maybe another marriage wouldn't be as glorious as her parents or maybe it could just be a different glorious.

But in the meantime, she could have fun with Nick. She thought about those warm brown eyes and the passion she'd experienced last night, and was relieved she was alone. She could feel the heat traveling up her body, tinged with the tingle of anticipation.

Clearly, he was thinking they'd make love again tonight. Certainly, they couldn't go back to the way it was yesterday morning. She felt too much heat to stay away from him.

Did he feel the same? She thought he'd at least had a good time. Otherwise, wouldn't he have avoided her? And there was no need to bring the calla lilies. She wondered if he knew this particular flower represented 'feminine beauty'.

But keeping him interested, keeping that spark. Lord, she was no match for his past, for the women, all the women, who had come before her. Who was she kidding? He'd be bored in a week.

She'd been restless, looking for a new challenge since the death of her mother and Megan. Nick was not quite what she had in mind, but really this could be a life-long skill. Maybe if she had a more experienced air, she'd attract a different kind of man this time. Trouble was there was no textbook for this kind of skill; no Academy of Sexual Techniques in which she could enroll.

Then the obvious popped into her mind. She had the perfect tutor. Bree pulled out her cell phone, punched in her sister's number, and left a message.

"Carly, can you give me a call? I need tips on seduction techniques. And don't mention this call to Dad."

Chapter Twenty-Two

N ICK STARED OUT THE PICTURE window of the Cusumano home at the house across the street that he had planned never to see again. A violent sensation swept through him. Part shock, part revulsion, it sent him back through his childhood in a few seconds, and shook him to the core: Waking Tory every morning for school. Bags of Doritos and soda for dinner on trays in front of the TV. His father in that damned recliner.

He turned around and caught Bree watching him from the Cusumano dining room. For a second, her face showed compassion he didn't want. He couldn't fight his feelings on two fronts—the love and affection in this house and the nightmare across the street that pricked at his soul. Bree saved him by shuttering her expression and heading back into the kitchen where everyone else had gathered.

Marie, of course, had prevailed in convincing Bree that she needed to come to Tory's going-away party. For such a kind, sweet person, Marie was a warrior when she decided she wanted something. People looked at her husband, Danny, who was more than a foot taller and had the steel of a man who had spent twenty years being a cop, and thought he was tough. But everyone in the family did what Marie directed.

Three of the kids—he couldn't remember if they belonged to Daniel's middle or older sister—ran out of the kitchen, jostled him, and continued screaming as they ran up the stairs to the second floor. One of the sisters called after them to go outside and play.

Not surprisingly, the Cusumanos had prepared a feast.

Danny had barbequed pork steaks, Marie had handmade toasted ravioli, and Daniel's youngest sister had whipped up a gooey butter cake from scratch. All the unique foods of St. Louis that no other state or country ever featured. Even Bree had filled her plate a second time.

He drifted back to the kitchen, and leaned against the doorway. Marie and Tory had their heads together as they washed dishes at the sink—just like they had dozens of times when Tory was little. Marie had always been a sentimental woman, and he knew that having Tory and him back made her happy. When he took off again, he'd have to send her more emails.

He caught Daniel watching his sister with a hard intense look on his face. Daniel and Tory had quietly skirted each other all night. What few comments they made to each other had an edge to them. Had others noticed the tension? The two of them hadn't seen each other in years so what did they have to be angry about? He'd have to probe the next time he got each one of them alone. When they were younger, Tory had worshipped Daniel just as much as she did Nick. Daniel had always treated Tory like a baby sister or even like a brother because she'd been such a tomboy. The idea of them being at odds with each other didn't sit well with him.

Bree was now in a serious conversation with Daniel's eight-year-old niece. He caught her eye, and she gave him a swift, small smile.

Contentment shot through him. Worse yet, he recognized the desire to keep this scene in his memory for a long time. And once again he was pummeled with so many emotions, he felt a tightening in his chest, in his throat. He struggled to breathe evenly. He didn't think he could blame this one on his recovery.

He headed back into the living room, but that only left him staring out the picture window at that damn house again. It tempted him the same way drugs, alcohol and women did. He'd be a masochist to go anywhere near that house. He knew he should go back in the kitchen, but he wasn't a strong man. He swore softly in three languages when he headed out the front door.

Nick crossed the street and halted in front of the house. It had been a pale green shingle when he'd lived here. By the time he'd left home, the green had long faded to gray. Some owner had changed it to tan siding. Maybe that was a blessing.

More memories assaulted him, and in his mind, he was standing in front of the pale green shingled house with its deep porch and big picture window. He saw Bernard sitting in his recliner, listening to the Cardinals or watching TV. Every night.

He didn't want to wonder again what he'd done wrong so his father didn't care enough about him, or why his mother had so little love for any of them that she'd taken off and never attempted to find him in almost thirty years. He was thirty-seven-years old, for Christ's sake. He wanted to tell the ghosts that he didn't give a fuck when all he felt was rage.

He started when Bree wordlessly slipped her hand into his. Nick looked down at her. This woman would offer him whatever he needed as long as he needed it. *As long as he needed it.* The thought banked some of his anger.

"Marie said a young couple with one baby owns the house now. She told them you were coming back," she shared. "They said they were going to a family event and to feel free to peek in the windows. Do you want to walk around back?"

<hr>

Bree could tell Nick was struggling, both wanting to do something, and to run as far away as he could. She tried not to rush him. When she felt him growing more remote, she tried to distract him with good memories.

"It must have been nice to have had your best friend live right across the street."

"Yeah," he murmured, still staring at the house. "It was a big deal when I got to cross the street by myself." He looked down at her. "That's the day I became a man."

She smiled because she knew he was struggling to lighten the mood. If only she had that gift.

"I think I was five."

He looked across the street at Daniel's house. "We spent a lot of time playing in the streets. We'd get up really early during the summer and stay up late, playing hide and seek and flashlight tag."

She smiled at him. "I bet you were a ringleader."

"Yeah, I was. As I got older, I flirted with some bad stuff so Danny had me kept overnight in jail once. Scared the hell out of me—which I'm sure is what it was supposed to do. Unfortunately, once I was away from the influence of Danny and Marie, I fell into bad habits quickly."

Bree wasn't going to mention that he'd already started falling into good habits in just the few weeks he'd been helping her. Goodness scared Nick. Her heart ached for the little boy, so clever and smart, who had no one to show him how to be happy. Bree had never been more grateful for her parents.

"And Marie, she signed Tory up for art lessons at the art museum when she saw that she had talent. She made sure Bernard wrote the checks each month."

Bree didn't say anything when Nick fell quiet. For a few minutes, she just let him work through whatever he was wrestling with. Eventually, she recognized his paralysis. Nothing more was going to be gained by letting him stand here and brood. She touched his sleeve gently, but kept her voice matter-of-fact.

"We're so close to Ted Drewes. Let's go get frozen custard. You've had just about every other St. Louis delicacy. You don't want to leave without having it at least once again."

They walked back over to the Cusumano house, where everyone protested them leaving early. The family gave Nick and Tory space for their good-byes, and watched as they clung to each other—silent and with their eyes closed—as if storing the feeling. Nick broke the tension by reminding her he was headed her way soon. However, he wouldn't look at Bree once he broke away from his sister.

Maybe she'd been naïve to think this would help. After all, what did she know about overcoming such deep-seated loss? The one time that she'd been thrown into the pit, she'd sunk.

Bree kept a lively chatter while she drove them the mile to the most popular spot in the city for frozen custard. It was eight p.m., but even so, the line was long. She brought him back a strawberry concrete. Little by little the haunted look left Nick's eyes as he ate his frozen custard, and she gave a silent sigh of relief. She looked over to find Nick staring at her.

"What? Did I spill chocolate on my shirt?"

He grinned, and she stopped breathing. She'd seen Nick when he had looked more devastatingly handsome; nothing could compare to those smoldering looks that he could cast. But he'd never looked more relaxed and happy. He leaned over and kissed her. A simple, gentle, loving kiss.

Her heart clutched with fear. It worried her that she couldn't get enough of him. With Nick, her body would always be exquisitely revered, but her heart . . . her heart would never be safe with this man. When he left, and she knew he would go, she just hoped she was strong enough not to beg him to stay.

Chapter Twenty-Three

NICK STOOD IN FRONT OF the French doors that stretched the entire wall of the family room of the Kincaid home as the sun began dipping below the horizon on Rachel Kincaid's garden. When he and Bree had returned from the Cusumano celebration, she'd convinced him to take a long walk. He had to admit he felt better after they walked, though he'd never be able to keep up with Bree when she ran.

He was strangely content. Bree did this to him. She anchored him. Being with her was never boring. She had such high standards, though. If he stayed with her long enough, she would force him to be a better man than he wanted to be. He thought about all the scribbling in cheap notebooks he was doing now, all because she'd planted the seed about writing again. This woman, she was going to change all the rules; none of his old standbys would work with Bree.

He blew out a breath as he stepped into Rachel's garden. Rubbing his forehead, Nick closed his eyes and heard the soothing trickle of the two small fountains. The gentle sound of the water eased the tension from his shoulders and the sultry May evening caressed him like a sexy woman in flirty invitation. When he finally opened his eyes, he saw yellow, purple, and hot pink blossoms as stirring as a woman's lush mouth. A slight sweet scent beckoned as he walked among the flower beds. Who could resist such a woman? Certainly not Nick Mancini.

He didn't have a clue what any of the flowers were named, but they all looked delicate. Like Bree. And he laughed, then laughed harder when his moment of domesticity struck him as absurd. Next thing you know he'd be mowing the lawn or barbequing.

"This will be stunning in another month," Bree called as she came out of the house with lemonade. "See any you like?" she asked as she joined him.

Taking Bree's hand, he kissed it lightly. "I like whichever ones you like."

He'd meant it as a light-hearted comment, but he was learning when it came to Bree and flowers, there was no such thing as a rhetorical statement. She contemplated the flower beds with a fierceness Nick now found endearing, so he waited patiently.

"It's so hard to choose. So many interesting flowers. My mom did an incredible job. But," she paused, "I'd still have to go with the roses."

He smiled, and Bree returned a mischievous grin.

"What? You thought I was going to say 'pink carnations' so the next time you send flowers, I could get two dozen pink carnations?"

"Canny woman. Show me those roses."

She stepped to the right, but Nick wouldn't let her break their touch as Bree led him to a large bed of roses. She described them as floribunda of yellows and reds, hybrids in pink and whites, and multi-colored tea roses. Her words meant nothing to him, though now that he looked closer at the roses, he was ensnared by their beauty.

Bree leaned over to smell a few, showcasing those exquisite legs and trim tush beneath her Capri pants.

"Stunning," he murmured, pulling her into his arms, kissing her tenderly. He trailed soft kisses up her cheeks, and flicked his tongue over her eyelids. Her breath caught.

When she opened her eyes, he saw absolute trust in him. He didn't deserve it, but by God, he wanted it. He wanted her. Her trust was as pure as a child's prayer and so misplaced, but he wasn't strong enough to resist its pull.

Wrapping his arms around Bree, he lowered her to the grass. She started to speak, but he gently placed a finger on her mouth, then traced around her lips, barely touching them.

Those mesmerizing eyes that saw everything so clearly, that never shut him out, now looked at him with anticipation. He saw the future in her eyes . . . what could be . . . and he didn't want her to blink. She made him feel strong and whole. Nick craved her softness against his skin, and started to peel off her gauzy top but she resisted.

"The neighbors," she whispered.

"It's getting dark, their houses are far away, and they're your father's age. They can't see us."

She laughed. "My father's in his early sixties. Trust me, he has a knack for seeing things when we don't want him to."

"Your father's not here," he murmured.

Nick persisted, and this time, she didn't stop him as he tugged her shirt off and undid her bra. He reached up and broke off a rose bud as they laid down. He brushed it lightly against one breast and she shivered. He teased the other with his tongue. With a moan, she tried to push him away, but Nick grabbed both of her hands and held them above her head while he flicked the rose over her nipples. She rubbed against him as he felt her spiraling higher, but he didn't want this to be over quickly for her. Instead, he switched to ravish her soft, warm lips.

Her kisses tentative, she let him take the lead. Nick thought it was a sign of how out of his mind he was that he didn't mind her inexperience. To his jaded heart, it made her seem innocent and fresh. He wanted to please her.

He pulled down her capris and panties, and ran his hand up her tight, lean body. The perfume of the roses swirled around them like a cat rubbing against a leg. Reaching between her legs to stroke her with the rose, Nick kept his touch light. He couldn't see her now in the dark, but felt her quivering as one tender bud brushed another. She arched against him, breathing rapidly, and he had to work to control his growing excitement. He continued to slowly stroke her with the soft petals, then abandoned them to lick her into ecstasy.

"Nick," she begged.

He grew harder as she thrashed against him, but still he wouldn't let her come. Going slowly, sensually, he built her tension, switching from his tongue to the petals and back, always letting her get close, but never taking her over the edge.

"Tell me what you want," he whispered. "I'll do whatever you tell me to do."

Both trembling and panting, Bree gasped, "Come inside me now. Now, Nick."

Nick couldn't deny either of them at that point. He shed his pants, and with one smooth motion, entered her. Still, he resisted her urging to go fast, keeping his thrusts slow and teasing until finally, finally, he let her peak. Once she was sated and satisfied, he found his own release.

Gathering her in his arms, Nick rested his chin on her head. They didn't speak, just watched the stars and kept each other warm. In Bree's arms he found a contentment he never expected, and he pulled her closer, tighter.

"I don't think I'm ever going to be able to look at a rose again with a straight face," she finally purred.

They laughed softly and fell back into a comfortable silence, listening to the crickets.

Finally Bree broke the silence with a groan. "I still need to get online tonight to get a birthday present for my sister, but I don't want to move."

"How about sending flowers instead? I have it on great authority that women love flowers."

He felt her smile into his chest. "Carly takes her birthday—or at least the presents—very seriously."

Nick thought of all of Tory's birthdays he missed. He sent her presents whenever he found something he knew she'd like. She could get her birthday present three months early or nine months late.

"Carly's pretty easy to buy for. Sports stuff. Well, now it's sports and babies."

He felt rather than saw her shift her head to look up at him.

"When is your birthday?" she asked.

Unerringly, he found her lips in the dark and gave her a swift kiss. "December. Why? You want to plan a scavenger hunt here for me?"

She laughed softly, and he liked the sound of a relaxed Brianna Kincaid. "No, you're safe. But it can't be fun to have a birthday in December. I bet it gets lost in the holidays."

"Don't know. Haven't celebrated my birthday since I was six."

She went still in his arms. "When your mother left? Jesus, Nick, I'm sorry. I didn't think. I'm sor—"

Unerringly, Nick found her mouth again in the pitch black and silenced her with a tender kiss. "It's OK, Bree."

"No. No, it's not. Everyone should have a day when the world celebrates them. I hope," she said fiercely, "I never run into your mother."

"Shred her to little pieces for me?"

"That would just be the start."

The darkness made it easier for him to share himself. "When I was twelve or thirteen, I used to lay awake, planning what I'd do if I ever met her again. I was old enough then to understand what she'd really done to us. How much she'd really screwed us up. That's when I figured out that living in the past sucked, and I haven't looked back since. 'Live-in-the-moment', that's my theory."

"I can't even imagine that. I mean what about the future? Isn't there any big goal you want?" she asked softly.

He liked her better when she scowled or was tart-tongued because he discovered he had no defense when she spoke softly. When she was soft, she found a tenderness and vulnerability he didn't know he had. When Bree spoke, he could hear concern . . . caring. He was, he realized, drowning in his own mission of mercy.

"I'm not asking about us, Nick. I just think—" She hesitated, then because he'd never known Bree to hold back, she plunged on. "I just think you have more good qualities than you give yourself credit for. You could do a lot once you set your mind to it. There has to be something you really want to try."

Nick had no answer. To cover his uncertainty, he rolled so she was under him again. In the darkness, he thought he could see those clear violet eyes staring knowingly at him as he attempted to distract her from this uncomfortable line of questions. But as his lips trailed down her neck to find the sweet spot at her collar bone, he felt her acquiesce, and Nick lost himself in her so he didn't have to think about an answer.

Chapter Twenty-Four

N ICK WAS HOT. THE WRONG kind of hot. Not because he was in bed with Bree, but because he was standing at the entrance to the Garden on the first day of June that mistakenly confused itself with August. And it wasn't even noon.

He'd woken in Bree's bed, hours after she'd left for work. He'd fixed himself breakfast, which he ate on the back patio, under the shade of giant oak tree. At least he thought it was an oak tree. He'd scribbled ideas and passages for his novel.

Later, he wandered through the Kincaid house because, well, the chance to snoop was just too great to resist. He found old trophies of Bree and her sister from their days as high school athletes. He saw the many legal awards that Scottie Kincaid had received and the honors for Rachel Kincaid for her leadership at the Garden. And more of those damn pictures of happy people that he'd noticed weeks ago when he first visited the home. The accomplishments didn't faze him. He'd known enough politicians to know that garnering awards was just a trick. No, what made him irritable was the sense that he'd missed out on something. Something rare that this family had had and he'd never known. He found himself examining his life, and too many times veered near the feeling of regret, so he'd fled the house, only to find himself drawn to the Garden.

By now, Garden staff recognized him, even if they weren't sure what he did. He'd stopped at the admissions counter and the security office, making sure to subtly drop that Dr. Kincaid had lost something weeks ago, and had given up finding it. Even if only half the message drifted back to the killer through gossip chains, he would most likely call off his quest to kill Bree too. After all, if she wasn't looking, she wouldn't be a threat to him. There was no need to go after her.

Nick went to the upper level of the visitor center and entered the café, where he ordered a chicken sandwich, chips and soda. He sat near the window and made sure he chatted up the food service employees he had spoken to when he'd eaten here previously. Once again, he laced the conversation with the news about Brianna Kincaid; she had recovered from all the sadness in her life these past few months, and was looking forward to a quiet period of research out of the country.

As Nick gazed out the windows, he was aware of the one flaw in his plan. This guy had killed once, and almost gotten away with a second murder. Was he growing overly confident that he couldn't be caught? Would he try another attempt on Bree to silence the only person who might be a threat to him?

Nick set down his sandwich. He could protect Bree when she wasn't at work. But it was here in this paradise where she was most vulnerable. He looked around at the lush colors. The scarlets, yellows, whites, nature's display meant to dazzle and allure. The irony that such a beautiful setting could be lethal wasn't lost on him.

He had been right to wave her off the search. Their lives weren't worth the answers she sought. Now, as he thought through a plan to protect her, Nick wasn't sure she would be safe until she was away from this place. He *had* to keep her safe.

The notion shocked him, but not as much as his next thought. He was beginning to care *too* much for her. No, not this one, he thought. A blonde . . . a dumb blonde with big tits . . . not this feisty, honest shrimp. Too many brains . . . too much heart. He was not wired to be in a long-term relationship. He had no idea how it was done. His guilt kicked up a notch. She didn't deserve what he would do to her. He would hurt her, and she wasn't the ice queen that he had originally thought. You are such a shit, he thought.

It would never work. He could not live in St. Louis. Nope, couldn't stay in one place, much less *this* place. He would simply pretend that he hadn't made this horrible discovery.

The best thing to do was find those damn clues and solve this mystery so he could leave. Because Bree had made him review the clues so many times, at this point he'd memorized them, just as she had. Maybe he didn't have her analytical mind, but he was observant. And he'd read that romantic drivel of Megan Harper's so often that he thought could understand how she thought. Maybe he could bring a fresh pair of eyes to the search. After all, Bree had been wandering through this Garden since she was a child; maybe she couldn't see the obvious any more.

His mind made up, he finished his lunch, and headed outside. The clue they thought they had the best chance of exploring was about tears possibly meaning 'fountains', the clue they'd started before he'd been poisoned. In their conversations, they'd narrowed their ideas to three—the fountains in the Ottoman Garden, the Temperate House, and the Boxwood Garden.

He'd also spent so much time staring at the visitor's guide that he'd memorized the map too so he headed left to the Ottoman Garden, one of the newer gardens, tucked away in the northeastern corner. Not everyone found their way here so it would be a perfect spot for Megan to have hidden a clue because it was less likely to be disturbed.

The Ottoman Garden was a walled one, patterned after imperial gardens found hundreds of years ago in what was now Turkey. But when he arrived, a workman was fidgeting with the fountain, which was turned off for repairs.

Nick sat on a bench in the shade, and watched the repairs. After a few minutes he casually struck up a conversation with the guy, who said his name was Marty. Marty had stories to tell, Nick learned. Lots of stories. But Nick was both a good listener and knew how to shoot the breeze. Saying everything while saying nothing was an art, Nick believed, and he'd perfected it over the years. It was one of those talents that most people dismissed, but Nick knew its value.

Marty told him all about this garden. It had two unique sundials—one showed western solar time; the other showed Moslem prayer times, Italian hours and Babylonian hours. St. Louis and Istanbul were roughly at the same latitude, he said, so they could grow the citrus plants and Turkish tulips, and herbs found in such gardens.

Nick worked the fountain into the conversation. This fountain had been running non-stop since all the fountains had been turned on in late April, Marty said.

"Ever find anything really weird?" Nick asked.

"All the time," Marty said. "Mostly pennies. People can't resist making a wish. Lots of kids' binkies. An occasional condom. Last two really clog the fountain's motor."

"I imagine caring for all the fountains can be time-consuming and expensive. Some years are probably better than others. Any of the other fountains been down for repairs in the last couple of months?"

Nick hoped his question sounded casual. If Marty thought it peculiar, he didn't stop his work. Then again, the guy probably spent most of his day by himself, and he seemed to be a talker. Maybe he was just happy to have someone besides himself for company.

"Yep, it was a bitterly cold winter. Motors at a couple of the fountains had to be replaced."

Nick thought better of asking specifically about the two he was interested in. Calling attention to them surely would look odd. He shifted the conversation to how difficult it would be to care for the garden plants if the summer was a blistering one. Within a few minutes, Nick disengaged himself, and headed toward the Temperate House. Bree had explained those displays were of warm temperate-zone species requiring special protection from St. Louis winters. He expected it to be balmy and uncomfortable. It wasn't.

The entrance landing looked down on a steep stairway that led to a wall from a Moorish garden. At the center of the displays was a blue and white tiled patio, and in the center of that patio was a blue and white fountain.

There were few other visitors. From his high vantage point, Nick studied them. Had he seen any of them before? Had any of them been at the previous fountain when he spoke with Marty?

Was he getting paranoid?

He memorized their faces in case he needed to recall them in the future. His brush with death, and the resulting intense pain had given him a fragile appreciation of life that he'd taken for granted before. Sure, he'd been in tight spots on assignments, but seldom had he thought he would die. He shocked himself at how much he wanted the bastard who attempted to end his life to have a slow, painful physical experience too. If they could find him. And if they could find him before Nick took off.

He headed down the stairs to the fountain. A wrought iron bench sat on the southeast side of the fountain, and he plopped down to study it. In the quiet, he listened to the water. He didn't expect it to be soothing. However, after a few minutes of reflection, he got bored. Meditation was never going to be his thing.

Checking to make sure no one was looking, he moved to the edge of the fountain and sat there. He didn't expect anything obvious, and he didn't find it. If he could see it easily, it would already have been discovered. He moved around the fountain, staring at its base, checking under the rim. Looking for dirt that could have been disturbed more than seven weeks earlier when Megan planted the clue, but now would look less obvious. Nothing.

Somehow sticking his hand in the drains and the motor did not seem like the smartest idea. However, buying a six-pack and offering it to his new friend, Marty, if he would turn off the fountain and let Nick examine it seemed like an excellent idea, and that would be his approach if his search of the remaining fountain didn't reveal anything.

He headed towards the Boxwood Garden. The day had only gotten muggier so there were fewer visitors now. Mostly he passed people in their sixties and early seventies or heard the voices of children screaming in delight as they played in the circular water spray that he and Bree had ruled out.

The Boxwood Garden was in the shadow of the English Woodlands, and the boxwoods gave off a distinctive scent. At the fountains, Nick watched the water arc from one fountain to the next to the next so it looked like the water was jumping when, as Bree had pointed out, each of the four fountains was on a timer. It was a clever idea, however. One that never failed to delight and impress.

Nick walked from fountain to fountain. He sat on the ledge of each, looked under them. Looking around to make sure no one was coming, he tried lifting the drain of each, but they were secured. Of course, they would be. The Garden couldn't have the liability of people sticking their hands down anything. He didn't think he'd be able to access the fountain pumps either for the same reason.

Maybe they were thinking too literally. Maybe *tracks of our tears* referred to tracks and not tears so the model railroad where Bree had found the wedding ring would be the more likely site. Maybe Megan had grouped several of the clues in the same location to make it easy for her lover. Then again, a guy who most likely had advanced degrees should be smart enough to figure out the clues.

He rose and headed to the Boxwood Garden exit. He wouldn't mention his search to Bree. That would only set her off again on her quest. Right now, she seemed to be obeying his 'strongly worded' suggestion to lay off looking for clues. He didn't want to give her any incentive. That woman was a capital T for Trouble. They should name a flower after her, the Trouble flower.

Nick stopped. Hadn't Bree mentioned there were hundreds of roses and other flowers with the word 'love' in the name? He pulled out his phone and typed in 'flowers with tears in the name' and did a search.

Up popped half dozen names:

Job's tears

Baby tears

Angel tears

Widow's tears

He sat back down on one of the fountain ledges, and scrolled through each one, then moved about the boxwoods reading the names of all the annuals filling in the intricate scrolls formed by the boxwoods. None of the references to tears were in this garden. Maybe they were near the two fountains he had already looked at this morning.

As he prepared to head back the way he'd come, he caught a sweet smell. The last traces of the spring plantings in the boxwoods were fading. The horticulturists had planted summer flowers—saliva and marigolds—next to the tiny white bell-shaped flowers. He remembered the sweet, sweet smell from grade school. What had those little white flowers been called? The girls carried them as part of the local First Communion tradition. Lilies. Lilies of the valley. He typed 'lilies of the valley' in his phone and scrolled through various explanations.

The flower bloomed early in springtime, right about the time Megan would have planned her hunt. According to one source, lilies of the valley also symbolized Eve's tears after she was booted from the Garden of Eden, and the Virgin Mary's tears that she shed at the cross of Christ.

The train of tears.

Unfortunately, all of the boxwoods had lilies in them. Nick moved to the flower bed closest to him. The summer flowers were tightly planted. Made a better visual impact he guessed, but harder for his purposes. Especially since he didn't know what he was looking for. He couldn't get to the middle of the plantings, but then again, he doubted Megan would have considered trampling flowers, even in pursuit of love, acceptable.

He moved to the next bed, irritated by the sun beating on his back, and his hands getting dirty with soil from the sprinklers that had soaked the flowers that morning. He paused when he heard voices. An older couple strolled into the Boxwood Garden. He smiled. They smiled back.

Unfortunately, they parked themselves in the pavilion that transitioned the Boxwood Garden from the English Woodlands. Great. He could either come back later, give up entirely, or keep searching. The wonderful thing about being charming, he thought, was that you were always confident your charm could get you out of a mess. Plus people always trusted other people who were upfront, even if they were lying. There was just something about spilling your soul that made people cut you some slack.

"Hey, folks," he said, approaching. "My girlfriend dropped something sentimental into one of these beds. She was so upset, but she wasn't sure which one it was, so if I look a little odd as I poke around, please know that I don't mean any harm to the flowers."

Fortunately, the world was filled with good, kind people, and these two were sympathetic to his cause.

Nick went back to digging through the second flower bed, but turned up nothing. He moved onto the next bed. Halfway through pawing through the dirt, he felt a shadow and looked up to see the couple standing over him.

"We'll help."

"Oh, I couldn't ask that of you."

"Nonsense. We've all been together for a long time," said the man. "We want you to have a happy ending too."

"Your poor girlfriend. She must be beside herself," said the woman.

"Yes, she's very distraught. It's not expensive, but it meant a lot to her. To us."

"What is it you're looking for?"

"Oh, you'll know it when you see it."

They nodded and moved over to the next bed. Nick finished the bed he was searching through with no luck. Only one left.

"Is this it?" asked the woman. She held up a locket.

Nick moved to her side, and she placed it in his palm. The heart-shaped locket was cheap. It had rusted from sitting in the flower bed and being sprayed with water daily for months now. But he could still make out an ornate M etched on the outside. *Megan.*

"Yes, this is it. Thank you so much."

"She probably has your picture inside the locket," said the woman.

A picture.

He fingered the necklace for a moment. Was it possible after all this trouble that the answer was sitting in his hand, trapped between these two heart-shaped pieces of metal? A picture of her lover was one of the romantic gestures Megan had planned.

Nick realized he was holding his breath and let it out in a puff of air. He looked up to find the couple watching him expectantly.

"I'm so grateful you found this," he said. "My girl will be thrilled."

"Happy we could help," said the man.

"We love happy endings," said woman.

Nick crushed the locket in his palm. "I'm going to find her right now, and give her the good news. You have no idea how excited she'll be. Thanks again," he said as he moved past them.

Nick waited until he had left the Boxwood Garden to find a bench where he stared at the locket. It could finally be over.

With a start, he realized if this quest of Bree's was over, he'd have no reason to stay. Well that would be perfect, wouldn't it? It was time for him to move on. He'd stayed way too long. St. Louis was feeling little and stifling. He needed to find some place new.

Nick waited for the thrill of the new to grab him. All those possibilities of a new locale. He loved possibilities. So endless. After New York City and Tory, he'd try Michigan or Canada. Both would be cooler than this ridiculous St. Louis heat and humidity. Yep, he would start preparing. It was settled.

And he didn't need to feel guilty about leaving Bree. He'd told her he was leaving soon. He'd been honest all along. Besides, she would be headed to a new assignment in the next few months anyway. It would work out for the both of them. Yes, it was okay to go.

His gaze drifted back to the necklace in the palm of his hand. *Time to find out who you are, you bastard.*

He slipped his nail between the joint of the locket to pry it open, but it didn't open as easily as he expected. He looked at the tiny hinge that held the locket together. It was rusted more that the locket itself. He rubbed it against his jeans, hoping some rust would flake off. Nick tried putting nails from both thumbs in the joint, and this time, the locket opened.

Damn.

If there had been a decent photo of Megan's lover in the locket before, it was now nothing but mushy pulp. Sitting in the flower bed, getting sprinkled every day, had destroyed the photo.

He knew a smattering of swear words in Italian, Spanish, Turkish, and Swahili—and he used them all. Another dead end.

It was almost as if Megan was protecting her lover from her grave. She'd been an infatuated young woman in life; she was proving to be a frustration even in death.

Nick rose from the bench and headed toward the visitor center. When he passed a trash container, he threw in the necklace.

He would not mention the locket to Bree. It would just rile her up to search again. Right now, he had put a little fear of God into her to stop looking. He didn't want to do anything that would encourage her because who would be here to protect her when he was gone?

Chapter Twenty-Five

BREE STARED AT THE ENVELOPE sitting on the nightstand next to her bed. She didn't have to open it to know what it said.

Nick was gone.

She'd texted him twice today, but he hadn't responded. Hadn't she known in the back of her mind that his lack of responsiveness meant something had changed?

Had he been different last night, and she was now so comfortable with him, she overlooked the signs? Thinking back, his love making had an intensity she didn't understand—until now.

Even though she expected this at some point, staring at the note was like a punch in the stomach. The unexpected blow left her with no air to breathe. Bree sank onto her bed and fell backward. She waited to feel something. Heartbreak? She couldn't command any tears to fall. Rage? Fury would be a welcome shield, but she couldn't summon the energy. Instead, she sunk into a void, a limbo where she drifted with no thoughts, no feelings. Merciful numbness. Blessed nothingness.

When she came out of her stupor enough to sit up and grab the envelope, the shadows in her room had changed. Had she really blanked out for an hour?

For a second, Bree was tempted to just shove the envelope in the nightstand. Of course, he'd left a note. It was the easy way out, and Nick always took the easy way out. He hadn't had the guts to face her. Did he think she was going to go into hysterics or attack him? He could have given her some closure. They could have promised to be friends, and keep in touch, and drift apart gradually. Now she was going to have to deal with this all on her own.

Was there really any point in reading the note? It wouldn't change anything. She could ignore it for six months, take it out when it wouldn't hurt, and then continue on with her life.

Who was she kidding? It would *always* hurt. If she thought losing Mitch had been painful, having Nick walk out on her was excruciating. She wasn't sure how she was supposed to go on without him. In less than two months, Nick had become her heart and soul. What was the point of going on? When Mitch had left her, she felt like a failure. With Nick, she felt her heart break. The man she loved didn't love her enough.

She stared at the envelope. She didn't have to open it right now. After all, if she waited another day or two, the results wouldn't change. He wasn't coming back.

She changed out of her work clothes into her workout clothes, and headed outdoors for a run. She understood the symbolism of running away from her problems. Screw symbolism.

An hour later, sweaty and exhausted, Bree climbed the stairs back to her room. She picked up the envelope.

How would he do it? Would he be funny? Sincere? No likely, he'd be a smart ass—not easy when you knowingly were blowing up someone's life—unless, of course, his point was to make her hate him.

Long or short note? It was Nick. He'd go short. Again, the easy way out.

She ripped open the envelope.

Pink rose petals fell out.

Being with me would be no bed of roses. You deserve better.

That's right, you bastard. He would never be good enough for her. He would constantly fail while she was headed to the top of her profession.

So why was she so sure her heart would never mend?

Chapter Twenty-Six

B Y THE TIME BREE PICKED up her father at Lambert International Airport on Sunday, she told herself she had worked through her feelings about Nick. For sure, she'd had issues every time she had looked at her bed because they'd made love there. She couldn't bear to eat in the kitchen where they'd shared so many moments. The bastard had even ruined her mother's garden for her because he'd made love to her there too.

It seemed now that the whole world conspired against her for she saw little reminders of him every day—when she ate lunch in the café or walked past the Tower Grove House. Every day, there were little losses, and it hurt like hell.

Sadly, she had still craved his touch. They'd been together such a short time, but his touch had comforted her, excited her and brought her a feeling so powerful that she doubted that she would ever know it again. A pang of longing had clawed at her until it threatened to overwhelm her.

She had been disgusted with herself—she had no pride. Didn't she have any say in this? Why was her heart paying absolutely no attention to her head? There was a darkness in her that she didn't think would ever shine again.

But Bree had experience in boxing up grief, and by Sunday, she convinced herself that Nick had been a fling. Necessary to help her heal from Mitch, but she would not let him damage her. She would *not*.

As she stood at the TSA checkpoint waiting for her father to appear, she put on her game face, which was very important when handling her father. After all, as a top criminal lawyer, he was not only brilliant, he was also sensitive to a jury and could be incredibly insightful when he wanted to be. Appearing routine and normal would be critical so her father would never suspect anything had happened while he was away.

She hugged her father when he appeared. Mercifully, he carried the conversation on the drive home. He regaled her with stories of her sister and niece, and stories of weird legal issues.

She'd been so wrapped up in Nick and the search for Megan's killer that she had forgotten about all the changes she'd made to the bedroom her parents had shared and the removal of her mother's personal items. After unpacking, her father was subdued for the rest of the day, though he never said a word to Bree. At the end of the day, he simply gave her a kiss on the forehead and headed off to bed.

For the next month, they said good morning and good night to each other as they went about their business. Bree had always prided herself on how hard she worked, but her father made her feel like a slacker. He settled back into his normal work pattern—twelve-hour days filled with either all work or work and civic meetings. As a Kincaid whose family had played significant roles in state and national politics, he knew what St. Louis expected of him. On weekends, though, her father, who was a social creature, sat in front of the television.

Bree went for long runs and walks—so long and so often that her clothes started hanging loosely on her small frame. As guilty as she felt about leaving her father alone, she couldn't bear small talk right now. She had to leave her phone in the kitchen when she ran or was in her bedroom alone so she wasn't tempted to dial Nick or reach out to Daniel Cusumano to see if he knew where Nick was. She kept reminding herself that she had too much pride to be so pathetic. And besides, she was over him. So over him.

On a Saturday morning, she went down to the kitchen, where her father sat, reading the *New York Times* and *the*

Washington Post.

She opened the cabinet door for a coffee cup, only to discover that there were none. She glanced down at the sink, loaded with rinsed off bowls of cereal and numerous coffee cups. She opened the dishwasher, but was crammed with dirty dishes. She turned back to the cabinet and grabbed a clean wine glass and poured decaf coffee into it. She popped cinnamon raisin bread into the toaster and grabbed an orange.

"You know, counselor, I think there are some people who would say that you and I are slobs."

Scott Kincaid looked around the kitchen, and sheepishly caught his daughter's eye. "I think we'll have to plead guilty and hope for early parole."

"I don't suppose we could throw them all away and just buy a new set?"

A memory of her mother sparked, and she turned to her father who was smiling broadly.

"Just like your mother, huh?"

"That's still one of the best Rachel stories ever, Dad."

"Nothing shocked me more than when the first plate went sailing by my head, darlin'. I didn't think your mother could have a temper like that."

"I just remember that you were laughing at the end."

"Well, once I got over my shock, I couldn't help but tease her. And in the end, she did get the new set of dishes she wanted." Her father smiled. "People always think I'm the wily one, but they underestimated your mother. She was a special woman, though sometimes I forgot that."

"What? Never."

"We were married for thirty-eight years, Bree. It wasn't all wine and roses. It was tough while I was going to law school. We were poor, and we had you. I was determined to make it on my own and not use the Kincaid name." He rolled his eyes. "Youth."

He got a far-away look in his eyes. "But we were happy.

We were always happy. Well, I was always happy because I had so much with your mother and you girls. The hardest time for your mother was after Carly left home. She was a nurturer with no one left to nurture. That's why getting deeper into photography was so good for her."

She better understood the emptiness her father must have felt this past six months. To lose your light left only a horrible darkness in the heart.

"I still miss her, Dad."

"Me too, sweetie. But the pain isn't quite as sharp as it used to be, is it?"

Bree couldn't tell if he meant that or if her agreement would reassure him that he was coping better.

"I can see now that you and Carly were right to make me visit Boston," he said. "It helped. You've got your mother's wisdom, Bree."

Bree could feel herself tearing up. "Actually, Carly gets the credit for the idea. We were so worried about you so we made up a story about how Carly needed your help so I could take a crack at mom's things."

"I know, sweetheart. I couldn't let any of her go, but it made me stuck in time. How could a father be so lucky to have two such perfect and conniving daughters to rescue him? You get that from my side of the family, you know."

He kissed the top of her head. "I've been thinking a lot lately, and I believe it's time to put the house up for sale.

"I decided it's too big, even with the two of us. And let's face it. We know it's only a matter of time before you go back into the field." He paused, watching for her reaction.

"We want whatever will make you happy, Dad." She meant the words, even as she struggled to picture holding Christmas or the family's big July Fourth celebration someplace besides this house.

She looked at her father. His smile didn't reach his eyes. Scottie Kincaid needing reassurance. That was a new one.

"We can make new memories. It's not the place, it's the

people, right?" she said.

"Exactly." He headed to the kitchen island to get his mug. While he was refreshing his coffee, he said, "Your sister also suggested that in another six months, I might want to try online dating."

"Tell me she didn't." Bree went over to the sink and began organizing the dirty dishes.

"She explained that I wasn't meant to be by myself. And that your mother wouldn't want me to be alone for the rest of my life, especially with the two of you so far way."

Bree frowned as she squirted detergent on a new sponge and began cleaning the less dirty dishes. "Why don't you start with a baby step, sell this house and look for a condo?" She looked over at her father as she handed him the wet plate. "I'm not sure I'm ready for you to start dating. What if I don't like the person you like?"

"How could I like someone whom you and Carly don't like?" He grabbed a towel and began drying the dishes. "What about you? You ever tried this online dating?"

Bree stared at him suspiciously. "Did you come up with this online dating line of inquiry yourself, counselor, or did Carly put you up to this?"

"I understand online dating is how your generation meets people now."

"Dad, don't think that after years of hearing you talk about trials at the dinner table that I don't know when I'm being manipulated."

Her father raised his eyebrows and shrugged, not looking at all remorseful that he'd been called out. "I'm just trying to figure out what bastard I have to hurt because he broke my baby's heart."

"Just a guess, but I don't think it goes well in prison for a lawyer."

"Don't change the subject, young lady."

Bree could feel him studying her, but didn't have the strength to stare him down.

"You know I adore both my daughters. I don't understand you as easily as I understand your sister, Bree, but I know it's not like you to retreat for so long. Usually you figure a solution to a problem and attack it with a ferocity that's part of your Kincaid DNA." He leaned against the counter and folded his arms. "The only problems that a fierce will can't overcome involve love and other people because they may not act the way you want them to."

Bree rinsed off another dish and handed it to her father. As much as she loved him, she couldn't explain her relationship with Nick. It had been too brief to be meaningful, she told herself again. More importantly, he had been right. Life with him would have been no bed of roses. It would have been messy, and at times, painful. And glorious all the other times, her heart protested.

She squared her shoulders. "You don't need to worry about me, Dad. I'm determined to put him behind me."

He put the dish away. "Honey, you can't plan your emotions the way you can your calendar." He grabbed her hand. "You know I would take on your sorrow if I could, and make it go away, just like your mother used to kiss your boo-boos when you scraped your hand on the thorns of the roses in her garden."

In the warmth of his love, Bree was so tempted to talk about Nick. However, how could she make her father understand why such a scoundrel should be the one to break her heart?

"I know, Dad." Bree kissed her father on his cheek. "While we're talking about changes and mom and new relationships, we need to talk about her scholarship at the Garden."

"Is there a problem with the money? Not enough to cover Megan's salary?"

How much to tell him? The less, the better.

"Megan died in a car accident, Dad, right around the time you left for Boston. We need to interview new candidates for the scholarship."

He absorbed the news in silence. After a few seconds, Bree pushed on. "And I've decided to have a small sculpture erected in the Garden to honor Megan."

"I'll contribute too," he said absently. "What a tragedy, Bree. She was so young."

The sorrow Bree had kept at bay for the past months came crashing down on her like a tsunami striking shore. Once again she was drowning over the loss of her mother, Megan and now Nick. She muttered the right words to her father, but escaped to her mother's garden as soon as she could without arousing his suspicions. However, being by herself under the shade of the big trees and with the riot of scarlet and neon pink geraniums and the sweet scent of the oriental lilies only teased her senses. She couldn't see her mother's handiwork, only that night with Nick. And there were so many restaurants she'd never be able to go back to because they reminded her of Nick.

Screw you, Nick Mancini. You coward.

Someday, he would drift back to this city, and he would follow his temptation to check out what had happened to her. He would find she was happy. Happy, dammit. She would not let him haunt her. She could resume her search for Megan's clues and killer because nothing she did could get him hurt since he wasn't here. Thank goodness she was free now, and no longer had to worry about or protect him.

Chapter Twenty-Seven

WHAT, EXACTLY, DOES A KILLER look like?
Bree looked around the conference room table. If she was right, one of these men had taken a life. One of them had carefully thought out how to kill Megan to save himself. That someone would commit a sin so evil, and now sat in this room acting totally normal both baffled and infuriated her.

As Emery began the meeting, her insides trembled. If she resumed trying to smoke out the killer, she would change the normalcy of this world, the one on which she'd built her life. She could damage the reputation of her beloved Garden, and for the first time, she faltered. Would she be wiping away all that her mother and Emery had spent a lifetime building?

She paid no attention to what was being said, but instead scrutinized each person at the table, calculating if each could be the killer. Mercifully, she could rule out the other three women who were the heads of human resources, education and communications. However, twelve men still remained. Nine of whom were Caucasian. Her eyes swept over Emery, and onto the next department head, but then swung back to Emery. Her stomach curdled at the thought that this man to whom she had looked up to since she was a teenager could possibly be a killer, but she needed to look at each man with critical eyes.

Why was it that in her quest for justice for Megan, she had to doubt everything and everyone in her life? Next time she got a brilliant idea, she would think it through before she committed herself. Because once she committed, there was no backing away.

The more she considered Emery, though, the more unlikely she decided he was involved. He was only about five-foot-nine, not tall like Megan had portrayed her lover. And wouldn't the neighbor who had spotted Megan with her older boyfriend have noticed if the man had looked old enough to be her grandfather? In all the years that Bree had known him, she'd rarely heard him speak anything but affection for his wife. A late-in-life fling seemed a stretch.

She ruled out the controller. He only knew money, not plants. Ditto the chief information officer. He would know algorithms and bytes, but poison was unlikely.

That left the chief operating officer, vice president of conservation, vice president of science, the vice president of living collections, the two vice presidents of Garden subsidiaries, and the head of applied research.

Since she had always planned to go back out in the field again, she hadn't invested a lot of time or energy getting to know them well. Now she had to treat them all as potential murderers.

Certainly, each one was intelligent enough to plan and execute a murder. Stories circulated had about three of them because they'd lost their temper at the wrong time. They'd been reprimanded, but not terminated. Ultimately, their career had recovered. Would one of them risk it for Megan?

Maybe it was never about Megan, but maybe about the sex. Or maybe . . .

With a pang, she realized she missed bouncing ideas off Nick.

By the end of the meeting, she'd narrowed her list of likely candidates to five men: Klaus Heinrichs, director of conservation in Central America, who like her, had been back less than a year; Stephen Almy; Michael Singleton; Abe Brodeur, director of biodiversity; and Charles Davidson.

Abe and Klaus were in their fifties while Stephen, Michael

and Charles were in their late thirties or early forties, but all of them matched the height and build Megan had described in her clues. And they all had the blue eyes Megan had called out.

Her sense of justice wanted it to be Charles. She wanted the universe to prove karma existed, and that his self-absorption and snarky attitude towards the rest of humanity would eventually catch up with him.

The others—she just couldn't imagine them being so . . . so evil. Hadn't that been exactly what had gotten Megan killed, though? Her lover had masqueraded as a tender, caring man until she didn't meet his needs, and then with no feeling, he'd eliminated her.

She couldn't investigate them herself as she remembered her promise to Nick. Wait, she didn't answer to Nick Mancini anymore. But she could make a list for Daniel with clear reasons why each man should be considered or rejected. Certainly Daniel trusted her more now than the first time he had visited her home.

At the end of the meeting, Stephen headed back to their building with her.

"Do you want me to ask how it's going?" she asked. "I noticed Emery didn't say anything about your departure."

He smiled. Surely no killer could send such a genuine smile. "Abby and I have reconciled. We're going to give it another try."

"I'm so happy for you."

"Thank you. How about you? Ready to go back into the field?"

"Yes, I'm looking for the right opportunity now that my father seems to be past the worst of his grief. I'm hoping something opens up in the next couple of months."

At the entrance to her building, he left her. She no longer approached her office with fear or trepidation. Mercifully, the killer seemed to understand she had abandoned the search and was no longer a threat to him, or maybe it was he had been unsuccessful in killing her or Nick. With each day, she felt more comfortable she was in no harm. However, this would disturb the truce the killer seemed to have put in place.

Worse, she had no back-up with Nick gone. If anything had happened to her, he would have suspected immediately and taken action. If she decided to pursue Megan's killer again, she would be entirely on her own. Her heart beat too fast and her breath hitched. She wasn't sure she could continue. She pounded her hand against the back cushion of her visitor chair. She hated to give up. She hated to admit she was scared. She hated to retreat and not take the risk.

However, the objective scientist in her realized the danger she would in if she decided to continue. She placed both hands against her lips. As miserable as the last few years had been, she did not want to die. There were still so many things she wanted to do.

Oh, Megan, I'm so sorry.

Bree slipped out of her dress shoes to put on her running shoes. She took off her cream jacket covering a tan sheath so she wouldn't sweat, and told her assistant, Cheryl, that she was taking a short break. She walked past the home demonstration gardens, heading for the Japanese Garden. It was marketed as the garden of pure, clear harmony and peace. Couldn't she use that right now?

In truth, the fourteen-acre garden was not one of her favorites, though it was not politically correct to voice such an opinion. Built around a huge lake, it was meant to inspire serenity when Bree thrived on the vivid colors provided by flowers. But today, she needed to think, and reds, hot pinks, oranges and yellows would only distract her. The bridge over the koi pond was crowded as usual, but Bree wove her way through the children and adults feeding the fish. It wasn't long, however, until she'd distanced herself from the crowd and found herself walking by herself along the path around the lake.

Movement made thoughts come easier. Nature gave her clarity. As a teenager, when she had decided to go into botany, she had memorized lines from Emerson: *Nature never wears a mean appearance. Neither does the wisest man extort her secret, and lose his curiosity by finding out all her perfection. Nature never became a toy to a wise spirit.*

She didn't feel like a wise spirit right now. She needed direction. She needed to make a decision. Suddenly, she missed her mother with a sharpness that knocked the breath out of her. Her grief was followed by a second wave of sorrow. *Nick.*

Would this pain never lessen? Bree took a deep breath. Then another. Then another. With each breath, she fought to regain her equilibrium. She would not let grief swallow her. Her mother would not want that for her, and she wanted to honor her mother. As for Nick, surely what she felt was fury, and she wasn't going to waste any more energy on the man.

Bree walked onto one of the short wooden docks that periodically poked out into the lake. Japanese water iris bookended either side of the dock. Perhaps if she was quiet and relaxed, she could channel the wisdom of her mother.

Think, Bree, think. There has to be a way to do this.

Megan's killer knew a lot about poison. Most of the botanists on staff would know about some poison. She wondered how she could finagle access to employee records to see who had been in South America in the past five to ten years.

She should use professional investigators. Certainly, she could call the members of her father's legal team to get the names of some private investigators. No doubt they would mention the call to her father, though, no matter what she instructed. Her father would carry more weight with them.

She needed another plan.

Chapter Twenty-Eight

BREE STOOD OUTSIDE THE POLICE station. Gathering her courage, she entered the building. Mercifully, there was a different desk sergeant on duty from when she visited yesterday, and Daniel had not been in. This time, he was available.

When she reached his desk, to his credit, he didn't flinch or look uncomfortable. Daniel Cusumano, she decided, should play poker with Emery.

"Bree. What can I do for you?"

"I am still working on Megan Harper's death."

Daniel's expression turned to stone. "I thought Nick's poisoning would have been enough to make you understand you should leave this to the professionals. I also thought you promised him you would stop."

She blinked several times, then realized he was probably being harsh to scare her off. Then she realized he had referenced Nick, and she had to bite back the retort 'well, he isn't here anymore, is he?' But that wouldn't get her what she wanted or needed so she counted to five before she answered.

"That's exactly why I'm here, Daniel. I want to hire a private investigator to do background checks on several of my colleagues."

"And why would you want to do that? We already looked into the background of the people who worked directly with Megan." He looked her in the eye. "Including you. And no one had any trips to South America or where the poison would be found."

"Based on Megan's clues about what the father of her

child looks like, I've come up with a list of five guys. I'm only interested in their background. Scout's honor, Daniel. This is strictly paperwork. I have no intention of personally putting myself in danger."

"Give me the list. We can look into them."

"Daniel, you're overworked, have little time, and have made no progress."

She left out 'even after Nick was poisoned' because she knew that would sting. Daniel was determined to do everything possible to find the person. He was a straight shooter like her. In theory, he would be perfect match for her. So why didn't she feel any tug of attraction?

"I'm not faulting you, Daniel. I understand you're trying. But I can help in ways that you can't."

The set of his jaw clued her in that he didn't feel the same way, but was too composed to tell her off.

"What if I make you a promise? I will turn over any findings by the private investigator every two weeks so you can see them. *And* I will not do anything that interferes with your investigation."

"Or that puts you in danger."

"Exactly." Didn't she sound reasonable? "Besides, I'm here asking for the names of investigators that you know and are comfortable with. Surely this would make them more likely to reach out to you than if I went out and hired someone off the internet."

He studied her. "Why aren't you going through your father or his firm? He has to know top-notch investigators."

Damn Daniel. He was too smart.

"The types of investigators my father works with are too . . . too polished."

"Too polished?" Now Daniel looked slightly annoyed. "You said you were interested in background checks. That's mostly paper and electronic searches."

"Well, the more polished they are, the more expensive they are. The people my father employs can be as much as two hundred and fifty dollars an hour. I can't afford that."

"I thought you had a deep trust fund."

"I can only draw on the interest and dividends without my father's approval until I turn forty. I've had a number of rather unexpected expenses this spring."

Had Nick told him that she'd picked up most of the bill for his hospital stay? Nick certainly had been right that he had lousy healthcare insurance. When she added in the cost of the sculpture to honor Megan, she would have reached the maximum amount she could withdraw this year.

"I heard you were also going to have a sculpture created in Megan's honor."

So Nick had shared more about their efforts with Daniel than she had expected.

"My father agreed with me, and he's contributing some of his money as well." She leaned down, closer to his face. "Come on, Daniel, I'm being upfront with what I'm doing. I could have done this without reaching out to you. Just give me two to three names of people to interview. I promise we will share the results with you."

"And if they come up with nothing? You'll let this go?"

Was this his way of saying she was edging toward being a fanatic? Would she give up?

"Yes," she said softly. "I will not pursue this further if the investigators come up empty handed."

"Bree, there's no shame or guilt in that. You're going above and beyond what anyone else would do."

Except someone's going to get away with murder, she thought. She kept that thought to herself, and simply nodded.

Daniel pulled out his phone and texted her the names of three contacts. "These people are reliable, and reasonable with their fees. They're very different, though. That should make your choice easier."

"Do you want to tell me a little about each one?"

"Nope. You need to pick one you can work with, not one

that I like."

"But you'd recommend all three?"

He nodded.

She held out her hand and thanked him. He took her hand and held on to it.

"If you do anything or instruct your investigator do to anything that remotely looks like breaking the law, I will file charges, Bree. You shouldn't think your father can protect you."

As she withdrew her hand, she understood his threat was out of concern. He was trying to scare her so she didn't take foolish chances so she smiled sweetly.

"I promise. No felonies or murder."

"Well, I can sleep so much better at night."

She gripped her purse. Nick would have a sarcastic comeback like that. She had to bite her tongue not to let the conversation take a wrong turn. Instead, she nodded, smiled again. She thought she did a fantastic job of walking out and never looking behind her. With any luck, next time he talked to Nick, Daniel would share that she'd come by and never asked about him.

Chapter Twenty-Nine

BREE SAT AT A TABLE near the door of St. Louis Bread Company, waiting for the final investigator to show up for their meeting. Her hopes for this last meeting were both high and low. She had been uncomfortable with the first two men. Bobby Meyers was a former police officer. Of stocky build, he had worn a black suit and white shirt, looking very much like someone who would work for her father. But he'd had poor grammar, and didn't seem that smart. She needed someone smart to outfox the fiend who had poisoned Megan.

Zane Bolton had been so silent that the interview had seemed painfully long. Bree wasn't used to carrying an entire conversation herself. However, his answers to her questions and the few things he had suggested seemed like good ideas. If this interview didn't go well, she would chose him, and plan on communicating through texts and emails.

Of course, each had asked if she was related to Scottie Kincaid, though neither had met her father. In her field, few people connected her name with a well-known lawyer so she'd not had to carry the burden of living in her father's shadow. She had mentioned repeatedly during each interview that her father was not involved in this matter.

Bree glanced at her phone for the time. A representative from O'Shea and Sons should be arriving in the next few minutes. She paid no attention to couples or families who passed by her table. She was looking for a lone man. She wondered if she had time to refill her cup with decaf coffee without causing him confusion if she wasn't seated near the front door when he arrived.

"Dr. Kincaid?"

Bree looked up to find a young woman in jeans, biker boots, a black leather jacket, and carrying a motorcycle helmet, standing at her table. The woman looked to be in her mid-twenties with black hair, delicate features and deep green eyes.

"Are you Dr. Kincaid? I'm Riley O'Shea."

"You're with the investigation firm?"

"Yes, I must have beaten my father." She turned to look out onto the parking lot. "Oh, he's pulling in right now."

Bree saw an ancient Volvo pull into a parking spot. Huh, not what she was expecting, and she resigned herself to going with the barely audible Zane Bolton. When a tall, but out-of-shape man in workout clothes got out of the car, Bree wondered if she could get away with a twenty-minute meeting without seeming rude.

Bree rose when Jack O'Shea joined them at the table, and shook hands with each as introductions were made. Jack already had a couple of coffee. Riley declined Bree's offered to buy her something to eat or drink.

"I imagine everyone you meet with asks the obvious question. O'Shea and Sons. Are there any sons?"

Jack smiled. "Two. Dylan is a CPA. Tim is a former cop like me. He's the one who knows Daniel. My boys are working on other cases." He nodded towards his daughter. "Riley is our computer scientist."

He leaned forward. "Dylan can analyze financial records. Tim knows the law, the city, and where to look for people and things that may not want to be found. Riley searches social media, scours the dark web, and finds records for Dylan. As you can tell, we can provide a full range of services to meet your needs."

"What I need most is discretion, Jack. I don't want anything I ask you to do to reflect poorly on an institution I love and that does so much good work. I also don't want to damage the reputation of any of the men I consider suspects. If they have peccadillos that aren't related to my issue, I don't want to know."

"Two things to know about the O'Shea agency," Riley said. "We don't break the law to get you information. That only happens on television. We're just smarter than the people we're investigating."

"I don't want you to break the law so no problem there. What's number two?"

"If we find something that does break the law, we turn it over to detectives like Daniel."

"Of course. I just don't want the Garden to get caught in any bad public relations. The organization is innocent, and it does too much good work around the world."

Bree lowered her voice to explain she was trying to find Megan's killer. She laid out the events, including Nick's poisoning, and why she had a list of five men.

"Why not use the investigators at your father's firm?" Riley asked.

Well, of course, the computer scientist would have researched her before this meeting. "I prefer to keep my father's affairs separate from mine."

She didn't elaborate further, though from the way Jack O'Shea looked at her, he wanted to know more. Given his clothes and his car, she might have dismissed him as an incompetent slob except for the care with which he listened and the intelligence behind his green eyes. She wasn't sure if she was interviewing them or if he was deciding whether to take her on as a client.

Jack outlined what actions they would take, expenses he anticipated, as well as a time line, if she decided to hire them.

"It would also be wise if we plant some cameras in your office for your own safety," Riley said.

Bree sucked in a breath. "You think he'll come after me again? From what you've described, your first steps will be background searches by Riley and Dylan. Won't that give us a clue who I really need to worry about?"

Jack shook his head. "The key word there is 'worry'. A person who has killed thinks only of protecting himself. A person who attempted murder twice is dangerous. Very dangerous. You need to be on your guard at all times. Maybe even take some vacation.

"And if it's one of the men on your list, he probably knows where you live. For your father's sake, you might want to clue him in."

Bree was sure all the color drained from her face.

"Your father will be fine," Jack said. "He's no stranger to being threatened. He needs to know, though, so he can be on his guard."

Bree gripped her coffee mug tightly.

Jack O'Shea took a sip of his coffee. "I can tell he's shielded you from the underbelly of what he faces. You think someone takes on high-profile cases, and doesn't piss off one side or the other? Talk to him."

Bree nodded absently as she had a flashback of one spring when Carly and she were escorted to elementary school by men her father had said worked with him. She realized now they'd probably been a security team, and she'd been too young to know it.

"I imagine your house has an excellent security system," Riley said. "Make sure your security system is on *all* the time, even when it's daylight and even if there are others in the house with you," the younger woman emphasized. "It may buy you critical time."

Deciding Jack O'Shea knew what he was doing and she liked the idea of a team investigating, Bree offered them the job. Unless something urgent cropped up, O'Shea and Sons would give her their first report in two weeks.

Chapter Thirty

BREE OPENED HER EYES TO sunlight streaming into her yellow bedroom. She loved waking up to the light, cheery color. It gave her a sense of energy. Then she waited for the familiar heaviness to settle in her heart. It came, but much lighter and gentler than it had in the three months since Nick had disappeared.

I'm healing.

The knowledge amazed her. She would not sink this time. She'd fought back. No pulling the covers over her head and letting a failed relationship leave her broken.

Take that, Mancini. I can get along very well without you. Now.

She doubted he'd been either holed up in a room or working so hard that he had no extra time to think as she had these last three months. Was he with someone else now? Of course he was! The new woman in his life was probably beautiful.

With her father home, she had managed to banish Nick's ghost in this house, in this room. Occasionally, she would have a flashback to him sitting in her office guest chair and drinking her drinks. She found the only way she could cope was to get up and leave her office. There were nationalities of foods she avoided now because they reminded her of him; she certainly hadn't been to Thai, Indian or Mexican restaurant since he walked out on her.

Several times a day, when she was furious with him, she imagined him showing up at her front door. She didn't slam it in his face. Certainly not. In her mind, he begged his way in, then begged her forgiveness, and produced a two-carat diamond ring before she sent him away. Sometimes, she was so scathing that Nick left bereft when it was obvious that she would never come back to him. From there, her daydreams varied. Often, her latest imaginary lover, who made Nick look ugly and scrawny, beat Nick up. Invariably, they would meet again years later when she'd just accepted the first Nobel ever awarded for botany and he was a broken-down drunk.

And he'd implied that she wasn't creative.

Well, she was going to be happy, damn it! And today was the first day in a new direction, a new Brianna Kincaid.

She started this Sunday off with the same prayer that she had been saying every day since June. *Please give me the grace to look at all that I have and be grateful. Let me love those around me. Let me go forward. Let me not miss Nick Mancini today.*

Three out of four—at least it was a passing grade.

She rolled out of bed, and drifted down to the kitchen where Scottie was making an omelet. Her father had already played a round of golf this morning. She realized the hum of energy that she associated with her father was back. Maybe they were both healing.

He had made hazelnut coffee, and she kissed him on the cheek on her way to the coffeemaker. He offered her half of his cheese and veggie omelet if she'd butter the cinnamon toast that was about to pop up.

<hr>

Scottie watched his daughter as she worked on the toast. Blessedly, she was not buttering it as if it was the head of this Nick Mancini that she was slicing off. Scottie shook his head. She was so contained and fearless, his oldest girl. He'd given both his girls his determination, his drive to change things, only Bree had mutated the traits into a desire for perfection . . . impossible standards. Except for the one time they'd talked in the last few months, she had said little about this guy, except to finally share his name, and to extract a promise from Scottie to let her deal with it.

He divided the omelet on two plates. Bree added the toast and orange juice, and asked about his golf game as they sat at the table. Although neither of his daughters shared his passion for golf, they had been elite athletes in their sports and understood the highs and lows of competing.

As they finished eating and talking, he said, "Good to have you back, sweetheart."

Bree understood what he was saying and tilted her head. "I'm getting there, Dad." As she took their plates to the sink, she said over her shoulder, "Turns out you and Mom are a hard act to follow. I'm not sure I'll ever have a relationship like you two had, but I'm not going to let Nick or Mitch or any guy steal my happiness.

"Bree, you were gone, off to school, or in your jungles, when your mom and I hit rough patches. In my mid-forties, I had a mid-life crisis that was so stereotypical, it's laughable now. But back then, my wild streak flared again, and I caused your mother grief."

Bree frowned. "Was this when you got the little red sports car?"

Scottie nodded. "Clichéd, I know. I'm usually so much more original. Anyway, that was only a small part of it. I felt old . . . I had kids in high school and college . . . I wanted my old fire back. The same one that I remembered from my twenties.

"I know that you miss your mother, Bree, and God knows that she was a one-of-kind woman, but what made her so special was that she was so very human. She understood the heart so well because she felt not just love, but envy . . . despair. And she understood forgiveness."

Scottie could see tears welling up in his daughter's eyes, while he felt his own throat tightening as he tried to smooth over the emotion in his own voice.

"It may be time to you forgive yourself. You're awfully harsh on Brianna Kincaid. At some point, it may even time to forgive that bastard Mancini so you can be free."

"I'd be happy to forget him entirely, Dad," Bree said flatly.

Scottie was silent while Bree rinsed the dishes. When she came back to the table, he said, "You know, I can understand your Nick and his running away in some ways."

"Dad," she said sharply.

Scottie held up his hand. "I didn't say that I wouldn't beat the living hell out of him if he showed up on our doorstep today because he hurt you, sweetheart. You're one of the three most precious things in life to me. But I do understand how he could have been so scared by his feelings for you that he had to run away."

"I wouldn't want any man who runs away from his feelings. If he's so stupid . . . We were good together. I know it," she said fiercely. "And he threw it all away. The ass."

"Well, I ran away from your mother—or I scared her away—when we first started seeing each other because I was so scared. The thought of loving someone so much . . . of realizing that you have no control over this love, and that this woman holds your life in her hand, is not the most reassuring thought for a man, Bree."

"But what's life without love, Scottie?"

"I can only answer that question now, sweetheart, because I'm a smart sixty-two-year old. But when I was younger, it took me time to come up with that answer. I finally realized I couldn't live without her. Your mother saved me. I think women save most men."

"Apparently Nick didn't know that he needed to be saved," she said. "And it's not an issue that I intend to worry about again."

It was moments like this that Scottie fervently missed his wife. Would she have let the remark go by, and hope that their eldest would pull herself out of this funk? Or would she encourage her with words of wisdom?

He sighed. He hoped she might consider the kick in the rear that he was about to give their daughter, because he didn't think patience and encouragement were going to work any longer.

"So what are you going to do? Stay wounded for the rest of your life, Bree? Never get in another relationship? Are you going let these two relationships skew you so much that if the right guy comes a long at age fifty that you'll pass the opportunity by? Let him go for good."

His daughter looked at him, and he held her gaze. Scottie watched the anger drain out of her. He took her in his arms for a long hug.

"There is someone out there for you, Bree. He will find you if you keep your heart open."

Chapter Thirty-One

NICK KISSED THE YOUNG WOMAN'S cheek and rolled off her. The brunette snuggled up to him and sighed. He said something in Greek that made her laugh, and she started talking. If only he felt like listening.

The sex had been great. And the brunette, sweet. She was a bit young for him. It disgusted him that he even considered that, but after spending time with Bree, he was very aware of his habits. He still felt a restlessness that even this twenty-something beauty couldn't soothe.

He gently told his babbling companion that he needed some sleep. She complied easily, turning over and falling asleep herself. That was the wonderful thing about younger women, he thought. He blamed his inability to fall asleep on the music played by the live band in the hotel bar.

He should feel so good. Yet he barely felt anything. Fuck. He'd tried every vice known to man, but none of them made him feel as good or as alive as he had when he'd been with Bree those few months.

He'd had the strength to leave her, so why the hell couldn't he forget her? It wasn't like she was that special. The woman in his arms was certainly more beautiful. He hadn't been able to find one smarter, but that wasn't a surprise. But who in his right mind would want a smart, determined woman? God, she would forever be testing him simply by being Bree.

In the darkness, it was easier to admit that he missed her. Bree had given him a sense of peace with himself that he had never found anywhere else. But he knew that it wouldn't last. Jesus, how could it? He got restless when he stayed in one place too long. He could never be faithful, and the woman had impossible standards. She'd probably insist on kids too, and he'd really screw that up. Look what he had turned out like after his own childhood with Bernard and without Elena. He couldn't stand it if he did that to an innocent child.

So where did that leave him? He eased out of bed so as not to wake up his sleeping Greek goddess. Pouring himself a shot of ouzo, he moved onto the second-story balcony of his hotel room. At two in the morning, the night was starting to cool off, and he could hear the Mediterranean as the tide went out.

He was almost finished with a piece on migrants for *National Geographic* that he'd been working on. Tory had called him that morning. She was catching a flight back to St. Louis to spend the Labor Day holiday with the Cusumanos. They had both avoided mentioning Daniel's name. He worried about her after they hung up.

Surprisingly, his various editors had liked his work more in the last few months as he'd branched out into writing stories for the *Huffington Post*, then caught the attention of the *Washington Post*. He even had made progress on the novel he had started. The last couple of weeks, work had been his salvation. He sure wasn't finding any peace in screwing or drinking, so he threw himself into his work until he was so exhausted that he slept. Though it was getting to the point that he almost preferred to sleep by himself.

That thought pissed him off so he went back to the bed, and woke the brunette. While she looked innocent, she either had a gift from the Gods or the boys in the village had been very good tutors. When they finished, he dozed for a couple of hours and woke just as the dawn began slitting the sky in two.

But he woke with a hollowness that wouldn't go away; just like there was a third person crowding the bed. He just needed more time, he told himself. He couldn't pretend that he didn't care. In fact, he cared so much that if anything happened to her, he wouldn't be able to go on. That's why he'd left. What man wanted to give a woman that much power over him? What guy with any balls turned his destiny over to something that he couldn't control?

He slid out of bed, picked his clothes off the floor and shrugged into them. He let himself out of his room so as not to wake the young woman and wandered down to the street. He was in a small city with an ambitious young mayor who wanted to modernize it, yet was shrewd enough to know that the old part was what lured the tourists. His small, old-fashioned hotel sat in that old part of town with cobble streets, white-washed buildings, and beautiful window boxes of flowers.

He strolled aimlessly, passing fisherman, shop owners and delivery men who were starting their day and paid no attention to him. Without realizing it, he ended up at the beach, and watched the sun rise.

Damn Bree, he thought angrily. He stood in what should be a postcard-perfect scene, and all he felt was intense loneliness. This constant thinking of her . . . of missing her . . . made him feel vulnerable and defenseless. Then it slammed into him. Shit, she'd turned him into his father! What was the difference between him and Bernard except he'd swapped the recliner for a sandy beach? Well, he sure as hell wasn't going to end up as pathetic as his old man.

Stoked by anger, he stomped down the beach, back towards his hotel. Starting right now, he would never think of that bossy Twig again. He'd cut her out of his life with a ruthlessness that his spineless father had never had the backbone to show.

He returned to his hotel, and woke the brunette up again. He kept her in bed for hours, fucking her harder every time that Bree threatened to creep into his mind. When the young woman finally needed to leave for work, Nick immediately headed for a bar. He drank heavily through the rest of the day, and by night time was looking for a fight. He was too drunk to care who he took on, but his luck held when he could only provoke two students from England who were taking a semester off, and were poor fighters.

He wasn't sure how he got back to his room, but the next time he opened his eyes—technically it was just an eye because the other one was swollen shut—it must have been late afternoon of the following day for the room was bathed in warm sunshine. He was conscious just long enough to realize that everything would really hurt when the alcohol wore off, then mercifully fell back into a fitful sleep.

When he woke up the next morning, his body was black and blue, his hands red and raw.

Bree wouldn't care what his face looked like, he thought, because she loved all of him. The thought had popped into his brain before he could stop it, and it depressed the hell out of him. Not to mention she'd give him a really long lecture about getting into fights at his age.

He called room service, ordered a light breakfast, and had the concierge send out for some first aid supplies. After he ate, and cleaned and bandaged large amounts of his body, he went back to bed with the hope that he could sleep off his growing sense of despair.

But his demon was still with him when he woke up, too sober, around six that night. Well, he sure as hell didn't want to sit in the room, thinking, so he gingerly shuffled back to the beach.

As he stood on the edge of the sand, watching the sea, he realized the facts weren't going to change. He loved Bree. He didn't want to, he thought wearily, but apparently he had no pride and apparently even less say in the matter. His heart was blithely running away even when his head screamed stop.

Loving her was sapping him the same way Bernard's love for Elena had sapped him. He would end up a broken loser like his father. All those years of hard living just to end up in the same place as his soft-spoken old man. If it didn't hurt so much, he would have laughed, a bitter laugh, but wasn't it just too ironic? He had been better off with fifteen years of running away, of destructive behavior, than to end up like this.

Well, here's to us, pop, he thought angrily. We finally have something in common. Brought low by loving the wrong woman. Obviously, the Mancini men had no gift for picking the right women. Unfaithful, careless Elena, and . . . and what? Unfaithful, careless Bree?

That brought him up short. She would never be so cruel as to abandon her children. He simply couldn't imagine a woman who knew the power of a loving family just walking out on her babies. And she would never be unfaithful. She might tell him that he wasn't doing his part in the relationship. Oh yeah, she'd definitely tell him that. Or she'd tell him that they were in a rut and needed a change, but he couldn't ever see her cheating with another man, especially since she didn't give her heart away easily.

Bree knew how to love; she knew how to give. Bree would always encourage him to write that novel, no matter how many he started. She would expect that same support back, but she would always be by his side, or in front, slaying dragons for him. Yes, Bree knew how to love. Unlike his feckless, selfish mother.

Still, while he'd spent so much of his life trying not to be like his father, he had the uneasy feeling that he and Bernard might have something in common. Like his father, he was letting his love for Bree break him. The thought made him sick to his stomach. He'd fought and fought these feelings for Bree, but he was in over his head. If he went back to her, he'd be just like Bernard. Bernard had given in and given up to his feelings. If he had fought more, if he just hadn't wallowed, but had moved on, maybe he wouldn't have ended up so defeated by love.

Nick frowned into a gorgeous sunset. What should Bernard have done? He should have picked himself up and gone on. Maybe if he'd just gone through the motions more. If he'd spent more time throwing himself into his two kids, instead of retreating. If he'd charged out, back into the world of love, would that have made a difference? Bernard hadn't even tried. He'd just withdrawn, never caring about anyone again.

Just like I've been doing since I left, Nick thought. The thought stunned him. *I'm just like Bernard. I've been retreating too; I just went farther away to do it.*

So if running away wasn't the answer, what was? He winced as he sat up straighter. Maybe, just maybe, he should do the opposite. If he gave into his feelings for Bree, what would happen? He'd probably end up with a loving family. Was he strong enough for that? Hell, he didn't know.

He sat on the beach, shivering as the sun went down, though it wasn't because it was cool. It was because he was scared. Gradually an idea formed, and then a feeling followed. With unsteady steps, he went back to the hotel and booked a flight.

Chapter Thirty-Two

THE SEPTEMBER HEAT CARRIED A slight breeze. The perfect weather filled Bree with happiness as she completed the first circuit of her noontime run on the paths. She relished the combination and studied the details of the Garden as she ran, knowing she wouldn't be here to see the changing seasons in a couple of months.

Her father had put the house up for sale, and it had sold much faster than the realtor had predicted, in large part because of Rachel's gardens. So now they were scrambling to get everything out of the house while Scottie searched for a condo. Downsizing had exhausted both her father and Bree, who vowed that she would move every five years so she didn't accumulate as many things as her parents had.

Still, she enjoyed the time with her father because she hoped to be overseas by Thanksgiving or Christmas. There was an opening to head the conservation project in Kenya as well as one in Vietnam, and she was perfect for both. The interviews had gone well, and either would be a step up from what she'd done before. Yes, she was being a coward to want to be gone on the first anniversary of her mother's death, but Carly had promised to visit so her father wasn't alone. Bree thought she was entitled to run away from reality after the year that she'd had.

Bree felt her body thrumming with energy; she was warmed up and felt loose. The next time around the same circuit would be both relaxing and invigorating as she settled into her rhythm.

Bree passed the Climatron, glanced up to make sure the path was clear and saw a man in the pathway. She took a second glance, and came to an abrupt stop. She struggled for her breath; she felt as if all the air had been sucked out of her.

Nick held a single red rose.

A red rose. *Love.*

To her distress, Bree felt tears pooling in her eyes. Not now, she pleaded with herself. Not now. She wanted to be angry.

———◆———

When it was obvious that she wasn't going to keep coming his way, Nick walked slowly to her. God, she looked more beautiful than he remembered. Her skin glowed from running.

He stopped a few feet from her. Her hatred was almost palpable, and she had such disdain in her eyes. This was going to be harder than he expected. He'd known that she wouldn't make it easy for him, but he had hoped that her anger would give way to hurt, which was supposed to yield to forgiveness. Fat fucking chance.

They just stood—Nick staring and Bree glaring—surrounded by silence.

It really doesn't matter what I say, he thought, she's not even going to hear it. For a second, panic flared—what if she didn't want to be with him? What if she really hated him? Or what if he misjudged her and she was with someone else now? Just say something to get started and get it over with, he told himself. He started to speak, but she shocked him by stepping past him and resuming her running.

"Great. Just great," he muttered, looking skyward.

Then he turned and ran after her. With his longer legs, it didn't take much to catch up.

"I'm sorry, Bree. I panicked and I screwed up. I love you."

She kept on running. He narrowed his eyes at her when she subtly picked up her speed.

"I know that I don't deserve you, but I can't live without you."

She stopped abruptly, and pushed him.

"You bastard. You think that you can just walk back into my life with your pretty words, and that I'm just going to fall into your arms?"

She pushed him again.

"You hurt me, Nick. You made every day of the last three months a living hell with your thoughtlessness." She shoved him really hard. "With your cowardliness. Why in the hell do you think that I'd want you back in my life?"

She turned away, but he grabbed her arm. She launched into him and they toppled onto the grass. She landed a solid punch into his stomach, which was still painful from his fight the week earlier in Greece. That someone so tiny could be so lethal surprised him. He struggled to get her hands and was rewarded with dirt in his face.

"That's it," he yelled.

They slapped and shoved until finally Nick wrestled himself on top of her and pinned her arms over her head.

"Are you going to listen to me, you pig-headed woman? I love you!" he shouted. "I've never said that before to any woman."

"Here's what I see as the Nick Mancini definition of a relationship. Love you one day, gone the next."

"OK, I'm the stupid one. We know that. I will probably always be the stupid one."

"It will never work," she said wearily, and he felt the fight go out of her.

"We can make it work," he said.

"What? For three, maybe six months? Then you'll get scared or bored, and poof, gone again. Go to hell, Nick."

He didn't think she'd believe him if he said he'd already been. If she knew how much he'd missed her, she'd be too hard to live with. And he didn't want to give her that much of an upper hand.

He smiled, a slow, devastating smile, and was rewarded when her face became wary. Her head might not want him, but her heart wasn't as cold as she pretended.

He stood, and offered her a hand up. They walked slowly toward the visitors' center.

"I love you, Bree," he said. "I know that you don't believe me or even trust me, but I do love you, and I'm going to stay with you until you believe me.

"I love everything about you, Brianna Kincaid. I love that you're smart, and loyal, and sassy. I know that when you love, you love with everything you've got. I want us to be together."

"Nick, quit saying that. You say it like it's going to be so easy, and it just shows how naïve you are, about what it really takes to make a relationship work."

"You think I'm naïve?" His grin was positively wolfish.

Bree frowned. "Just about love."

Nick knew how to use silence as they walked to the entrance of the Garden. Sure enough, she filled the void.

"Maybe you do love me right now," she said begrudgingly, "but the kind of love that I want is day in and day out. Romantic love fades; it's a sprint. I'm a long-distance runner. Romantic love is just a warm-up for what I want."

"I know. I'm ready to do that."

He took her arm and tugged her toward him. Those violet eyes were so stunning, and they looked at him with an honesty that would have made most men squirm. But she wasn't as angry; he still had a chance.

"Forgive me, Bree. Give me a second chance." He touched her face. "Think how good we can be."

"So you've been in a monastery, pining away for me these past three months?"

She must have seen the guilt on his face before he could mask it.

She sighed. "Nick, you're so out of condition for love, I'm not even sure that you can sprint more than a couple of yards in a relationship race."

"I'm a man who appreciates a good metaphor. But if I run around the whole Garden, will you have dinner with me?"

Like he could possibly even walk that far. In the end, it wasn't her decision. Nick started jogging.

"I didn't say yes, Nick," she called. "This is a trick. It won't work, and it doesn't count."

If he tried to run around the entire Garden, he'd have a heart attack, and she'd have to visit him in the hospital. Then she'd feel sorry for him, they'd spend time together and he'd charm her all over again. If by some miracle, he actually made it around the Garden and she accepted dinner with him, it would be the same fate. She frowned. So typical of life with Nick. Then again, she felt a spark now that she hadn't felt in the last three months when life had been monochromatic.

He kept on jogging. She turned around and walked the other way. She'd go back to her office, call security so they could keep an eye on him, and just go about her business. He'd get discouraged in just a few days and disappear again. But at least now, she'd have the chance to tell him everything she'd thought over the past three months.

She warmed to the idea. She'd scribbled plenty of hateful letters to him in the ninety-four days since he'd left. She could use the best of the best, and write a letter to sear his tiny, black heart. She'd leave it with Daniel and ask him to give it to Nick. By the time she was through with him, she'd scar him for life—just the way he'd ruined her. And she wouldn't have to fear being entangled by those heated brown eyes. Or the pouty full lips. The mere thought brought her great satisfaction; in fact, she felt happier than she had all year long, and she started jogging. Now was when she would start rebuilding the life she loved again.

She stopped abruptly. Except she couldn't bring back the life she wanted. She wanted her mother alive again. She wanted poor Megan back on this earth. And that dizzy feeling of being in love. Then she wanted the cozy warmth of a lifetime love like her parents had had, even if she knew it was unrealistic to hope she could duplicate it.

Frowning, she started running again. She was worth loving, damn it! There was a man—another man—out there that she could build a beautiful life with. She could feel it now; she could picture it. All these months, all she'd needed was just the chance to close this chapter with Nick. And then she'd be free.

Why wait? Why wait and write him a letter? Why not just catch up with him now, and hit him with her full fury? Then she could walk away, and start over fresh again in a new place with a new attitude and newfound peace. The perfect plan, she thought smiling, and savored having a plan again.

She cut across one of the rose gardens. Nick couldn't have gotten very far. By now, his legs would feel heavy, if he hadn't stopped running as soon as she turned her back. She got to the path on the east side of the Garden, near the Tower Grove house, and looked behind her towards the daylily garden. No Nick.

She turned to face forward, and her eyes widened. He was still running. She saw him ahead of her, in the English Woodlands. The idiot. He wouldn't be able to walk tomorrow, if he didn't die in the next fifteen minutes.

Bree raced after him, pouring on speed to catch up with him.

◆

Nick heard someone running behind him. He hoped to hell that it was Bree, because he was going to collapse in another ten or twenty feet. His lungs were on fire. He wanted to take huge gulps of air, but not let her know that he was fading fast.

Bree drew next to Nick and slowed her pace. "You screwed up big time, Nick Mancini. I was the best thing that you will ever find in life," she said vehemently. "And you were so stupid that you threw it all away."

Let her vent as long as she wanted because then he wouldn't have to say a word, which was perfect because he couldn't talk now, and he had a painful stitch in his side.

"We would have made a great team together. I would have stuck by your side while you wrote your novel. You would have helped me uncoil and smoothed over my tendencies to go overboard. We would have had fun!" she shouted, and stopped.

Thank God! Nick stopped too, facing his fiery dynamo. He was heaving, trying to suck in great gulps of air—without her noticing. Though she was so worked up, he didn't think that she would notice anything short of him collapsing at her feet.

"But you aren't right for me. I can see that now. I need someone who is not afraid of a strong woman. Someone who will put family at the head of the list. Someone . . . someone . . ." Bree sputtered.

"Well, fine. You just sit here waiting for the paragon of perfection . . . this dream that you have. I need someone who wants a flesh and blood man, not some fairy tale."

He started walking. He still felt like shit, but now he was angry too.

He turned around, walking backwards, and shouted to her, "I made a mistake. I didn't know what love was until you came along. It took me a while to realize what it was, and then how precious it was . . . you are.

"But here's news for you, Dr. Kincaid. I've changed. I've started growing up. And if you can't live with that change . . . If you can't forgive and forget, then maybe you aren't the woman for me."

He flipped around and stalked off.

Bree watched him, and fought with herself. Should she

run after him and give him another chance? God, could she bear the pain if he left her twice? But he could also bring her the love she thought they could build together.

She looked back toward her office. She would be free, now that she'd told him off. She could start a new chapter in her life; possibly end up running this magnificent Garden in a few years. Surely, she could find a stable, supportive man. They'd build a lifetime of pleasant memories. Then she thought of Nick. Pleasant wasn't the word that came to mind. Exhilarating, fun-loving, someone who could match her step for step, thought for thought.

"Take a chance on me, Bree," Nick said softly as he came behind her and put his arms around her. "We're worth it. Have some faith."

She glanced over her shoulder. The sarcastic mask he usually wore to hide his feelings was nowhere to be seen.

"You aren't the kind of woman to have a flimsy love," he said, gently touching her face. "You aren't the kind of person to give up."

"I don't know, Nick. Maybe you were the one who finally taught me to get over that particular weakness."

Well, that silenced him, she thought with satisfaction.

Finally, he shook his head. "No, you are as constant as the sun, Bree. You wouldn't get over me that quickly."

Her eyes blazed. "Well, aren't you just so confident," she snapped.

He calmly continued. "You wouldn't give up on me, even when I wanted to give up on myself. I can't live without you."

I couldn't live without her. Isn't that what her father had said about her mother? She looked into those deep brown eyes and felt the familiar tug. It hurt just to look at him, and remember those seven weeks of ecstasy. But those brown eyes didn't seem as cocky as they had in June. Damn, he probably meant every word he was saying. He was just saying them all too late.

She hated it that he could understand how tough it had been for her, and that she could feel his respect. She wanted to lean into him and have him put his arms around her because holding her would chase away all the bad. It was so simple, really. In his arms, she felt both loved and powerful. Nothing would ever be wrong in his arms.

He looked down at her. "And if there's anything that you are, Brianna Kincaid, it's a builder. I'm tired of running away from life. I want something to run to, and you're it."

Well, what did a woman say to that?

"I know how good you are with words, Nick Mancini, but you should know by now that I'm not a woman for sweet talk. I have expectations."

"Draw me up a list."

"And don't even think I'm going to sleep with you tonight. Or tomorrow or next week either."

"Understood. You know what the red rose stands for in the language of flowers, right?" he asked. "I mean in addition to 'I love you'."

"Home," she whispered.

"That's right. Home. When I'm with you, I have a sense of peace . . . a sense of happiness that I've never known.

"We'll be good for each other," he said, nuzzling her neck. "We'll make each other better."

She knew that he would only live up to half of what he said. That was enough. Bree turned around in his arms, and they silently clung to each other, absorbing the strength of being together again.

Chapter Thirty-Three

RILEY O'SHEA REACHED OUT TO her a few days shy of the promised two-week deadline. Nick insisted on going with her, and they arrived early at a Starbucks. This time, Riley was driving a black sedan. She'd traded her biker uniform for a cute sundress topped by a jean jacket.

"Well, hello," she said. "Who's this?"

"I'm her sidekick," Nick said.

Riley laughed as she sat down, and turned her body towards him rather than Bree.

Nick smiled, but there was no heat in his look and his natural inclination to flirt was banked.

Hmmm, maybe he really could change. "Don't let him fool you," Bree said, reaching for his hand. "He's actually quite smart."

Nick gave her the full wattage of his smile.

Riley rolled her eyes, then pulled a report out of her purse, and handed it to Bree.

"We almost feel badly taking your money," Riley said. "Compared to the people we normally investigate, these guys are pretty clean."

"There's nothing revealing? Damaging? How can that be?"

"Dylan looked into their finances. Aside from the usual mortgages, auto loans, and some credit card debt, not much. Charles has very expensive tastes. He also had financial troubles in his mid-twenties."

"I knew it," Bree said.

"Oh, he solved that problem. He married a rich, older woman."

"He's married? He's never brought an older woman to any work events."

"She splits her time between New York City and Boca Raton. She's in her mid-fifties. From his airline reservations, it looks like they see each other once every four to eight weeks." Riley flipped through her notes. "Michael Singleton also married a rich woman."

Bree nodded. "Paige." She looked over at Nick. "An old St. Louis family like mine."

Riley continued. "As a group, they like to blog or post about climate change and plant conservation on various social media. None of them are on the dark web." She went down the list. "No DUIs or other arrests. Stephen and Michael have kids. They coach their soccer and baseball teams. The two older guys, Klaus and Abe, are active in their churches or synagogue."

"You said they were 'pretty clean.'" Nick pointed out.

"Klaus had gambling issues throughout his twenties. It looks like he's now able to channel that. He invests in wine and cryptocurrencies. Michael likes extreme sports and to take risks. Abe's teenage son is wrestling with drug issues so unless Megan was an escape for him, he's got his hands full at home.

"And Stephen Almy?" Riley shrugged. "Outstanding student who didn't seem to experiment with anything in his teens or early twenties. Settled down with his college sweetheart in his late twenties. They went into marital counseling a year ago, separated briefly, but recently reconciled."

"So he might be a good candidate if he's adrift," Nick said.

Bree gave a small sigh. Her faith in humanity would be shattered if Stephen had ensnared Megan. He seemed so authentic.

Riley looked at her notes. "The timing is a little off. Stephen and his wife separated after the timeline that you gave us about when Megan moved out of her other apartment."

"What about their access to the drug that killed Megan?" Nick asked.

Riley leaned in and smiled at him. "For a sidekick, you ask the right questions."

"He's not just a pretty face," Bree volunteered.

Nick looked at her and grinned.

Riley leaned back as she pulled another sheet from the stack of papers on the table.

"I had to dig really hard to put this one together because none of their travels for the Garden put them anywhere near where the poison is found. Anyway two of them— Charles and Michael—were on projects with other botanists who had traveled to the two locations where the poison is most commonly found."

"But no one else, especially any young women, died when they were on these assignments?" Nick asked.

"Correct."

Nick gazed off into space, thinking, before he refocused on Bree and Riley. "So at best, one of them obtained this drug and was saving it for a rainy day when he wanted to kill someone?"

"Charles and his rich older wife," Bree suggested.

Bree and Nick began debating different ideas. After a few minutes, Riley broke in, saying she had nothing further, handed the report to Bree, and asked if Bree wanted O'Shea and Sons to look into any of the men or situations further. Bree demurred, saying she needed to study Riley's notes before deciding.

The young woman stood and pulled out another sheet of paper. "Our bill. Let us know if we can be of further service, Dr. Kincaid."

She winked at Nick, then left them.

Chapter Thirty-Four

———◆———

"VIETNAM OR KENYA?" BREE ASKED Nick as they sat on the small balcony of Daniel's apartment. The September sun was setting, capping a perfect day in the mid-seventies. She had been offered both jobs for which she had interviewed before Nick's return. He was all in for traveling.

"I can get a better journalism gig in Vietnam."

"Okay. Looks like the start date is in two months."

He smiled. "I can be ready in a day. All I need is that laptop—and you."

"Oh smooth. You may just get lucky tonight."

He held up his hands. "No pressure. I'm a mature man now. I'm sure I can go months without sex."

"You've only been back for two weeks so let's temper your bravado, Mancini."

"But you will spend the night? I've been good about respecting your boundaries."

She loved waking up in his arms or finding him curled around her. Such a simple act of intimacy.

She leaned over and kissed him. "Absolutely." She laughed ruefully. "I need to text my father, though. If I don't come home by midnight, he'll have the police out looking for me."

"You don't think he's figured out by now that your work doesn't require as much 'overtime' as you've worked in the last few weeks."

Remembering the conversation from months earlier with her father, Bree had insisted they wait until they were sure this was going to work before she introduced Nick to Scottie.

She could tell Nick had become uneasy at the mention of her father. Fathers never took to him well, he explained. They took one look at him, and remembered all the things they'd done with girls when they were younger.

"I'll tell him I'm spending the night with a friend. It used to work for Carly all the time when we were in high school. I'm sure it will work for a thirty-six-year old," she said dryly. As she reached for her phone, she said, "Do you think Daniel minds me being here so much? I feel like we've taken over his apartment."

Nick shook his head. "He basically just uses the place to sleep. Besides, we bring excitement to his life—and good food. He probably would have starved if not for us."

"Oh, is that what we do? I would think Daniel has enough drama in his job that he'd want peace and quiet when he got home."

"I think we're a nice break from his routine. He's been living alone a long time. I've never heard him mention dating or women since I got back. Either time that I got back," he amended.

"He's such a nice guy. And good looking."

"You think he's handsome?"

"Not as handsome as you, of course. But certainly easy on the eyes." She tilted her head. "I can't understand why he doesn't have a steady girlfriend. Do you think he's gay, and afraid to come out because his father was a tough cop?"

"Uh, no in both cases. I can testify from when we were teenagers that he liked girls. And his father's mellowed. Danny would accept Daniel no matter what." Nick shrugged. "Maybe he doesn't have time for a relationship. He's in such a crazy field."

"Yeah, but you'd think there must be at one female cop in St. Louis whom he could date and who would understand his job."

"Well, he's certainly a one-woman man. When Daniel commits, he commits."

"A wonderful trait in a man."

"So noted." He hesitated. "As long as we're talking about traits and commitment, we haven't discussed . . ."

Bree waited. When Nick didn't continue, she cocked her head, spread her hands and looked expectant.

"We . . ." He stopped. "Well, we've talked about a lot of things, but . . ." Once again he trailed off.

He was uncomfortable, Bree realized. Unsure of himself. Her concern must have shown on her face because he rushed on. "Well, we haven't discussed kids."

It wasn't a subject she ever expected him to bring up.

"Knowing how you feel about your family, I imagine you'll want one. Or two."

"I was thinking nine. For a baseball team."

Nick looked stunned. Why did it always work when he made these droll comments, but not when she did it?

"Kidding, Nick. Keep breathing."

He couldn't have disguised his relief if he'd tried.

"But you do want some kids," he persisted.

Would it terrify him if she said yes? Would she wake up tomorrow and he'd be gone? Would she be happy if the next forty years were only Nick and her?

"I think I'd like at least one," he said.

She was so shocked, she didn't know what to say. It didn't matter, though. Nick clearly had been thinking about the subject and wanted to say his piece.

"It scares the hell of out me to even think about kids, Bree. But I want a chance to be the father that Bernard never was. I want to build what I never had."

She didn't think words were what he needed to hear. She looked into his eyes, hoping he saw her utter faith that he could be a good father. She moved over onto his lap, took his face between her hands and kissed him. Not a passionate kiss, but a slow kiss of love. He wrapped his arms around her waist. She leaned against him.

After a minute, he said, "What if it turns out that I'm horrible at fatherhood? What if the child drives me nuts? Puts too many restrictions on my life? What if I don't *like* my own child? How will you feel if I decide I only want one?"

How would she feel?

"I don't know how I'll feel. But I think we figure it out as we go. We're good together." She looked up at him. "Besides, what if it turns out that I'm poor at parenting? What if I'm an overbearing mother?"

"Well, if he or she grows up to be a serial killer, I'm going to blame it on you."

She chuckled. "Of course you will."

Content and happy, she felt a spark stir. She'd held back part of her heart since his return, but with each day, she believed they had more in common than she ever imagined when they first talked about Megan, and she thought he was lightweight. Every time they had a conversation like this, she decided their strengths and differences complemented each other. In short, Nick made her life better.

Bree moved out of his embrace to straddle his legs. She nuzzled his neck. For a second, he did nothing. Then he took her face in his hands and kissed her passionately. And it felt so wonderful. Oh, what he was doing to her lips.

"Let's go inside," she whispered into his ear. "I have something I want to teach you."

"Well, if you want to tell me about the birds and the bees, you're a little late, Dr. Kincaid," he drawled as they rose.

"Stamen and pistil. I'm going to teach you about stamen and pistil, the parts of the flower that mate." She began unzipping his jeans as she pushed him inside Daniel's apartment. "You can't believe how well they fit together."

"I was horrible at science."

Bree smiled. "A slow learner. I like that. We'll have to practice more."

She saw heat in his eyes too, and with wonder, realized that he was just as excited by her as she felt about him. A sense of power like she'd never felt before surged through her. Imagine, Brianna Kincaid being able to turn on Nick Mancini.

In one fluid motion, he swung her around and toppled both of them onto the sofa bed.

They landed with Bree under Nick. She surprised a laugh out of him when she flipped him over. She knew making love was about giving, but all she wanted to do right now was to take.

If there was one thing Nick Mancini had a gift for, it was making love. She was so well pleasured, she really didn't care where he'd learned such a gift. He was every woman's fantasy—tender, then passionate the second time they made love, then playful, the third time. And he'd made her feel tender, passionate and playful—things that she hadn't felt in such a very long time. She fell asleep in his arms.

Hours later, half asleep, Bree rolled over, and a wonderful warmth cocooned her. Nick! His musky scent reminded her of the night, and she was content just listening to his even breathing. Finally, she stole a peek at him. Even in his sleep, he looked sinfully handsome, with a little bit of stubble and long, black eyelashes that rivaled her own.

She heard a noise, and for a second, her pulse raced with fear until she realized it was Daniel moving in the kitchen.

"Hey," she said drowsily.

He came over to the sofa bed, but didn't say a word.

"Daniel, I'm so sorry. If me being here is an—"

She felt Nick stir next to her.

"It's not you, Bree," Daniel said, sitting on the edge of the sofa bed. "There's no easy way to break this news. Stephen Almy committed suicide. Car accident. Same way as Megan died. And he left a note, admitting he killed her because he couldn't live with the guilt anymore."

Chapter Thirty-Five

A S THE SUN BEGAN TO dip behind trees, the sky was streaked with purples and oranges bouncing off the large patches of clouds. Bree sat in one of the rose gardens, waiting for Nick as had become their end-of-the-day routine. It was been another Goldilocks day—not too hot, not too cold, but just right. The majesty of nature almost overwhelmed her.

It also helped to counter her confusion and pain as she contemplated how she had misjudged Stephen Almy's character. She could understand Megan's attraction to him, given his kindness. She could understand him turning to her when his family began to crumble. But murder and suicide? She didn't understand those at all.

News of Stephen's death had spread through Garden staff this morning, once again jarring her colleagues. Emery and human resources had scrambled to make grief counseling available. Only Bree knew the circumstances surrounding Stephen's death. She found comfort in knowing she had kept her commitment to find justice for Megan, though the price for justice was higher than she ever thought would have to pay.

She felt blessed that she was at peace with her own life. Bree knew what she wanted to do with her career. She found this unexpected surprise of a relationship with Nick. Her grief over her mother was ebbing. They would be starting a new chapter in their lives that let her put all of this behind her.

When Nick texted he was stuck in traffic, Bree decided to stroll through more of the Garden. After all, she wouldn't be back here very often. As she walked, her botany training couldn't let her help but notice which flowers had done well this season, and were still beautiful even in September. She passed the Linnean House and the Ottoman Garden, and turned left to the Sensory Garden with the unique hands-on sculpture of a bronze tree formed by Soleri bells. She closed her eyes and moved her hands down the tree's bells, striking different tones. She took in a deep breath for the Sensory Garden drew on sights, smells, textures and sounds to enhance the experience for those who were sight impaired. She caught a whiff of basil.

Her eyes opened wide.

The beauty we can and cannot see.

Bree couldn't help it. She'd been living with Megan's clues for six months.

The beauty we can and cannot see.

One of the clues was hidden here. She just knew it.

"Let it go," she muttered to herself. "You don't need to do this. It won't bring Megan back."

But now she felt if she found a clue, it would honor Megan's plan. And Bree had to admit, provide some closure for herself. But what were the chances the clue had survived after six months? Time and water would have eroded anything Megan had left behind. Eroded, but perhaps not destroyed.

Bree moved over to the raised flower beds where each plant was labeled with Braille and raised letters. Lavender, garlic, and other flowers and herbs filled the beds meant to tease the senses. She moved over to the lamb's ear, with its white silky fur-like coating, its texture another way to help the visually impaired feel the garden.

The beauty we can and cannot see.

Was she referring to a plant that was regarded as beautiful, but had unexpected medicinal benefits? Lavender would check that box. Or was Megan hinting that garlic, a vegetable people seemed to love or hate, had hidden value.

Or was it all simply a metaphor for Megan herself? A woman whose heart and brains would be overlooked because she was not beautiful to look at, and this man that she loved had taken time to see, really see her?

Bree glanced around the garden again, looking for any other plants that might fit the clue. She ruled out the bell tree. Anything Megan hid there would most likely have altered the sound. Not to mention, how many families stopped to make it sing every day. If the clue had been there, it would have been found by now.

Garlic. She would start with the garlic plants. If Megan wanted to hide a clue, but not have it disturbed or found by chance, garlic seemed a perfect choice. Bree moved dirt around with her hands, digging deeper and deeper until her left hand felt something metallic. She scooped away more dirt in the area until she saw a flash of metal, and then dug deeper to reveal a key. She pulled out the old-fashioned skeleton key about one and a half inches long and wiped it off as best she could. The handle of the key was an intricate heart within a heart. Of course, it would be heart. Megan had been madly in love. No doubt it was meant to represent the key to her heart. Was it meant to be symbolic or did the key really open something important, like the next clue?

Although it was old-fashioned, the key was smaller and more simplistic than the one she had borrowed to open the Tower Grove home so she doubted that it lead to a clue there. After all, there were still three clues she hadn't deciphered: *Amazing, the happy times we will show our child, and our love is worth a fortune.*

A key wasn't worth much in a maze because there was nothing to open. The other two clues were so vague—

"Hey, didn't your mother tell you not to play in the dirt?"

Bree looked up to see Nick and Michael coming toward her. She fought the temptation to shove the dirt back around the garlic. She moved in their direction, hoping they wouldn't notice her dirty hands or the disturbed dirt.

"I found Nick coming into the building," Michael said. "I thought I'd seen you leave so we tracked you down together."

"It's such a stunning day, I couldn't resist a walk in the Garden," she said.

"My favorite time of the year," Michael said. "I love living in St. Louis at this time of year."

Bree thought Nick choked back a laugh because that's what he'd said months earlier about what people always said about living in St. Louis.

"Sorry about the traffic," Nick said as he kissed Bree on the forehead. "I'm starving. I've been hungry for an hour."

"Well, I'm ready, so let's go."

The three of them headed to the employee parking lot, politely chattering about nothing, and parted ways at their cars. Michael waved to them as he drove out of the lot.

"Okay, hand it over," Nick said.

"What?"

"Whatever it is you're hiding."

Bree held out her hand with the key laying in her palm. "I didn't mean to find it. I was not looking for it."

"One of Megan's clues?"

"I think so." She explained how she found it. "You two showed up just as I was going to dig to see if she left instructions or words for him."

She stared at the ground, then peeked up to find Nick studying her.

"You do know it's over, right? Justice was served. There's no point in tormenting yourself any further, Brianna. Let it go."

"Of course, I can let it go. I'm a well-adjusted adult. Let's go eat."

Nick sighed—the heavy sigh of a put-upon person. He took her arm and steered her back to the Garden.

"Come on. Let's at least look so you won't spend dinner overthinking."

"You think I overthink things?"

He smiled down at her. "All the time. It's my job to save you from yourself. Besides, I'm counting on wild sex after dinner, and 'wild sex' and 'overthinking' just are not compatible."

"Well, I'm only doing this for you then," she said, grasping his hand. "Because I care so much about your happiness."

He squeezed her hand as they headed past the security guard and back into the Garden.

When they returned to the Sensory Garden, Bree was able to resume digging where she'd found the key while Nick leaned against the brick raised plant bed. After a minute, she pulled out a blue ribbon. Although soggy and grubby, it was the same kind of ribbon that Megan had used to attach her messages to all the other clues they had found. Attached to it was a glob.

Bree looked over at Nick. Clearly a clue had been attached, but they were six months too late. He wrapped her in his arms, and she rested her head against his chest. She was grateful he didn't say anything. Too late. Always too late.

Gradually, the warmth of his body and security of his arms eased the ache in her heart and the lump in her throat. She stepped out of his embrace, and began loosely repacking the dirt around the garlic.

"So what's the plan for dinner?" she asked.

"Let's not be adults tonight. Instead, let's eat chocolate ice cream and chocolate cake for dinner."

"Deal. Lots of chocolate may get you that wild sex you so look forward to."

Her father had headed to Seattle for a trial, so they were setting up camp at the Kincaid home to give Daniel some privacy. She was planning a nice dinner when her father returned from the trial to introduce him to Nick.

She had to admit the cake and ice cream did the trick in reviving her spirits. Nick did his best to distract her with funny stories about some of his assignments around the world. She was so relaxed that she responded to Nick's smoldering glances and subtle touches. His touch—how she craved it. Something so simple, yet it set her on fire. It traveled down to her toes, to the tips of her fingers, but most importantly, to her heart. Nick settled for a night of slow, luxurious sex. He was trying to make her feel better without saying a word.

At least until the next morning. He must have decided the sting of not finding a clue had worn off.

"I have time to check with the sculptor on her progress on Megan's piece if you want me to," he offered. "It's going to be fabulous piece, Bree. It will make Molly Harper and her mother happy. Takes an extraordinary woman to have something good come from something bad, you know."

She kissed him, and feeling the glow of his words, headed out the door to the BMW. It was only when she was about to open the car door that she realized he had subtly reminded her to focus on the positive, what she had accomplished, and to stop obsessing over clues that would lead to nothing anymore.

She looked over to her home to see him standing in the kitchen doorway, coffee in hand. He lifted the cup and offered the trademark Mancini smile to tell her he'd outfoxed her. She laughed, and he disappeared back in the house.

Chapter Thirty-Six

HER ADMINISTRATIVE ASSISTANT STUCK HER head in the door, interrupting Bree's meandering thoughts.

"I need to leave, Bree."

"Thanks for everything today, Cheryl. I know it's been a long day, but the proposal is looking great. We should be in good shape for tomorrow."

"You're the last one here. Why don't you shut down your computer and walk out with me? It's almost eight."

It wasn't what she said, but the tenseness in Cheryl's voice that made Bree look closer. Cheryl could always be counted on to find the positive. Maybe because her world was simpler. Her life revolved around her church, and her children and grandchildren. The deaths of Megan and Stephen had sliced into the cocoon she knew. Rumors were flying about the connection between the two deaths, though Bree kept what she knew to herself. She didn't even know if Emery knew the truth.

"It will be OK now, Cheryl. Stephen's dead. If the gossip is true, he can't hurt anyone anymore."

"I never thought he could hurt anyone in the first place." Cheryl walked further into Bree's office to rest her hands on the back of Bree's visitor's chair. "All this has made me so sad. He was so smart. And kind. I keep asking myself why he would do it. Why didn't I see anything?"

"I don't think any of us saw it so I imagine we're all struggling, just in different ways. The loss of two people we worked with in six months. It may take us all a long time to work through it."

Cheryl was silent for a moment, before she asked, "Do you think it was his kindness that drew Megan?"

Bree responded with a simple nod. She had never shared her thoughts about Megan's craving for love, just like she had never revealed Megan's pregnancy to anyone at the Garden. The pregnancy wasn't her secret to share, nor was it time to shred Megan's memory.

Cheryl heaved a sigh, then shook her head. "There was nothing more important to that girl than family. It just breaks my heart . . . I can't even bear to think about her, Bree. And her poor mother! What she must be feeling. Then I start thinking about Stephen's wife. Poor Abby. She must be going through hell."

"Maybe in a few weeks, you should call her. I imagine she's numb right now, and consumed with making sure her kids are okay. But in a few weeks she would probably appreciate someone to talk with. You're a good listener. I know from my mother's death that the months right after are even harder sometimes, once the numbness wears off."

Cheryl's face brightened. "Good suggestion."

"See you tomorrow."

"OK then. But don't stay too late, Bree."

"No worries. Nick is coming in about half an hour."

Cheryl patted her heart as she left the office, and Bree laughed.

"Remember, sleep a little later tomorrow," she called after Cheryl. "We deserve it after the long days this week."

The only good thing about working under a proposal deadline was that she could wear jean, a t-shirt and her running shoes. But after an eleven-hour day even jeans felt grungy.

She turned back to her computer. "All I have to do is read eighty-seven more e-mails," she muttered.

She'd been working on the proposal for two days straight so hadn't had time to answer any. She responded to ten of the easy ones, deleted a few spam, and marked two to read later. The rest would have to wait until tomorrow. She pushed back her chair and stretched. Her eyes landed on Megan's skeleton key that she'd found last week. Picking it up, she traced the two hearts on the head of the key. Alone, she could admit to herself that when she and Nick moved to Vietnam, when she was not walking through the Garden every day, she would be relieved not to have constant reminders of her mother and Megan. Maybe Nick's habit of running away wasn't always a bad one.

She stood and walked over to her mini-refrigerator to pull out a bottle of lemonade, then hesitated. What if Stephen had been feeling so desperate before his suicide that he sabotaged her drinks again? She listened to the silence. She was all alone until Nick showed up. No one to save her. She put the bottle back in her 'fridge, and went to the hallway drinking fountain. When she finished drinking, she turned around and gasped.

"Oh Jesus." She put her hand on her heart. "You scared me, Michael."

"Sorry."

"I thought I was the only one here."

"You are. I'm just dropping this off on Abe's desk, then I'm out of here."

He followed her back to her office. "You in good shape on the proposal?"

"Yep. Nothing to do tomorrow, but review it one more time, and FedEx it."

"Not surprised that you're not rushing at the last minute. You are one of the most organized people I know." He picked up the skeleton key. "A present from Nick?"

Bree shook her head. "I'm not quite sure what it is." She smiled. "It's a long story."

"One I'll have to hear another time. I promised to read to the kids before they go to bed. See you tomorrow."

Michael took such pleasure in his kids. Nick would probably be a wonderful father to small children. After all, they would have so much in common, she thought dryly. Despite what he said, she did not want to start a family soon. He need a more time in their relationship before they brought a new life into the world.

Bree thought of her father and mother, of all the advice they'd given her about running the student council, all the sleepovers they had let Carly and her have. How her father never missed any of Carly's basketball games, no matter how busy his schedule. Her life would have been so different without either of her parents.

A strong family. Nick had never had it. Megan craved it. Bree was so lucky she'd had it.

She picked up the key. Somehow that seemed fitting that she have it and the wedding ring planted underneath the base of Megan's sculpture. She stuffed it in her purse, and left her office, figuring she'd meet Nick at the visitors' center.

The sun had already dipped behind the horizon. What a long day. She was going to take her own advice and sleep in tomorrow. As she strolled towards the public entrance to the Garden, she saw the sculpture of the exuberant family with the mother, father and child. She would have that someday. The family that she and Nick had would be different than she imagined when she was married to Mitch, but it would be a family filled with love and joy.

Bree stopped. A family. A joyous family.

Oh the happiness we will show our child.

She couldn't help it. She walked over to the statue to examine it, which was not easy to do in the fading light. No places that she could see where Megan could hide a clue in the sculpture itself as the father, mother and child figures were arched to convey motion and relatively thin. She bent over to examine the base of the sculpture. Nothing that she could see in the dim light. She ran her fingers over each side of the square base until her fingers felt a small opening. She pulled out her phone and hit the flashlight app to see a tiny key hole.

She fished the brass antique key out of her purse. Was there any point in seeing if it fit? They already knew who killed Megan. They'd proven Megan had not taken her own life.

Let it go. It won't bring anyone back.

However, perhaps this clue was something tangible like the ring and the key, and could be buried with the other items under Megan's sculpture. More closure.

She stuck the key in the hole and turned it. When a small plate opened, she pointed the flashlight beam at it. The beam bounced off something metal, and she pulled out the object. Megan had had a picture printed on metal. Of course, she would have made created something permanent. In the picture, she looked adoringly up at—

"I really admired your intelligence and tenacity, Bree," said Michael Singleton. "Until those qualities started causing me so many problems."

The flashlight on her phone showed the gun he pointed at her. It looked like a small pistol, similar to ones she had had to protect herself on certain overseas assignments.

"I'm sorry. I can't afford a subtle and prolonged approach to death this time. You're going to have to die quickly, unlike Stephen and Megan."

Bree felt both a spike of anger and a chill of fear, and decided she could afford neither.

"Hand me whatever you've found and your phone. Then get up and head towards the back of the Garden. Towards the Japanese Garden."

She needed to stall and distract him because even an idiot could probably kill her if he fired a gun at this close range.

Bree started walking slowly. "Did you ever love her?"

"Of course. Megan was so warm and friendly. Not like Paige, the bitch. We could have had such a great time. But she got pregnant on purpose. I would have lost everything. The money. The kids. The chance to be the next Emery."

Bree realized if he got her as far as the Japanese Garden, she would die. There would be no one to hear or see anything.

"Everything was working perfectly until you decided to nose into this. In your next life, perhaps you should be less persistent, Bree."

"You took Stephen's life?"

"That's your fault. You and the boy toy you've hooked up with just wouldn't go away. I already knew how to use the poison. The hard part was the suicide letter."

He went into detail about getting a sample of Stephen's writing, and practicing over and over, and Bree stopped listening as she realized she was running out of time.

Think, think, think. She knew every foot of this Garden.

She couldn't try to wrestle or hit him—he outweighed her and the gun was so close that he wouldn't miss. What could she do that he couldn't? Her only hope was to outrun him, and hope he was a poor shot if there was distance between them. She could run farther into the Garden and double back to the visitors' center to get help. But she needed him off balance or distracted.

She could barely make out the oldest chestnut tree in the Garden. Another thirty feet and they'd split off to the path that lead back to the Japanese Garden. She pictured the path as she'd jogged it for so many days, and then it came to her. It might be her only chance.

Imperceptibly, Bree started edging to the right. She felt the gun poking her more persistently, but then Michael unwittingly adjusted several inches to the right. Another few feet and she shifted to the right again. He did too.

She felt like she was moving in slow motion. She could feel her heartbeat pounding, and her senses sharpened they did when she was in the flow of running.

Distract him, she thought as she got ready to shift again.

"Do you really think that you can get away with murder? Three bodies is one too many don't you think? No one will believe that I killed myself, Michael. Three bodies will arouse suspicion. Detective Cusumano and Nick Mancini won't rest until they find you. And my father will use ev—"

"I've gotten away with two murders, Bree. It's easier than you think."

She hoped that he couldn't see the fear on her face when she thought how casually he said that. But it explained the steadiness with which he held the gun in her side. Did he know how to use it? At this range, it didn't matter.

Only a few feet.

Michael lurched when he stepped into the hole in which she had sprained her ankle earlier in the summer, and Bree pushed him at the same time. Out of the corner of her eye, she saw him go down on his knees, and used both hands to break his fall. She sprinted, thanking God that she wasn't in heels.

She heard a crack, and realized that he hadn't lost the gun in the dark. She waited for the pain. When nothing happened, she put on more speed. She heard a pop, and then a ping as the shot hit in front of her.

She sprinted to the home demonstration center, where there were numerous small gardens. The plants weren't as high as they would be in full bloom in the summer, but it gave her more cover than running along the pathway. Without the tapping of her shoes on the pavement, she should be harder to find. Her only hope was to elude him and find a way to double back to before Michael did. While she'd bought herself more chances, she'd also upped the stakes. He had no choice now but to find and kill her to protect himself.

She started for the Prairie Garden because the wild grasses were the highest right now, but he would think of that too. She only had precious seconds to make a decision, and she swerved right toward the bird garden. Lots of low growth. She threw herself under a beautyberry bush.

Between the darkness and the branches, she couldn't see

Michael, but she could hear him moving across the bricks. She thought she heard him breathing hard, but maybe that was her.

"Bree, I know where you are. I can see you," he said softly. "I'm going to put a bullet in your heart—or maybe in that smart head of yours."

She held her breath as if this would hold her fear in. Still, he didn't shoot. Maybe he was bluffing.

"I'm going to kill you with much more pleasure than I killed Stephen Almy. He was always so trusting. He reminded me of Megan. I almost couldn't kill her. She was so sweet. But she was going to tell Paige everything. Paige is a cold bitch, but she's a rich bitch. Just like you, Bree.

"You know, on second thought, I may torture you because you're causing me so damn much trouble. Or maybe I'll kill that stupid boyfriend of yours."

Like hell, Bree thought. He was playing mind games with her. Maybe he couldn't see her at all. She forced herself to listen for any telltale sounds of his movement. She slowly slithered away from Michael, feeling the gray dogwood and green hawthorn bushes catch on her jeans and top as she moved. She stopped, straining to hear any noise that he made. She could hear crickets, frogs, some birds. She hoped that was all he could hear too.

She slid out the other side of the bird garden and scrambled up a slight incline. That's when she heard another shot, which thudded into the dirt to her left. Then he fired again. Five shots. Five shots and he hadn't hit her yet. She hoped his gun was a little thirty-eight with only eight bullets.

She only had to outrun three more bullets.

Chapter Thirty-Seven

———◆———

NICK WALKED INTO THE VISITORS' center and spent a few minutes shooting the breeze with the two security guards. With the Cardinals not in the World Series, they talked about Blues hockey. Not surprisingly, the conversation turned to Stephen Almy's death. It was still the talk of the Garden, they said. They bickered like an old married couple as one maintained he'd heard all sorts of dark stories were coming to light about Dr. Almy now that he was dead. He did drugs. Had fathered several children in other countries in which he'd worked. Nick wondered what people would say about him when he was gone. So little of it would be kind.

The other guard said he couldn't believe nice Dr. Almy would kill that sweet Megan Harper. Nick felt uneasy when he heard the exact same thing that Daniel had said. It wrapped Megan's murder all up neat and tidy. A little too neat and tidy. However, given there was a suicide note, the department would not invest any more time and considered the case closed.

Nick was all for that. He didn't want to think about Megan Harper or Stephen Almy or poison or petunias anymore. He wanted to start in a new place with Bree, and happily forget St. Louis and all it had cost the two of them.

He wanted that feeling of contentment in the pit of his stomach that Bree brought him. It was such a new feeling that he wasn't sure that he trusted it, but he wasn't afraid of it. That amazed him as much as his feelings for Bree. She wouldn't give an inch on some things; she'd call him on all the thoughtless crap he did. But when she was in his corner, he felt invincible.

Nick asked the two guards if they'd seen Bree, and both said they hadn't seen her leave yet. He let them buzz her extension, but she didn't answer. She wasn't answering her cell either. She'd told him they were done with the proposal. What the hell could be so important that she didn't take a second to answer her phone? Was she wandering around the Garden again?

Finally, the older of the guards, a retired St. Louis cop, stood and said he was going to make his rounds. Nick said he'd amble out with him, walking to one of the rose gardens. Outside the visitors' center, the guard headed left while Nick veered right towards the now-silent trams. Damn, it was getting dark out here. He could barely see; he hoped to hell that the guard didn't come around the other way and accidentally shoot Bree.

Nick passed the statue of the family that she liked so much, but no Bree. Where the hell was the woman? He had plans for her tonight and they didn't include playing hide and seek. Maybe she'd gone around the other way and run into the guard, and would retrace her steps to find Nick.

He passed one of the rose gardens, and was at the Mediterranean House when he heard a crack. He'd been in enough war zones and bad sections of cities to know the sound of a gun. In the fading light, he saw Bree sprinting towards him

"Nick, run. He's got a gun!"

Instead he ran toward her.

"No, Nick! It's Michael. He killed Megan. Run away."

She dragged Nick the other way.

"We need to get away and tell Daniel . . ."

Bree heard the crack of the pistol again, and cried out. She grabbed her arm and stumbled.

"Keep going," she screamed.

But he stopped and bent down to help her up, and they heard the whistle of another bullet.

"Jesus, Bree," said Nick, "Are you hurt? Stay down."

"I believe that I got her in the arm," said Michael, stopping about ten feet from them, and pointing the gun steadily at them.

Nick couldn't tell what kind of gun it was. He put his hands up, and slowly rose, stepping in front of Bree.

"Move away from her," Michael said.

Nick stayed where he was, but heard Bree behind him.

She stood and slipped her right hand into his left, and squeezed it. Would the woman never do what he told her?

"He's fired eight shots, Nick. He can't kill both of us."

"I reloaded," said Michael. His voice was filled with disdain.

"I don't think you did," she said coolly and stepped toward Michael.

What the hell was she doing? Nick thought wildly.

"You always were so cocky, Bree."

"And you were never quite good enough, Michael." Without taking her eyes off Michael, she said, "Nick, somewhere on him, Michael has a picture of him and Megan, which she inscribed *To the Love of My Life. The Father of Our Son.* He confessed that he poisoned her because she was going to destroy his reputation when his wife found out about the baby. And then he wouldn't get Emery's job as head of the Garden. He killed Megan and his own child over money and a job. A damn job."

Nick's tongue was so heavy that he couldn't speak. She was trying to get herself killed and save him. He could lose her, and that idea terrified him as much as the gun.

"Any way you look at it, Michael, I bet you get life in jail. Probably two life sentences. He killed Stephen Almy too, Nick."

"Put the gun down, Dr. Singleton," said the security guard as he came up behind him.

"You stupid bitch," he screamed at Bree. "You ruined everything."

And he pulled the trigger.

Nick flinched while he threw himself in front of Bree, and then realized that nothing happened. She'd been right; Michael was out of bullets.

He threw the gun at the guard, who ducked. Michael sprinted back down the path toward the Climatron. The three of them ran after him. Bree was in the best shape, and quickly outdistanced the other two. She was drawing up on Michael to tackle him, when he abruptly stopped and turned on her. She tumbled into him, and they went down on the pavement. Michael put both hands on her throat, but she pummeled one of her fists into his balls. He gasped with pain, and released her just as Nick and the guard caught up with them. Nick punched Michael in the face three times before Bree could pull him off Megan's murderer.

The guard was able to slap handcuffs on Michael, and then pulled off his belt to bind his feet. As the guard pulled out his radio, and called his partner, Nick pulled Bree into his arms—and then heard her gasp.

"Oh my God. Did he hit you?"

"I think he just grazed me. Although it hurts now that the adrenaline is wearing off."

He asked the guard to summon paramedics. Once she reassured him no organs had been hit, he pulled her into his arms again, careful not to hurt her, and felt her melt into him.

Oh God, he could have lost her.

"Just what the hell did you think you were doing?" he asked.

"I was pretty sure that he was bluffing."

"Pretty sure? Pretty sure?" Nick cursed in four languages.

It must have dawned on Bree how he was furious with her. She tried to put his face between her hands, but he pulled her hands away. He ranted. He swore some more. And then went back to ranting again. Eventually he wore his anger out, and pulled her back into his arms, though he didn't seem to care that she winced.

"I'm sorry," she said in a little voice.

"Damn. That's not good enough, Bree."

"I will never do such a stupid thing again."

"You understand that I can't lose another woman in my life. *The* most important woman in my life, right?"

She nodded, then pulled back to look at him. "But we solved Megan's murder. Her soul can be at peace now."

◆

When, exactly, was the right time to box up a life?

Bree doubted if there was an 'exactly', but she understood now that there was a time to let go, to move on if the life had been well-lived, or pray for one that hadn't been happy. Maybe the 'exactly' was different for each person left behind, but at some point you had to stop looking behind and start looking forward.

Epilogue

T HE SWEAT AND GRIME OF three days in the jungle clung to Bree when what she really had in mind was clinging to Nick. She couldn't wait to get back to the hotel and a hot bath, soft bed and warm husband.

She patted her slightly protruding tummy. "Bet your daddy misses us big time," she told their baby. She knew Nick wasn't as cavalier about his pregnant wife trekking into the mountains as he pretended, but he was smart enough to know that arguing about it with her would only make her more determined to go.

"Your daddy is one smart man," she told the baby. "We are so lucky."

And a romantic one too. No doubt he planned something amorous to celebrate their third anniversary.

They'd melded their lives together rather effortlessly, Nick writing wherever her job took them. With her encouragement, he'd finished that novel, and his agent had sold it to a publisher. It had been a modest success, so he was working on a second book.

She ran no matter what country they were in, but more often than not, she swung by to pick up Nick who would jog the last half-mile with her. Some of their best talks were during the long cool-down when he tested his characters and plots on her, and she told him about her conservation efforts or they talked about their families. They rarely talked about Megan.

She waved to the clerks at the front desk as she headed to the third floor. The hotel wasn't elegant, but it was the best available in this rural part of Vietnam.

She called out a perky greeting as she let herself in their room, but stopped short when she saw Nick's stricken face as he sat at his laptop.

"Oh, honey, did the battery die again? Did you lose part of your story? I know the humidity here—"

"Tory's been arrested for murder," he croaked.

She froze, her comprehension as still as her feet. "What?"

"Daniel sent me an e-mail. The day after the opening of her exhibit at the St. Louis Art Museum, she was accused of murdering her lover."

Bree didn't even process what he said. All she knew was that her husband was in distress, and she scurried across the room to Nick's side.

"She was arrested yesterday and is being held without bail," he said.

Nick's hands hadn't moved from the keyboard since Bree had walked in. He was in shock, and she took over planning.

"We can get there in twenty-four hours," she said, picking up the phone. She took one look at her husband and set the phone down. She came back to him to put her arms around him. He sank into her. For a minute, they simply held each other.

Then Bree moved out of his embrace. Looking up at him, touching his face gently, she said softly, "Luckily, we know one of the best lawyers in the country. Let's go save your sister."

Author Bio

NJ Litz is a former journalist and communications director. (Litz is a college nickname.)

She is a member of Sisters in Crime and a former member of Romance Writers of America. She writes romantic mysteries about strong women who seek justice for those who can't get it themselves.

She lives with her family in St. Louis. Not surprisingly, given her books, she is an animal lover and an avid gardener.

37275545R00146

Made in the USA
Lexington, KY
26 April 2019